The yellowbacks... classics of popular fiction

The yellowjackets or yellowbacks were a great series of bestselling adventure and crime thrillers that had its origins in the mid to late 19th century following on from the 'penny dreadfuls'. They virtually began the mass market revolution of the early 20th century with a clear standard format and imprint/series livery (what would today be called branding). Hodder & Stoughton published the yellowjackets in two main series with series run dates of: 1923-1939 and later 1949-1957.

As the tagline ('where thrillers really began') on the back cover implies, the imprint and series focused on thrillers that were the bestsellers of their time. This current reissue or retro revival if you will, brings back many of these masterpieces, now classics in their own way and extends it further by including key titles from that period that were either great crime or thriller or even general commercial fiction (including sub-genres of noir, horror, gothic, romance, westerns, etc.) influences of their time. There are some perennial favourites and many rarities either lost or not easily available being revived in the current series. Writers and characters ranged from adventure heroes like Bulldog Drummond, Allan Quatermain, Richard Hannay or the Saint through thriller grandmasters Edgar Wallace and E. Phillips Oppenheim, crime and mystery maestros like Patricia Wentworth, GK Chesterton, Agatha Christie and the Detection club, to western and swashbucklers like Zane Grey, Max Brand, Captain Blood and even romance or general fiction classics like Hermina Black, Denise Robins, Marie Corelli or Stella Morton. These were books that had storytelling at their heart and always entertained.

The yellowbacks had both hardback (with varying design elements) and paperback (which built the series look) versions with the latter still carrying the imprint 'yellowjacket'. The current reissues pay tribute to both and use an amalgam of elements from both editions while retaining the complete yellow (or 'mustard-plaster') livery with the author's name in blue beveled type with a 'simulated emboss' effect and a white outer 'outline', and the book title in black. These reissues retain the distinctive size of the original mass market paperback and follow the three main category variations—the thrillers (crime, westerns, mystery, adventure) had blue lettering for the author's name, while Romance and softer general fiction had red; and other categories like humour had green.

For more detail and a full list of titles visit https://www.hachetteindia.com/home/yellowbacks

THE NOVELS OF SOLAR PONS

Terror Over London

and

Mr. Fairlie's Final Journey

THE NOVELS OF SOLAR PONS - TERROR OVER LONDON AND MR. FAIRLIE'S FINAL JOURNEY

August William Derleth (February 24, 1909 – July 4, 1971) was an American writer and anthologist. Though best remembered as the first book publisher of the writings of H. P. Lovecraft, and for his own contributions to the Cthulhu Mythos and the cosmic horror genre, as well as his founding of the publisher Arkham House (which did much to bring supernatural fiction into print in hardcover in the US that had only been readily available in the UK), Derleth was a leading American regional writer of his day, as well as prolific in several other genres, including historical fiction, poetry, detective fiction, science fiction, and biography. Derleth wrote more than 150 short stories and more than 100 books during his lifetime.

THE NOVELS OF SOLAR PONS

Terror Over London
and
Mr. Fairlie's Final Journey

August Derleth

hachette
INDIA

The Novels of Solar Pons : Terror Over London and Mr. Fairlie's Final Journey

Terror over London first published in 1998 in *The Final Adventures of Solar Pons.*
Mr. Fairlie's Final Journey first published in 1968 by Mycroft & Moran

(Registered Name: Hachette Book Publishing India Pvt. Ltd.)
An Hachette UK Company www.hachetteindia.com

1

The texts in these editions in most cases have been reprinted as is, with minimal editorial changes and by and large no bowdlerizing for political correctness; though in some editions, a few words and phrases considered archaic, or those considered offensive now, along with archaic punctuation may have been modified in places to make the text more accessible to today's readers. The narratives, language, beliefs, social mores and/or cultural depictions, in these volumes are a reflection of their times and must be viewed as such. They may also contain certain cultural, racial and gender prejudices and stereotypes that may be outdated or clearly wrong then and wrong today; but their removal would be tantamount to claiming these prejudices never existed. The Publisher does not endorse or support those depictions or stereotypes; and these books have been made available for a discerning audience that will read it for entertainment value and a chronicle/record of popular fiction of past times.

Cover design by Priya Singh adapted from the original classic yellowjacket by Hodder & Stoughton.

Cover illustration by Ishan Trivedi.

Series note: Some of the books in the series (unless otherwise credited) may have cover or inside illustrations from the original yellowbacks or early editions, and while full restoration has been attempted, some images may be grainy or faded due to the condition of the original material. The end notes or bonus material or blurb details may have been sourced from the public domain or free use publications such as Wikipedia and attribution is hereby made also allowing similar free use reproduction from here. Sources requiring further specific attribution may write in and further detailing and/or corrections shall be made in subsequent printings/editions.

Reprint specifications may be subject to change including but not limited to finishes, paper, colour sections.

ISBN: 978-93-5731-183-0

Hachette Book Publishing India Pvt. Ltd.
4th & 5th Floors, Corporate Centre,
Plot No. 94, Sector 44, Gurugram - 122 003, India

Typeset in Electra LT STD 10/12.5 pt by Manipal Technologies Limited

Printed and bound in India by Manipal Technologies Limited

FSC www.fsc.org MIX Paper from responsible sources FSC™ C043100

CONTENTS

Mr. Fairlie's Final Journey

A NOTE ON THE ORIGINAL LANGUAGE

Over the years, many editions of August Derleth's Solar Pons stories have been extensively edited, and in some cases, the original text has been partially rewritten, effectively changing the tone and spirit of the adventures. Belanger Books is committed to restoring Derleth's stories to their authentic form – "warts and all". This means that we have published the stories in these editions as Derleth originally composed them, deliberately leaving in the occasional spelling or punctuation error for historical accuracy.

Additionally, the stories reprinted in this volume were written in a time when racial stereotypes played an unfortunately larger role in society and popular culture. They are reprinted here without alteration for historical reference.

Foreword

MASTERY OF THE FORM

BY DAVID MARCUM

While the exact number of Pons stories is debated – as some of the Apocryphal tales may or may not be counted as individual stories, depending on whom you ask – it's a fact that there are more original Canonical Solar Pons adventures than there are of the original Sherlock Holmes. But it was always lamented that there was only one Pons novel, *Mr. Fairlie's Final Journey*, as compared to the four Holmes novels, *A Study in Scarlet*, *The Sign of the Four*, *The Hound of the Baskervilles*, and *The Valley of Fear*. However, in 1995, friends of Solar Pons were electrified to learn that a second Pons novel had been discovered, along with a number of other previously lost stories. So even if we didn't have an equivalent four Pons novels, we now had two.

In that magical year, Derleth's daughter April gave Pons scholar Peter Ruber two boxes of Derleth's papers to sort, and these were found to include several additional unpublished Pons adventures, including the 30,000-word Pons novella, *Terror Over London* (originally titled *Mr. Solar Pons of Praed Street*). Also included in the box were manuscripts for "The Adventure of Gresham Old Place", and a more complete version of the previously discovered "The Sinister House", now entitled "The Burlstone Horror". Additionally, there were two more Pons adventures co-written with science-fiction author Mack Reynolds to complement the two collaborations between Derleth and Reynolds that had already been published. (There is much more about all of these stories in the foreword to *The Apocyrpha of Solar Pons.*)

These discovered adventures were copyrighted in 1998 by Derleth's children, April and Walden, and subsequently published that year as *The Final Adventures of Solar Pons.* Thankfully, as the rights to these stories are still completely owned by the Derleth Estate, currently consisting of his grandchildren, we are able to present them as a part of this volume.

Terror Over London was clearly written very early in Derleth's career, very probably before much of the Pontine Canon had been established. While this adventure in long form is somewhat different in tone than the rest of the Pontine Canon, it's a very important part of it, and it continued Derleth's tradition of excellence, while showing his mastery of the Golden Age form. *Terror Over London* doesn't have the polished feel of later Pons adventures. It's also very much influenced by Sax Rohmer's narratives of Denis Nayland Smith and his nemesis, Dr. Fu Manchu – as was the Poirot novel *The Big Four* (1927), written just a few years earlier. Its conclusion has some similarities to a later short story included in *The Reminiscences* – although I won't reveal which one, as finding out here would spoil the fun. It's of interest because it specifically states that Pons knew Sherlock Holmes – although it's quite incorrect in referring to him as "the late Sherlock Holmes", because Holmes was still very much alive when this adventure took place in 1928.

After the Stock Market Crash of 1929, and the death of various pulp magazines that published the early Pons stories, Derleth mostly set aside The Sherlock Holmes of Praed Street until the mid-1940's, when, with the encouragement of Ellery Queen, Edgar W. Smith, Vincent Starrett, and other noted Sherlockians, he resurrected Pons in his notable volume *In Re: Sherlock Holmes.* After that, he continued to write steadily over the following decades, collecting Pons stories every few years in treasured volumes. The count of Pontine short stories continued to rise, but during his lifetime, Derleth never went back and revised or published *Terror Over London*. Had he forgotten about it? We'll never know. But towards the end of his life, he again composed another Pons novel.

Mr. Fairlie's Final Journey (1968) is a curious volume, for many years believed to be the only Pons novel. I wonder if, with this book, Derleth had a complicated story that was simply too long for the short form, or if he intentionally set out to craft a Pons novel, and expanded the plot to fit. Derleth scholars, or perhaps members of the August Derleth Society (ADS) might know, but I haven't been able to discover much about the writing of this tale.

Like the previous Pons books, it was published by Derleth's own Mycroft and Moran. Three-thousand-five-hundred copies were produced, which was five-hundred more than *The Chronicles* (1965), and quite a bit more than the two-thousand copies each of the books before that. Curiously, the cover of this slim volume didn't feature any atmospheric illustrations of Pons or Parker. Rather, the dust-jacket is completely white, and the front of the book is a simplified map of the story's setting, Frome, located in Somerset in England's West Country.

When I first read *Mr. Fairlie's Final Journey* as a teenager, in the Pinnacle paperback edition, I recall that Pons and Parker are clearly themselves. There are no unusual character deviations. This is to be expected, as Derleth had been writing about them for decades by this point. In addition to being written late in Derleth's life, the story is also one of the latest Pons adventures to be presented chronologically. It takes place in September 1938, and it refers to another recent adventure, "The Orient Express", which occurred just weeks before. (This adventure, published in the subsequent posthumous volume, *The Chronicles of Solar Pons*, is not to be confused with the famous Hercule Poirot adventure which occurred in 1932. But perhaps the fellow with the amazing mustache who crosses Pons and Parker's path while on the train might be...?)

Only one other story from the Pontine Canon occurs chronologically after this one, "The Golden Bracelet", also contained in *The Chronicles* and set in July 1939. These stories are at the very end of the twenty-year period (1919-1939) that includes the "official" Pontine Canon from Parker's Literary Agent. Pons is fifty-eight years old during *Mr. Fairlie's Final Journey*, and Parker is sixty – and yet, there is no diminution in either of their abilities.

I've read this book a number of times. During many earlier readings, my imagination created Frome in my head as Pons and Parker carried out their investigations. Gradually I began to read Pons (and Holmes) while referring to maps, and this pinned things down and made them more real in my head. For this re-reading, during the preparation of this volume for publication, I made use of Google Street View and was amazed. Locations in Frome that were visited by Pons and Parker are still there, and one can see the streets that they walked and the hotel where they stayed. Some sites have changed a bit since 1938, and for a few others one might need to make a few assumptions, but I recommend doing a little Google Map research while reading this book. It will really add an amazing and different aspect to the story.

Something else to consider while reading it is making a chart of the families involved in the story. I must admit that, even having read it multiple times, I still have to make an extra effort to keep track of the connections between many of the similarly named children and which from which branch of the family that they come. When I re-read this book in college in the early 1980's, I made a small card with the family relations diagrammed, and it's still tucked into my Pinnacle paperback copy. I considered constructing such a chart for this volume, but in the end I rejected that notion, in favor of presenting it as

Derleth intended – letting the reader keep track of these people for themselves, just as Pons and Parker had to do in 1938.

Mr. Fairlie's Final Journey was the last Pons adventure published in book form during Derleth's lifetime. Before he passed away in 1971, he continued to write stories, some for magazines, that would eventually be collected in *The Chronicles*. Additionally, he provided some other Parker-narrated adventures in the Praed Street Irregulars Newsletter, *The Pontine Dossier* and also in his slim volume A *Praed Street Dossier* (1968). (These have been collected in *The Apocrypha of Solar Pons.*)

For those meeting him for the first time, Pons is very much like Holmes. He solves crimes by using ratiocination and deduction. He plays the violin, smokes pipes, and lounges around his rooms in dressing gowns, as well as occasionally conducting chemical experiments there. His brother, Bancroft Pons, is an important fixture in the British Government, rather like Sherlock Holmes's brother, Mycroft. His landlady is Mrs. Johnson, and his closest contact at Scotland Yard is Inspector Jamison. And his friend and biographer, in the mold of Dr. John H. Watson, is Dr. Lyndon Parker.

While most of Holmes's Canonically-recorded adventures stretch from the 1870's until his retirement to Sussex in 1903, Pons operates in the post-World War I-era, with his cases extending from when he and Dr. Parker meet in 1919, after Parker has returned to England following his war service, to 1939, just before the beginning of World War II. Pons had also served in the War, in cryptography, and when the two meet, Parker is disillusioned at the England to which he has returned. However, this is quickly subsumed as the doctor's interest in his new flatmate and friend grows when he joins Pons on a series of cases that he later records.

For too long, the Solar Pons adventures have been too difficult to obtain. Fortunately, these new editions will change that. Here's how that came about.

In the late 1970's, I had been a Sherlockian for just a few years, having found Mr. Holmes in 1975. Those were the early days of the Sherlockian Golden Age that began with the publication of Nicholas Meyer's *The Seven-Per-Cent Solution* in 1974, and has continued to the present. Meyer reminded people that there were *other* manuscripts by Dr. Watson out there, still waiting to be found – hidden in attics, filed away in libraries, or suppressed by paranoid individuals for a plethora of reasons. These began to be discovered, one by one. Meyer himself subsequently published the amazing *The West End Horror* (1976), along with an explanation as to how the appearance of the first book had led to the second. Other Sherlockian adventures continued to surface – *Hellbirds* by Austin Mitchelson and Nicholas Utechin (1976), *Sherlock Holmes and the Golden Bird* by Frank Thomas (1979), and *Enter the Lion* by Sean Wright and Michael Hodel (1979), to name just a very few. The Great Sherlockian Tapestry, after consisting of mainly just sixty main fibers for so long, was about to get much heavier.

And around that time, someone with great wisdom realized that Solar Pons should be a part of that.

Pinnacle Books began reprinting the Pons adventures in late 1974, just months after the July publication date of *The Seven-Per-Cent Solution.* In the world of book publication, at least in those days when things took forever, Pinnacle certainly didn't jump on the bandwagon at the last minute to get the books immediately into print, after seeing how popular both *The Seven-Per-Cent Solution* and Sherlock Holmes were. Rather, the re-publication of the Pons books must have been planned for quite a while, and it was just their great good luck that their

Pons editions appeared right around the same time as Meyer's *The Seven-Per-Cent Solution.* Planning and setup would have required a great deal of planning and effort, as would designing the distinctive "Solar Pons" logo that they would use on both their Pons books, and later on Sherlock Holmes books by Frank Thomas. And most of all, they would have needed time to solicit the wonderful cover paintings of Solar Pons and Dr. Parker.

It was these paintings that drew me into the world of Solar Pons.

Living in a small town in eastern Tennessee, finding things related to Sherlock Holmes in the latter 1970's was difficult. My hometown had both a new and used bookstore, and I regularly scoured them looking for new titles. Strangely, several of my most treasured Sherlockian books from these years were found – not in the bookstores – but on rotating paperback racks at a local drugstore. However, it was at the new bookstore, a few weeks before my fourteenth birthday, that I happened to notice seven books lined up in a row, all featuring a man wearing an Inverness and a deerstalker.

I grabbed them, thinking I'd found a Holmesian motherlode. Instead, I saw that they were about... *Solar Pons?*

I had a limited amount of Sherlockian research material then, and I don't recall if I found anything about Mr. Pons to explain why he dressed like Sherlock Holmes. (I had quite forgotten then, although it came back to me later, that I'd first read a Pons story back in 1973 – before I'd ever truly encountered Sherlock Holmes. That story, "The Grice-Paterson Curse", was contained in an Alfred Hitchcock children's mystery anthology, and I credit how much I enjoyed it then with shaping my brain to be so appreciative when I first read about Holmes a couple of years later, in 1975. That one is still my favorite Pons story to this day.)

Those seven books haunted me, and I somehow managed to hint strongly enough to my parents about it that they ended up being birthday gifts a few weeks later – along with some other cool Holmes books. And so I started reading the Pontine Canon, as it's called – the first of countless times that I've been through it. (It's strange what the brain records. I vividly remember reading and re-reading those books frequently in an algebra class throughout that year – particularly one story on one certain day, "The Man With the Broken Face". I was lost and behind for a lot of that year in that class, and instead of trying to catch up, I'd pull out a Pons book, which felt much more comfortable. The teacher, who later went on to be beloved and award-winning for some reason that escapes me, knew what I was doing and did nothing to pull me back. Pfui on her! But I did like reading about Pons.)

As time went on, I discovered additional Pinnacle paperbacks, featuring new Pons stories by British horror author Basil Copper. It was great to have more Pons adventures, but his weren't quite the same. Around the time I started college, I discovered that Copper had edited a complete *Omnibus* of the original Pons stories, and it was the first grown-up purchase that I made with my first real paycheck. (Many thanks to Otto Penzler and The Mysterious Bookshop!) I was thrilled to see that the stories had been arranged in chronological order, which appealed to me. (That kind of thing still does.) Little did I realize then that Copper's editing had been so controversial within the Pons community.

For it turned out that Copper had taken it upon himself to make a number of unjustified changes. For instance, he altered a lot of Derleth's spellings in the *Omnibus* edition from American to British, causing some people to become rather upset. I wasn't too vexed by that, however, as I was there for the stories.

Copper continued to write new Pons stories of his own, published in various editions. I snapped those up, too, very happy to have new visits to 7B Praed Street. Over the years, I noted with some curiosity that Copper's books came to take on a certain implied and vague aspect – just a whiff, just a tinge – that Pons was *his* and not Derleth's.

Meanwhile, the Battered Silicon Dispatch Box published several "lost" Pons items, and also a new and massive set of the complete stories, *The Original Text Solar Pons* (2000), restoring Derleth's original intentions. It was in this book that I read Peter Ruber's extensive essay explaining Copper's changes in greater depth, and the reaction to them within the Ponsian community. However, Ruber didn't mention what I found to be Copper's even more egregious sin. But first a little background...

Over the years, there have been various editions of the Pons books – the originals published by Derleth's Mycroft & Moran imprint, the Pinnacle paperbacks, the Copper *Omnibus*, and the Battered Silicon Dispatch Box *Original Text Omnibus*. (There has also been an incomplete set of a few titles from British publisher Robson Books, Ltd.) Only a few thousand of the original Mycroft & Moran books were ever printed, and for decades, Pons was only known to a loyal group of Sherlockian enthusiasts by way of these very limited volumes. The Pinnacle books made Pons available to a whole generation of 1970's Sherlockians – such as me – that would have never had a chance to meet him otherwise if he'd only remained in the hard-to-find original editions.

As time has passed, however, even these Pinnacle books have become rare and quite expensive. For modern readers who have heard of Pons and are interested in learning more about him, or for those of us who are Pons enthusiasts who wish to introduce him to the larger world, it's been quite difficult, as all editions of his adventures are now quite rare and expensive, unless one is stumbled upon by accident. The Mycroft & Moran books can be purchased online, usually for a substantial investment of money, and the Copper and Battered Silicon Dispatch Box *Omnibi* were always expensive and hard to come by, and now it's only worse. Finally, with these new publications, the Solar Pons books will be available for everyone in easily found and affordable editions. With this, it's hoped that a new wave of Pons interest will spread, particularly within the Sherlockian community which will so appreciate him.

In 2014, my friend and Pons Scholar Bob Byrne floated the idea of having an issue of his online journal, *The Solar Pons Gazette*, contain new Pons stories. Having already written some Sherlock Holmes adventures, I was intrigued, and sat down and wrote a Pons tale – possibly almost as fast as Derleth had written his first Pons story in 1928. It was so much fun that I quickly wrote two more. After that, I pestered Bob for a while, saying that he should explore having the stories published in a real book. (I choose real books every time – none of those ephemeral e-blip books that can disappear in a blink for me!) When that didn't happen, I became more ambitious. Bob put me in touch with Tracy Heron of The August Derleth Society, and he in turn told me how to reach Danielle Hackett, August Derleth's granddaughter. I made my case to be allowed to write a new collection of Pons stories, as authorized by the Estate, and amazingly, I received permission. I introduced Danielle (in this modern email way of meeting people) to Derick Belanger of Belanger Books, and then set about writing some more stories, enough to make a whole book. Amazingly, the first new authorized Pons book in decades, *The Papers of Solar Pons*, was published in 2017.

But that started me thinking...

Realizing that this new book had the possibility to reawaken interest in Pons, or spread the word to those who didn't know about him, I wondered if the original volumes could be reprinted. After all, interest in Sherlock Holmes around the world is at an all-time high, getting the word out by way of the internet has never been easier, and shifts in the publishing paradigm mean that the old ways of grinding through the process for several years before a book appears no longer apply.

The Derleth Estate was very happy with the plan. Now came the hard part.

Being fully aware of the controversy surrounding Copper's *Omnibus* edition, it was evident that that new editions had to be from Derleth's original Mycroft & Moran volumes – for after all, he had edited and approved of those himself. Thankfully, modern technology allows for these books to be converted to modern electronic files with only a moderate amount of pain and toil.

I had several friends, upon hearing of this project, who very graciously offered to help me to "re-type" the original books. I can assure you that, if these books had needed to be re-typed from scratch, there would have been no new editions – at least not as provided by me. Instead, I took a copy of each of the original Mycroft & Moran Pons books, of which I am a very happy and proud owner, and scanned them, converting them all into electronic files. So far so good – that only took several hours of standing at a copy machine, flipping the pages of the books one at a time, and hitting the green button. (And sometimes re-doing it if a scanned page had a gremlin or two.)

After that, I used a text conversion software to turn the scans into a Word document. That raw text then had to be converted into another, more easily fixed, Word document. Then came the actual fixing. Early on, it was decided to try and make the new editions look as much like the originals as possible. Therefore, many inconsistent things that niggled me as an editor-type remain in the finished product, because they were that way in the originals. For instance, Derleth's punctuation improved quite a bit from his early books to the latter – but it was very tempting to start fixing his punctuation in the earlier books. If you see something that looks not-quite-right, chances are it was that way in the original books.

There were times that a letter or a note, as quoted in a story, would be indented, while on other occasions it would simply be a part of the paragraph. I wanted to set up all of those letters and notes in a unified way throughout the various books, but instead I kept them as they had appeared in the original editions, no matter how much the style varied from story to story. Finally, some of the racial stereotyping from those stories would not be written that way today. However, these are historical documents of sorts, and as such, they are presented as written, with the understanding that times have changed, and hopefully we have a greater awareness now than before.

Since the early 1980's, whenever I've re-read the Pons stories – and I've done so many times – it's been by way of the Copper *Omnibus* editions. I enjoyed having them all in one place in two matching handsome and heavy books, and I was very pleased that they were rearranged for reading in chronological order. The fixing of British-versus-American spelling didn't bother me a bit. This time, as part of the process to fix up the converted-to-text files, I was reading the stories as they had originally appeared, in the order that they had been published in the original volumes. I hadn't done it that way for years. The conversion process captures everything, and that means some items do have to be corrected. For instance, when setting up for printing, original books from the old days often *split* words at the end of a line with hyphens, whereas modern computer programs *wrap* the text, allowing for hyphens to be ignored. When converting the text of the original books, the program picked up every one of those end-of-line hyphens and split words, and they all had to be found and removed. Likewise, the text-conversion program ignores words that are italicized in the original, and these each have to be relocated and re-italicized. (However, in some cases, Derleth himself was inconsistent, italicizing a word, such as a book title or the name of a ship, at one point in a story, and not at a later point. That had to be verified too.)

I have long been a chronologicist, organizing all of the thousands of traditional Sherlock Holmes stories that I've collected and read into a massive Holmes Chronology, breaking various adventures (book, story, chapter, and paragraph) down into year, month, day, and even hour to form a *complete* life of Holmes, from birth to death, covering both the Holmes Canon and traditional pastiches. It was inevitable that I would do the same with Pons. For several decades, I've had a satisfying Pons Chronology as well, based on research by various individuals, and largely on Copper's arrangement of the stories within his *Omnibus* – with a few disagreements. By re-reading the original stories in their original form, for the first time in years, I realized that, in addition to changing spelling, Copper had committed – as referred to earlier – a far bigger sin.

I discovered as I re-read the original stories for this project that a number of them weren't matching up with my long-established Pons Chronology, based a great deal upon Copper's arrangement in his *Omnibus*. Some of the stories from the originals would give a specific date that would be a whole decade different from where I had placed the story in my own chronology. A quick check against Copper's *Omnibus* revealed that he had actually changed these dates in his revisions, sometimes shifting from the 1920's to the 1930's, a whole decade, in order to place the story where he thought that it ought to go. Worse, he sometimes eliminated a whole sentence from an original story if it contradicted his placement of that story within his *Omnibus*.

As a chronologist, I was horrified and sickened. This affront wasn't mentioned in Ruber's 2000 essay explaining why Ponsians were irritated with Copper. I can't believe that this wasn't noticed before.

There has always been ample material for the chronologist with the Pons books, even without these changes. Granted, the original versions, as written, open up a lot of problems and contradictions about when various stories occur that Copper smoothed out – apparently without anyone noticing. For this reason, and many others, I'm very glad and proud that the original Solar Pons adventures, as originally published by Derleth, are being presented here in these new volumes for a new generation.

David Marcum
"The Obrisset Snuffbox", PSI
(excerpted from the Belanger edition reissues)

Terror Over London

I

"IF YOU SEE A HUNCHBACK..."

It is fortunate, I think, that what powers there are endowed me with a generous store of patience. If ever a man lived to try another's patience, that man is my friend, Mr. Solar Pons, the private inquiry agent, whose modest rooms at Number Seven, Praed Street, have long since become famous in the most out of the way places in the world.

Yet I am happy to be able to call him my friend, paradoxically enough. I know that he likes to exercise mentally on me, and I know that when he sometimes contemptuously refers to me as a "scribbler, even if a medical scribbler," he nevertheless has a considerable respect for the craft of writing. And his idiosyncrasies are more likeable than not.

Though he objects to being called a private inquiry agent or a detective, calling himself simply an observer of human beings and their habits, he nevertheless is in my opinion a first-rate detective. Indeed, I have gone so far as to say publicly in print that only the late Sherlock Holmes, whom Solar Pons knew, respected, and imitated, exceeded Pons in the art of deduction and detection. Pons is too fond of deprecating himself and his abilities, but he does not lack self-confidence, and seldom leaves an opening for his opinions to be challenged.

Solar Pons tries my patience in many ways, but in none worse than managing somehow to find some use for me whenever I have occasion to leave London, and sending posthaste to bring me back. There is a good deal of humour in the oft-repeated spectacle of Pons solemnly assuring me, "Parker, I strongly urge you to rest away from London for a few days," and even going so far as to remind me with all gravity that I have not had a regular vacation from my practice for years, seemingly forgetting that the reason in every consecutive year was none other than the interference, certainly not unwelcome, I must honestly admit, of Mr. Solar Pons.

In January of a year that must remain undesignated for reasons of State, I had gone to Madrid, had spent a week there, and had started for Paris on the Sud Express. My train crawled lazily out of the Spanish capital and northward toward the French frontier. I sat in a cramped space, suffering vaguely from the atmosphere, which seemed to me oppressive, and listening half-heartedly to the excited buzz of Spanish which came from all around me.

Occasionally I looked up at an especially vehement outburst of invective, which came invariably from a group of Spanish students not far behind me; when I had entered the *wagon-lit*, they had been condemning their government, and now they had managed somehow to get up to Austria, and half of them were supporting the policies of the late Monsignor Seipel, who was then in power, while the other half were denouncing them, none of them quite knowing anything about the theory of government, if their conversation could be looked upon as any index.

There was no one in the carriage who might be spoken to, and I, as the only Englishman, felt isolated and alone, though I reflected how much worse it would be if I could not understand Spanish. The Spanish landscape, despite what certain post-war American modernists have tried to make it in fiction, is not particularly breathtaking, especially from the windows of the Sud Express. And I had nothing to read, a stupid oversight on my part bringing this about. I dozed a little, but the movement of the train was not conducive to dozing.

Then, suddenly, I found myself wide awake. The Express had jolted to a standstill, and on all sides of me flew queries – "What is it? We don't stop here – we aren't supposed to stop here." Some inquiring eye must have caught sight of the reason for our stop, for suddenly everyone was saying, "It's the government – an order from the government!" And every occupant of the carriage looked suspiciously at his neighbor, as if one of the little group would suddenly emerge as a revolutionary fleeing justice.

I looked disinterestedly out of the carriage, and immediately my eye fell upon a tall gentleman in military costume standing at some distance down the track; indeed, I could not help seeing him at once, for no sooner had I popped my head out of the carriage, when he raised his arm, pointed at me, and gave a sharp command, at which two soldier-attendants immediately came forward at a run.

"Are you the *Señor* Parker?" one of them asked, upon coming abreast.

"I am Dr. Parker," I replied in Spanish, "but there must be some mistake. I am from London, and I do not know anyone here..."

The soldier, however, said no more. He motioned to his superior, and this officer now came forward, bowed with elaborate politeness, and addressed me.

"Dr. Parker?"

I admitted my identity a second time.

"Dr. C. L. Parker, of Seven, Praed Street, London?"

"Quite right," I replied.

"Will you step from the Express, Dr. Parker?"

"But surely the officer realizes – " I began to protest.

He looked at me sternly, and I ended rather lamely by muttering something about being an Englishman and certainly I had some rights; would he like to see my passport and visa?

I stepped from the carriage and confronted the military gentleman. My thoughts were very confused and troubled; I began to think that there had been another revolution, and that somehow I had got mixed up in the business. As Solar Pons has often pointed out, I am not of very much use in any sort of crisis because something doesn't function properly.

"Dr. Parker has baggage?" asked the officer.

"A small bag, that is all," I said.

"In the carriage, yes?"

I nodded.

The officer gave a command, and immediately a soldier entered the *wagon-lit*. The officer gazed vaguely off into the distance and appeared to be regarding some evening clouds on the horizon with unnecessary interest.

Presently the soldier emerged from the carriage, carrying my bag.

"That is your bag, Dr. Parker?" asked the officer.

"Yes," I answered.

"Very good."

Then, to my shocked surprise, the officer stepped back and gave the signal for the Express to proceed. Into my ears from the carriage I had just quitted came a chorus of disconcerted voices – "The English gentleman!" in a voice which might have added, "Who would have thought it!", and a hissing sound vaguely resembling "Government!" uttered with great scorn, at which I knew that the Spanish students would spend the next hour unanimously condemning the government over and over again.

The movement of the Express startled me into protest. "Look here," I said angrily, "I'm an English citizen, and I can assume you that this unwarranted action will give you no end of trouble." That is as far as I managed to get.

The officer smiled, bowed again, and with a single graceful movement reached into his inner pocket and handed me a cablegram. "We missed you in Madrid," he said. "Very sorry that this inconvenience was necessary."

For an instant I looked blank, and then the simple solution of the mystery burst upon me. My friend Solar Pons had once again found some use for me. I smiled, ungraciously I am sure, tore open the envelope, and read:

> BEARER IS VALLEVIA SPANISH GOVERNMENT OPERATIVE STOP TRUST YOURSELF TO HIM UTTERLY HAS BEEN KEEPING YOU UNDER HIS EYE FOR DAYS STOP YOU ARE TO BRING PAPERS TO ME AT ONCE – PONS

I looked up at Vallevia.

"Ah, Dr. Parker is assured," he said blandly, and he smiled, with a twinkle in his eye.

Somewhat disgruntled, I replied, "Quite. But is there not some mistake – if I am to bring the papers, this sending away the Express, surely..."

"Softly, Dr. Parker, softly. These papers are too important to travel so slowly." As Vallevia spoke, he tapped his breast significantly.

"Of course," I said, immediately disconcerted. Inwardly I blasted Pons for placing me in such an awkward position.

"You must go to London faster than the Express could get you to Paris," continued Vallevia. Then, with a quick nod, he indicated the twilight beyond me.

I turned and looked. In the soft dusk I saw outlined an aeroplane about which soldiers were standing. On its wings, strong in the twilight, were the insignia of Spain, marking this a government plane.

"But surely, I'm not to fly?" I protested.

Vallevia made a deprecating gesture with his hands. "And why not, Doctor Parker?" he asked. "You forget that Mr. Pons himself wishes you to travel swiftly. By morning you must be in London, at Praed Street – indeed, you must be with Mr. Solar Pons himself."

I nodded stupidly, even while realizing that since I knew nothing beyond the contents of Pons' cablegram and a few vague hints about "papers", I nodded in vain.

"But," I said, "surely something so important could be flashed to him in code, couldn't it?"

"Not this, Dr. Parker," replied Vallevia.

At this point I responded to Vallevia's gentle pressure on my arm and allowed him to urge me toward the aeroplane, where, when we arrived at its side, he took from his tight-fitting jacket the mysterious papers and passed them to me with a curt, "Here are the papers."

I took them, peered at them in vain, and then put them into my coat pocket, likewise on the inside in a pocket with a flap that could be buttoned – one certain way to prevent ordinary pickpocketing, as Solar Pons had years ago pointed out. Vallevia looked at me significantly, nodded curtly, and stepped toward the pilot of the plane to give him rapid directions. Then he returned to my side with the evident intention of urging me into the machine and seeing me off.

"Really, my dear sir," I said then, "I should like to know something of these papers. May I read them – in case something should happen to me?"

"Nothing must happen to you, Dr. Parker," said the officer in a vibrant voice. "You must be very careful, and not once may you touch those papers. They are vital – how vital we cannot yet know."

"You need have no fear," I replied.

"That is good," he said shortly. "When you come to Croydon in the morning, you must be very vary careful. It is possible that even now they know."

I jerked my head up. *They*? This is all like a penny dreadful, I thought, I looked at the officer, probably as I should have looked at a man who had suddenly turned out to be a violent lunatic. I swallowed.

"And do not stop for breakfast – nor indeed for anything. You may be followed from Croydon."

"How shall I know?" I asked.

"If you suspect anyone, lose him if you can," replied Vallevia. Then his eyebrows pressed downward in a grim frown. "But if you see a hunchback – then run – run for your life, Dr. Parker!"

Before I could say another word, I was shut in the aeroplane; Vallevia gave the signal to start, the motor roared, and the machine sped forward over the ground and up into the darkening night. Northward we went, and in a few moments, looking from the machine, I saw, far below to my right, the moving lights of the Sud Express, and I wished with all my heart that I might still be there, safe in the *wagon-lit*.

Vallevia's last sinister words drummed with ever increasing insistence in my mind – "If you see a hunchback – run for your life!"

II

AT THE FOREIGN OFFICE

We reached Croydon Aerodrome at dawn, and I took a taxicab for Praed Street at once. My fears of a sinister hunchback came to nothing, for nowhere was there a figure who could even vaguely correspond to such a definition. Nor, to my vast relief, could I discover anyone who seemed even remotely interested in my person. "Go very fast," I had said to the driver, and indeed he was doing so. We literally flew through the outlying districts of London, and in a short time me were speeding up Edgware Road. We rounded the corner of Praed Street and came to a grinding stop before Number Seven.

I put one tired foot out of the taxicab and then the other. I reached in for my bag, and was about to turn around, when suddenly the door of Number Seven flew violently open and revealed the spectacle of Solar Pons catapulting from the house down the outer steps. He came flying toward me, having seen the taxicab no doubt from our rooms.

"Back in, back in," he shouted.

I stood stupidly staring at him – what a queer figure he made, half-dressed, his dressing-gown slung loosely around him. But I had little time to reflect upon his appearance, for he came at me with the evident intention of tumbling me into the cab unless I went immediately of my own volition. Back I went, with Pons on my heels. As he slammed the door behind him he shouted to the driver, "To the Foreign Office!" and sat back in his seat, snorting angrily.

"This is madness," he muttered, "utter madness." Turning to me, he interjected, "I'm glad to see you back, Parker," he interjected, and stared out the window with deep concentration. "What can have happened?"

"I think," I put in, "that I ought to ask you that. What can have happened to send you to the Foreign Office in this condition?"

"Have you seen this morning's papers? No? I thought not. Well, look at this."

Then for the first time I noticed that he was carrying a paper in his hand; this he now thrust forward at me. It was folded, and the article he obviously intended me to read was uppermost.

"MYSTERIOUS INDIVIDUAL TERRORIZES CITY," I said. "Who is the Deuce of Clubs? It has just reached the press that in the recent murders of Lord Cantlemere and Sir Harry Mackenzie, a mysterious clue was found; this took the shape of an ordinary playing card, the deuce of clubs, and is thought to be the sign of an individual who is seeking to terrorize the city. It is certain that government officials and many C.I.D. men are utterly baffled by the depredations of this individual. Another question which seems to have arisen in connection with this matter revolves about the identity of a mysterious hunchback."

I looked again at the last line, and then up at Pons. "Hunchback," I repeated, as I handed the paper back to Pons, who took it without a word. "What is this business about a hunchback?" I demanded.

Pons looked at me in silence for a moment. Then he chuckled dryly, spread his hands deprecatingly, and said, "I wish we knew Parker." That was all.

The taxicab drew up before the Foreign Office. Pons threw a note at the driver, and ran toward the building. Before it stood a nervous little man who came forward at the sight of Pons.

"Good Heavens, Mr. Pons," he said. "Try to calm his Lordship. He is pacing the floor in there like a madman."

"Very well," said Pons. "I shall do what I can. He has seen the papers, then?"

"Yes, yes," answered the little man, who was clearly some dignitary from the Office, "and he is behaving like a madman. Discharging and recalling, and discharging again. It is quite frightful."

Without a further word, Pons plunged into the building. I followed, docilely enough. Without ceremony, we went forward until we approached a room from which came the sound of angry voices raised in dispute. Pons threw open the door and entered, the paper in his hand.

"Pons!" exclaimed the tall gentleman in the center of the room. "Pons! And you have seen the paper, too!"

His Lordship put on his pince-nez, took them off, rubbed them nervously with a cloth from his desk, and put them back on. Then he began to pace the floor again and said, "Well, well, well?" in a voice which might have made any of the remaining gentlemen in the room tremble. Pons said nothing, but strode forward into the room, and took up his stand next to the table, fixing his eyes on the Foreign Minister, waiting patiently for him to stop his pacing. This he presently did, coming to a stand before Pons and looking at my friend expectantly.

The two other gentlemen in the room were High Commissioner Steele of Scotland Yard, and Sir Landon Hatry, Secretary to the Foreign Office. They looked at Pons expectantly, thinking perhaps that the mere presence of Pons should immediately soothe.

"Well, gentlemen, well," said the Foreign Minister, and would have begun his futile pacing again, had not Pons stopped him.

"How did this get out?" he asked, tapping the paper.

His Lordship threw up his hands. "Get out?" he snapped. "If someone would only tell me. How did it?"

"You do not know," said Pons. "Then you have done nothing, I daresay?"

"Done nothing?" repeated the Foreign Minister. "I have discharged three of my men – those who have to deal with the press. I have given orders that absolutely no news from this Office is to reach print until given my personal approval. What else can I do?"

"I think it would be well to recall the men you have discharged," said Pons.

Lord Norton stopped and stared at Pons. "Recall them?" he snapped. "What good will that do? I've recalled them once, and discharged them again. Why, to look at them makes me ill. Such a batch of men. Inefficient – I flatter them."

"Your Lordship has sent himself into a needless distemper," said Pons icily. "I suggest that you recall the men immediately! Explain to them that some error has been made. Then discover who it was that gave out the information."

"Very well," said the Lordship, and banged out of the room.

"The men are still here," interposed Sir Landon Hatry. "His Lordship does this quite often."

"Good Lord!" exclaimed High Commissioner Steele. "It would drive me mad to listen to him for very long."

"Very unfortunate, this," said Sir Landon, and shook his head dolefully.

"Very," assented Pons, "but it could have been much worse. The papers are evidently not yet aware that this matter is internationally significant; that is gratifying. They have put the gang on guard here in London; that is all. But even that is a serious break to have been made."

The High Commissioner nodded glumly, and at the same moment the Foreign Minister burst into the room.

"I have found the wretch, gentlemen!" he exclaimed. "He is being detained for your questioning, Mr. Pons, but I daresay it will be useless; the affair appears to have been an accident after all."

"Very well," said Pons.

"But it is maddening that this should have got out – utterly maddening. It is gratifying that the papers do not suspect a fraction of this terrible crime ring. But it is maddening... maddening..." Then suddenly the Foreign Minister stopped speaking. He had moved around the desk, at which he had evidently not yet been that morning, and had picked up a packet of papers which lay there. As he picked them up, something fell from the packet and fluttered to the desk. It lay there for a moment before his Lordship's eye caught it.

"My God!" exclaimed his Lordship, and sat down suddenly in his chair. "What is it?" asked the Secretary in evident alarm.

In answer, Lord Norton, British Foreign Minister, reached forward and took between his finger and thumb the object which had come from between his private papers. He held it up for all of us to see.

It was an ordinary playing card – the Deuce of Clubs!

III

PONS EXPLAINS

At our rooms in Praed Street once more, Pons at last consented to answer my repeated questions. What was this thing that hung over London? What was this business about the Deuce of Clubs? And who was the hunchback?

"As to the hunchback," said Pons, "I only wish we knew, as I said before. He seems to be an important part of the business, but it is difficult to say just where he fits.

"But let me start from the bottom of the matter. We are after the directing genius and aides of an international criminal organization known as the Clubs. Their object seems to be a gigantic system of espionage, and we know that they will stop at nothing to accomplish their designs.

"Two months ago, the first intimation of the organization crept into England. Scotland Yard received a wire from the German Government Secret Service requesting England to be on the lookout for a gentleman known as Dr. Heinrich von Storck. A full description of the gentleman was given, but the matter was given only routine significance. A week passed, and another wire came from Germany. This time it came through the Foreign Office, and its content made officials look upon the search for Dr. von Storck with more attention. Germany hinted at the espionage system we now know to exist, and the search for the mysterious Herr Doktor was redoubled. I daresay that I need not state that he has not been found to date. At the same time, the Foreign Office found itself literally swamped with code wires from Spain, France, Austria, Italy – from almost all the Continental countries. Their content was in each case the same – Did the Foreign Office know of The Clubs?

"The Foreign Office began to investigate more actively. Full details were demanded from all Continental countries. In time, these came. It appeared that this organization was known as The Clubs; that its leader was the Deuce of Clubs; that its principle aides were in ranking order the Deuce, the Ace, the Trey, and King, the Knave, the Queen and so on, following the playing card system. Their sign seems to be the deuce; when this is found, it is equivalent of a warning. We have since verified all these data; the head of this organization communicates with his aides through the Agony column of the *Times*. He uses a variable code, which we have difficulty in deciphering. Twice we have found messages. The first, when decoded, read: *'Knave: Cantlemere: Deuce'* – just that; the second, *'Knave: Mackenzie: Deuce.'*

"The significance of these communications becomes apparent when you glance back over the events of the last months. On the day that you left for the Continent, I was called into the case; on the same day, Lord Cantlemere announced that he was working on a very important discovery relative to the Clubs. This was, of course, a private announcement, for the press was strictly muzzled – the outburst of this morning is the first that has leaked to the public. On the following day the first message appeared in the Agony column; late that night Lord Cantlemere was found dead in his library. He had been stabbed, and his papers had been taken from his desk. Before him, on the desk, we found the first deuce of clubs. Lord Cantlemere's secretary remembered that his Lordship had mentioned a suspicious hunchback who appeared to be skulking about the premises. From that data we can deduce a number of pertinent facts. The message, for instance, can be taken to mean roughly, 'Lord Cantlemere is dangerous and must be removed. The Knave is to do it.' Is the hunchback, then the Knave? It seems so, for the case of Sir Harry Mackenzie almost parallels the Cantlemere murder. Sir Harry, too, had found something, and indiscreetly announced his discoveries. The Agony column again functioned, the hunchback was seen, and Sir Harry was found dead, the deuce of clubs clutched in his hand.

"The whole affair reads like a sixpenny novel. If it were not for the dubious activity of a certain foreign power, I should be inclined to think that the matter is somebody's ghastly joke. But it has gone too far. This morning I first came to realize how far-reaching the influence of the Clubs really is; it is incomprehensible that the deuce could have been found in Lord Norton's private papers – yet it was there. And that can mean only one thing – someone on the inside; someone important, for it was he who reported the announcements of Lord Cantlemere and Sir Harry Mackenzie.

"It is significant that an important piece of information comes from Tokyo. Chief activities thus far seem to have been in Vienna, Rome, Berlin, Paris, Madrid, and London. But Japan announces that trouble in Manchuria is definitely traced to the activity of the Clubs. Japan's intimation is patent: is Russia involved, or not? It is true that we have had no message from Leningrad, but that in itself means nothing. We have had no message from Washington, but there is not the slightest suggestion of American hands in this business. And I suspect that it will not be long before we hear from both of these countries. The Continental governments are thoroughly aroused. The murder of M. Raymond Ladoux in Paris has put the *Sûreté* on guard; the hunchback is known in France, in Spain, and in Germany. Italy and Austria have said nothing of the hunchback, though those countries have not escaped without atrocities.

"We cannot underrate the power of the Clubs. They have put countless gentlemen out of the way, simply because these gentlemen have received some hint of the gigantic activities of the organization. Nor do they stop at espionage. They are robbers on a grand scale, swindlers, murderers, grafters – what more, we can only guess. They have operated at Monaco, and swindled the establishment at Monte Carlo – an affair that has its distinctly ridiculous side. There is no need to go into more of their activities – it would take up hours. In England, thank God, they seem to be comparatively new."

"Well!" I exclaimed. "You have a task before you. How will you go about the business?"

"I want the Deuce of Clubs," said Pons, "and I am taking no chances of missing him. Certainly he is in London, for I have checked up on the Agony column and found that these messages were sent through the post, accompanied by a banknote in payment. They were postmarked England – Belgravia, in fact, which puts us in the puzzling position of wondering what our gentleman is doing down there. It is my personal opinion that the postmark is deliberately designed to puzzle us.

"I have seen Frick, and another man we can rely upon, Howells. These two will pick up information in Limehouse, Stepney, Soho, and Wapping. I have two men moving in the highest circles also. But that is not enough. I am calling in a very distinguished helper, whose assistance I value very highly."

"Do I know him?" I asked.

"It is a lady," said Pons softly. "Have you ever heard me speak of the Lady Ysola Warrender?"

"Never," I said.

"She is the daughter of the Earl of Leicester, and, though you may never before have heard of the fact, she is my first cousin."

"Pons!" I exclaimed, leaning forward. I understood at this moment from where Pons' influence in higher circles came.

"Quite so," returned Pons. "She is one of the finest ladies I know. She has, I regret to say, an intense admiration of my methods; unfortunately, this tends to befog her mind on occasion. I have done my best to cure her of it, but it is no use. You will find her an interesting lady, Parker. Her mother, now dead, was a fiery Spanish lady, and of the Earl, my uncle, – well, perhaps it is better to say nothing."

"If she is anything like you," I said, "I shall be most delighted to know her."

"Be relieved, my dear Parker," said Pons, chuckling. "She is nothing at all like me; I should be all sympathy for her if she were."

"Nonsense!" I exclaimed. "When will she come?"

Pons looked at his watch. "It is now eleven-fifteen; I asked her to come at eleven. It is the prerogative of a lady to be late, but I daresay that is her car which I hear below."

In a moment, the outer bell rang, and we could hear Mrs. Johnson shuffling toward the door.

IV

THE LADY YSOLA WARRENDER

The lady who entered the room on the heels of Mrs. Johnson stood for a moment in silence as the door closed behind her and Mrs. Johnson beat a hasty retreat. Then she threw back her heavy veil, and revealed features of amazing beauty. Her face was aquiline, and very dark. Certainly she looked more Spanish than English. Her eyes were very dark, and her hair a deep brunette. She came forward and extended her hand to Pons.

"Dear Lady Ysola," said Pons, and took her hand.

"Solar," murmured the Lady Ysola, and I felt an indescribable sensation of pleasure at the sound of her low, sweet voice.

"You must meet my dear friend and colleague, Dr. Parker," said Pons, and immediately turned in my direction. "Lady Ysola Warrender, Dr. Parker."

Lady Ysola flashed her dark eyes, and murmured, "I am glad to know any friend of Solar's."

"Thank you, Lady Ysola," I replied. I took her outstretched hand and touched it with my lips.

"*Un gallant*!" murmured the Lady Ysola, and smiled.

"It is not natural," said Solar Pons, and chuckled.

Lady Ysola laughed deep in her throat, and turned away from me to Pons. "Now what is it that causes you to send for me, Solar?"

"As usual, something very serious has come up, and I am sure that you can be of help – if you will," said Pons.

"If I will!" exclaimed Lady Ysola. "Only tell me what it is."

"Very well, I will explain all I know," said Pons, and went on to relate to the Lady Ysola those facts I had already heard from his lips.

Lady Ysola sat for a moment in silence after she had heard the remarkable affair of the Clubs. Then at last she looked up at Pons and spoke. "You think it is someone up with us who is directing this thing, Solar?"

"Very likely," said Pons. "But at the most, it is all mere conjecture. Let us suppose that it is; even at that we do not know who it can be. I am going to let this fall to you. You must discover who among you might fit certain descriptions that I will give you. Is there, for instance, among your newer acquaintances, a tall, handsome man, with iron grey hair, soft moustache – which might have been shaved away, bloodless face, thin hard lips, undershot jaw, brown eyes? He has a reputation as a wit, is well built, considered good looking, and has a slight wen on the left slope of his nose. Usually wears dark clothes. Perhaps an accent, though it is doubtful."

"How exciting," said Lady Ysola. "Who is he supposed to be?"

"We have reason to believe that he may be the Trey or King of the Clubs, or he may even be the enigmatic Deuce; he was last known in public life as Dr. Heinrich von Storck."

"I cannot identify the gentleman from your description, unfortunately," said Lady Ysola, "but that does not mean that he is not active in my circle."

"He moved with the best class in Berlin," supplemented Pons, "and we have reason to believe that here in London he still moves with the best people. We want to determine that through you, Ysola."

"I shall try. Is there anyone else?"

"Yes," replied Pons quickly. "A hunchback. But our description of him is very meagre. He is a comparatively small fellow, and wears a beard; we cannot even say whether or not the beard is assumed for disguise."

"I know a hunchback, yes," said Lady Ysola with some hesitation. "But he certainly cannot be your man. He is old Sir Ronald Duveen. Walks around all the time with crutches, and..."

"Cannot be your man," Pons cut in. "Our hunchback is exceedingly active."

For a moment the Lady Ysola was silent. "Do you know, Solar," she said at last, "I have often wondered about Sir Ronald. He is comparatively new, he has a habit of coming and going at all hours of the day or night. For instance, last night our bell rang, and father said it was either old Duveen or a telegram; of course, it was a telegram, but it illustrates what is thought of Sir Ronald. He is an odd sort of man, and more than once I have wondered whether his crutches were not adopted to command sympathy. I feel sure that it is not impossible."

Pons chuckled. "There is no need to manufacture criminals out of your friends, Ysola. There are unfortunately too many skulking among them as it is."

"If I were the lady of quality I should be, I would draw myself up and look at you with flashing eyes and exclaim 'Sir!' at that. Lucky for you, I'm not, Solar." She laughed. "But I'm going to look into Sir Ronald anyway."

"Do as you think best Ysola. How new is he?" asked Pons.

"Over a year, but he managed somehow to get a baronetcy, and appeared suddenly at one of father's house parties. From that time on, I've run into him all over."

"Hm!" mused Pons. "He may be worth looking into, at that. It is well to remember that the Clubs have been active for over two years, from all reports of Continental countries."

Lady Ysola nodded. "Is there anyone else?"

"Not at present, unfortunately. You might keep a speculative eye on Lord Norton."

"Good Heavens!" exclaimed Lady Ysola. "Surely he isn't in this too?"

"Only insofar as he has come under the eye of the Deuce of Clubs. The card he received this morning is a warning. I have instructed him not to attend any parties, and to accept a C.I.D. man as bodyguard. He is just rash enough to disregard my suggestions. In case he appears at any affair you attend, I want you to let me know at once. Call me on the telephone, if you can, and I'll come over personally to get him out."

"Very well," said Lady Ysola. "I'll do that."

"It would not be exactly the best idea if you were to call here too steadily. If something urgent comes up, then come by all means. But use the telephone, or most preferably the post, and if you write, use the code we've used before; it is still good, I hope."

"You are in no danger yourself?" queried Lady Ysola.

"Dear Lady Ysola," said Pons dryly. "I may be effectively disposed of before you have reached your home – but of course, I look for the best always."

Lady Ysola smiled grimly, and rose to go. "All jesting aside, Solar, do take care of yourself. I should hate to report to that beastly bore, Lord Norton. The prospect is anything but inviting, I must say." She grimaced.

Pons chuckled. "Well, we shall see, Ysola. I have no great wish to depart this earthly sphere, and I am sure the Clubs will have to invent something new to trap me; I am too familiar with the old devices."

Lady Ysola moved slowly toward the door. “Which reminds me,” she said suddenly, “that father has a house party on for tonight – it will be a great relief not to see Lord Norton there. I know he has received an invitation.”

“For his own good, I hope he stays with his bodyguard,” said Pons.

“He is such a bore, and to cap it, he has been paying undue attention to me of late. You know he is a widower.” She grimaced again.

“Well, I do hope Lord Norton does nothing indiscreet,” murmured Pons.

“Goodbye, Solar. And goodbye, Dr. Parker.”

The door closed behind the Lady Ysola Warrender.

V

THE KING OF CLUBS

"Now, let us look at the papers from Vallevia," said Pons. He took up the papers from the table, where he had put them at our return from the Foreign Office. Very carefully, he undid the package and brought to light a small group of papers. These he picked up and examined, one by one, but for the most part they evidently contained only detailed reports on information already wired to the Foreign Office.

One paper, however, claimed his attention. This was written in close script, and he read it twice before he turned to me. He tapped the paper in his hand.

"A letter from Vallevia," he said shortly. "It appears that they have taken one of the gang in Madrid. A search of his person revealed a black metal seal, club design, with a gold '*K*' stamped on it. Vallevia assumes that they have the King of Clubs, and I daresay they have."

"It is one elimination for us, then," I put in. "For if their man is the King of Clubs, then our 'von Storck' must be either the Trey or the Deuce."

"Of course, that does not follow, but it is most probable, I should say," agreed Pons.

"What else does Vallevia say?" I asked.

"The identity of the fellow has not been established, though he is unquestionably a Spaniard. He was engaged in the government service – a minor position, evidently under a false name. Vallevia plans to grill him and find out what he can about the organization."

"Well, that should yield something," I said.

"Let us hope so," returned Pons. "Thus far, however, he has refused to talk – has not said a word, according to Vallevia's letter."

"How did they manage to get him?"

"It was accidental, I take it. He was gathered in by the orders of the Dictator, together with a group of revolutionists. The metal club found on him was brought to the notice of Vallevia, and Vallevia acted immediately, taking the prisoner from the jurisdiction of the Dictator."

I nodded.

"This accident may yield nothing, of course," continued Pons, "and I am frankly quite skeptical. Certainly the individual at the head of the Clubs has prepared for just such a contingency, and the King will know what action to take. His silence is no doubt prearranged."

"There are ways of making the man speak, if it must be done," I put in.

"Oh, I daresay Vallevia could establish an inquisition if he chose, but it is unlikely that he will get anything from the fellow that way."

There was silence for a few moments.

"It seems to me," said Pons at last, "that there must be something definitely in view in London, since we know that at least three, and most probably four head Clubs are centering on the City. Personally, I doubt whether there are any more head Clubs in Madrid; I am sure, on the other hand, that the chief Continental capitals are still being occupied by them.

The presence of the Deuce in London suggests a definite plan of action."

"Do you suppose they know of the Post-Vanbrunt Transport plans?" I asked.

"Lord Norton has already suggested as much. In addition, there is the matter of the far more important Ritchie-Carroll Super Aeroplane; I have no doubt but that this is what they are after. Acting on my suggestion, the Foreign Office has constructed a flood of dummy plans; of these, two have disappeared, but the original plans remain intact."

"Had Vallevia any idea of what they were after in Madrid?" I asked.

"Yes," answered Pons at once. "It seems the government has recently made some important discoveries about war tanks, and it is supposed that this information attracted the Clubs to Madrid."

"And the other Continental countries?"

"Oh, there are various reasons. These people, you must remember, are not alone spies, but also swindlers and thieves of a most accomplished order. Whenever they are short of funds a robbery occurs, or a swindle is carried through. The embezzlement of a huge sum from the important German *Reichsbank* last month is laid to them. So is the Monte Carlo swindle I mentioned before. And there are many others.

"In Germany, important diplomatic communications are being zealously guarded. It is rumoured that several very sharp documents regarding the Ruhr occupation would severely strain relations between the allies of the late World War. In Austria Monsignor Seipel has resigned the Prime Ministry; it was at first supposed that the Clubs had moved, but I have it on good authority that Seipel has been promised the Hat after a reasonable period of quiet life. But I can make a shrewd guess about the activity of the Clubs in Austria; you have only to remember that the young Prince Otto von Hapsburg aspires to the throne, and that the Clubs can easily cause trouble between the Austrian government and the Hapsburgs. The same is true in France, with the Pretender, the Duc de Guise, aspiring toward the throne of the Bourbons. But again, this is speculation, and it is better to leave off."

"Then, at last, we can look upon the capture of the King of Clubs as a lucky accident."

Pons nodded. "I look forward to Vallevia's next communication with the keenest interest. What he can get out of the King may help us to put our hands upon the entire organization, or at least may cause a temporary disruption of the gang's plans."

With this, Pons leaned back in his chair and took up the other Vallevia papers. He had gone through two of them with the most assiduous care, when the doorbell rang. Pons and I looked up as Mrs. Johnson peered into the room, holding out to Pons a wire.

"Vallevia!" exclaimed Pons, and took the wire eagerly from Mrs. Johnson. He opened it hurriedly, read it, and looked at a corner of the ceiling with a perfectly impassive face.

"Get anything?" I asked.

He smiled. "Only what I might have known." He looked at the cablegram in his hand and read. "'King found murdered in prison. Nothing learned. Vallevia.'"

VI

LORD NORTON IS INDISCREET

Sir Richard Huckins, seventh Lord Norton, drew on his gloves meditatively, adjusted his cravat and scarf, and stepped from the long hall of his house upon the veranda. A shadow rose from beside the door and confronted the Foreign Minister.

"Constable Cotton, your Lordship. Your Lordship is not going out, I hope?"

"Why not?" asked Lord Norton sharply. "My good man, stick here and watch the house – it takes more than a playing card to scare me off."

"I am sorry, your Lordship. But I have my orders, sir. I am to keep you in sight."

"My orders are of more importance to you that those of either Mr. Steele or Mr. Pons."

"Your Lordship is mistaken, permit me. I take orders only from High Commissioner Steele. Mr. Solar Pons saw fit to suggest to Mr. Steele that I be detailed to watch you, and this I must do. I have a car at my service, and this will follow you wherever you go."

Lord Norton looked angrily down the street, where he could see a machine drawn up to the curb. The Foreign Minister was for the moment disconcerted.

"Very well," he assented, "you may see me to my car. I am going to an affair at the Earl of Leicester's. If it is necessary for you to come, I suppose I shall have to do with you."

"Very good, your Lordship."

"You may as well go in my car," added Lord Norton, and strode angrily off toward the curb at his heels the redoubtable Constable Cotton.

"The old egg must have his way," thought Constable Cotton. He stepped into the shadow of a tall hedge, through which the Foreign Minister had just gone. "Oh, well," he thought, and at the precise moment he felt something come into contact with his head from the rear, and at the same time the Foreign Minister, his car at the curb, the hedge, and everything about him seemed to leap up into the sky. Constable Cotton collapsed awkwardly to the pavement. Two hands came from the shadow of the hedge and pulled the unconscious body away.

Lord Norton did not once look behind him. He stepped into his machine, thoroughly disgruntled, and glanced about to see whether Constable Cotton was coming. Lord Norton's chauffeur stood impassively at the door.

"Where is the constable?" asked Lord Norton, and bent slightly forward to look from the car. As he looked up the shadowy walk, someone suddenly emerged from the hedge, stood there a moment, and vanished. Short and squat, this figure and bent – a hunchback!

Lord Norton gave a sharp cry, made as if to leap from the machine, and felt suddenly that the chauffeur had jumped before him. He saw the fellow swing something, felt his hat being knocked off, and felt something strike him suddenly on his unprotected head; then he collapsed to the floor of the machine. The chauffeur slammed the door, ran quickly forward, took his seat at the wheel, and sent the car at full speed into the night.

The Lady Ysola Warrender stepped behind the screen, and found her father sitting restlessly on the lounge, patting his forehead with his silk handkerchief.

"Well, my dear," said the Earl of Leicester. "How are you enjoying yourself?"

"Very well, father," said Lady Ysola. "I was looking for Lord Norton just now – you haven't seen him, have you?"

"No, I haven't," said the Earl slowly. "Now that you remind me, that's funny. I haven't seen him at all tonight – not once."

"He sent no regrets?"

"None. He should be here. And I particularly wanted to see him, too. Could you call his home, my dear?"

"I think I shall."

The Lady Ysola moved into the adjoining room, closed the door carefully behind her, and drew the monophone toward her. For a moment she hesitated. Then she called a number.

"Could I speak to his Lordship?...Not in?...Could you tell me...? At the Earl of Leicester's...an hour ago? Very well, thank you."

Lady Ysola called another number. "Hello, Solar...I'm afraid Lord Norton has done something indiscreet. He left for father's affair an hour ago and hasn't yet shown up. I think something must have happened to him... I don't know; if you wait a moment, I'll see."

Lady Ysola went quickly from the room and ascended a small balcony overlooking the ball room; there she stood for some moments, scanning the people below. She returned to the monophone. "Are you there, Solar?...No, Sir Ronald Duveen is not here. I remember sending him an invitation, yes."

Solar Pons shoved the monophone away from his elbow and looked over at me. "Well, Parker," he said, "things are beginning to happen. Lord Norton has just disappeared. I wonder what has happened to Constable Cotton."

Our concern over Constable Cotton was answered by no less a person than the constable himself. He was a sorry-looking spectacle as he presented himself to us not long after Lady Ysola's call.

His story was soon told. Someone had hit him over the head with a sandbag. He had slept, he thought, for about an hour; the chauffeur had enjoyed the privacy of the hedge with him, but the chauffeur was quite seriously injured. Did he see anyone? No. But they had left him a playing card, the inevitable deuce of clubs. He had tried to keep Lord Norton from going, but it was no use. He'd run into it by himself. How did it happen that the man in the constable's car did not follow? He had waited for the constable's signal, and from that distance he did not know Lord Norton; so he did not follow the car. That was all.

"Well," said Pons, "there is nothing we can do. We shall have to rely upon the slim chance that Frick or Howells will pick up something; I see nothing else."

"It strikes me as a good sign that they took his Lordship away alive," I put in. "Perhaps we have scared them a bit, what do you say?"

Pons looked at me in silence for a moment. "I think I should much rather have discovered another corpse. Unless I am very much mistaken, this gang is going to use Lord Norton to find out what they want about the government plans hidden in the Foreign Office. And I am reasonably sure that they have ways to make Lord Norton talk."

"But look here," I protested. "They won't dare. There'll be such a hue and cry over his Lordship that they'll have to keep in hiding..."

Pons laughed sardonically. "There will be no hue and cry. The papers will announce that Lord Norton is temporarily indisposed, and the undersecretary will take over his work in the meantime. And that they know!"

"Oh, but surely something can be done..."

"The usual proceedings will go forward, yes. But nothing usual will find Lord Norton for us!"

VII

MR. HOWELLS APPEARS AND DISAPPEARS

Solar Pons did not err in his fears regarding Lord Norton. He spent the entire day following the Foreign Minister's disappearance, in Limehouse, but in vain. No one had heard of Lord Norton, and evidently no one had ever heard of the Clubs. Pons gave way to a fit of anger, blaming Lord Norton's indiscretion for the loss of twenty-four hours.

Both Pons and I retired early that night. I had scarcely dropped off, when I felt Pons' grip on my shoulder, and heard him hiss into my ear, "Visitors. Get up." I sat up sleepily, but a faint scratching sound on the hall door brought me wide awake on the instant.

Pons was in his dressing gown, and I hastily donned mine. "Who is it?" I whispered.

"Either Howells or Frick, I think," said Pons, and passed silently into the other room.

He stood for a moment before the door in the darkness, and as I listened, I heard two sharp taps, followed by a single tap; almost at once, the signal was repeated. Pons opened the door, and a dim shadow slipped into the room from the hall.

Pons closed the door and went rapidly to the windows, where he drew the shades. Then he moved to the table in the darkness, and in a moment the room was dimly illuminated by a small table lamp. Our shadowy visitor now emerged.

"Sit down, Howells," said Pons.

The man Howells sank into a seat well within the feeble light of the lamp. He was a slim, pale man, poorly dressed, but certainly not the typical Limehouse lounger. His face, pale and unshaven as it was, was that of a man of refinement. Nor was I mistaken, for his voice, when he began to speak, confirmed my guess.

"They've got Norton, I see," said Howells.

Pons drew in his breath sharply. "You know where he is?" he demanded.

"Not yet, I don't," answered Howells. "But I'll know by this time tomorrow night. The word's being passed. I got it from Frick; he doesn't know yet, either – but he'll tell me tomorrow. And – good news – Frick's joined the Clubs."

"Excellent!" exclaimed Pons.

"Strikes me it's a frazzled gang, Mr. Pons. Don't know much about each other, and every one of 'em scared to death of this fellow they call the Deuce. Head of the gang, all right. Frick carries a little black metal club – you know, clover-leaf, like the playing card design. Says all the members have 'ern. Only some have gold stamping on 'ern; that means they're the boys in the know, the boys higher up."

"That's first rate, Howells. Frick's on trial, I daresay?" suggested Pons.

"Or he'd have seen you before this, yes," answered Howells. "Have you got a fag, Mr. Pons. I'm dying for a smoke."

Pons silently handed Howells cigarettes and matches.

"Hm! Cork tips, too. Pretty nice, Mr. Pons." Howells struck a match and puffed reflectively on the cigarette. "You know, I used to smoke these things before I was sent down."

"I know," assented Pons. "There's no reason you couldn't be smoking them on your own again, if you'd care to put yourself back where you were before."

Howells made a vague gesture with his hands. "We're getting off the subject, Mr. Pons. It's Lord Norton we're talking about, not Mr. Howells."

"Very well," said Pons. "Go on with whatever you have to tell me."

"Frick says they don't intend to waste any time on Lord Norton. Seems there are some papers they want, and they're going to force him to tell where they are. Norton evidently fooled them before by having fake papers made, and the gang's pretty well worked up about it. They're going to take that out of him, too. They'll keep him alive only so long as he holds out; it won't be pleasant for him either way, I'm afraid."

"Torture, is it?" asked Pons.

"Torture it is, Mr. Pons," replied Howells. "They'll give it to him strong until he tells, and when he does, I think it's the River for what's left of him."

"Question is, will he hold out until we can get to him?" asked Pons.

"I don't know the man," mused Howells. "Frick seemed to think the sooner I got here, the better, though what he thought you might do without knowing where Norton was is somewhat beyond me. The good Frick evidently thinks very little of our Foreign Minister. 'Mud and water,' says Frick to me. 'Just mud and water, that's all he is.' And I'm thinking Frick was heavy on water. In plain words. Frick was afraid he wouldn't hold out until help came. Said he'd try to get a word to him if he could." He paused. "Much good that would do," he added.

"Is that all?" asked Pons.

"That's all for one day, but I'll come back tomorrow. Maybe I'll call you, maybe you'll hear by post. Too many trips to this place aren't going to be too good for me, that's sure. The Clubs know you're after 'em, and they'll not take any chances if they can help it."

"Yes," assented Pons. "I think it would be better to call or write; they'll be quite certain to keep Number Seven under observation from now on."

"I don't doubt it," said Howells.

"Do you need any money?" asked Pons.

"The stuff of life, Mr. Pons, the stuff of life. Have you got five pounds that aren't working? Ah, thanks. That will keep me in cork-tipped cigarettes for a while, eh, Mr. Pons?"

"Keep away from liquor, Howells, that's all I want to suggest."

"You needn't worry, Mr. Pons. I know how to stop the source when I want to; and I'm not gone in the head yet."

Howells tapped his head significantly, and rose to go. He stood at the threshold gazing moodily at Pons.

"I'm getting old, I guess," he said. "I'm forgetting things. You remember that hunchback you were telling about?"

"Identified?"

Howells chuckled. "You want too much all at once, Mr. Pons. They call him the 'Dove' where I come from; he only appears at night, never by day. 'Dove' is somebody's joke most likely, because the man's a killer all right."

"Hm!" muttered Pons. "Is he a double, by any chance?"

"Strikes me that way," agreed Howells. "He works some game by day, and another at night; sounds good to me that way. Shall I fix someone on him?"

"Someone you can trust, yes."

"All right, Mr. Pons." Howells thrust his hand into his pocket, and drew out a white strip of paper, which resolved into an envelope, as Howells came forward into the light. "Oh, yes," he said, looking at it. "Almost forgot this, too. I found it in your mailbox; you've a late post out this way, Mr. Pons."

He threw it to the table and went quickly to the door. "Well," he said, "I'm off." He opened the door noiselessly and closed it behind him. There was no sound as he descended the stairs.

Pons took up the envelope. There was his name, "Mr. Solar Pons," scrawled across the face of it, but no address; it had not come by post. He tore it open. Out of it fell a thin piece of cardboard. For a moment we looked at it; then our eyes met across the table. In the small patch of light between us lay the deuce of clubs.

VIII

THE LADY IN BLACK

I looked at the curious line of figures in the Agony column of the *Times* with intense interest; though the meaning of this cryptic message was utterly beyond me.

"2833151525:27262531:1415331315," it read.

"Well," said Pons, "Not a thing. Of course, I assume it is another message, but I couldn't decode it."

"It is comparatively simple, nevertheless," replied Pons. "Look at the key, and you can see it easily enough." He shoved a paper toward me; in his script was written:

1. a b c d e f g h i
2. j k l m n o p q r
3. s t u v w x y z

28 equals line 2, letter 8: q
33 equals line 3, letter 3: u
and so on.

"Then 2833151525:27262531:1415331315 reads *Queen: Pons: Deuce.*"

"In other words," added Pons, as I looked up from the paper, "I am the next gentleman to be removed. I am rather curious why they should send a lady to do it; for I am sure the Queen is a lady."

"After this, we can be sure that three of them at least are in London, to say nothing of all the small fry the organization has managed to attract."

"Quite so," said Pons. "It seems to bear out the theory that matters are coming to a head in London."

Whatever I was about to say in answer, was cut short by the sudden skirling of the telephone bell. Pons reached quickly for the instrument. There was a short conversation, and Pons pushed the instrument away.

"The Foreign Office," he murmured, "reporting the receipt of dispatches from the Continental countries. Secretary Hatry is jubilant; it seems that there has been some kind of clean-up and a great many head clubs have been taken. If true, that is welcome information."

"Do we go down?" I asked

"After lunch, yes," said Pons.

Immediately after lunch, Pons and I proceeded to the Foreign Office, where we found Secretary Hatry in a state of great excitement. The absence of his chief having been explained to him, he was fairly bristling with self importance in the position he had not been unwilling to assume.

"Well, Mr. Pons, well," he said, coming forward to greet us. "And Dr. Parker, too. We are getting on, even though the chief is no longer at the helm."

He chuckled and bade us be seated.

"Now, what is it?" asked Pons shortly.

"For one thing, we've heard from Leningrad. The Soviet have taken two Clubs; they say Ten and Five. And they want us to look for another, whom they now suspect of being higher in authority than either of those captured. It is a lady this time:

Tatiana Markovna. Of course, a full description of her is given, and she will most likely have changed her name."

He handed the dispatch to Pons as he spoke.

"And you were right, Mr. Pons, about the Ritchie-Carroll Papers; Leningrad reports that several officials of the government have been approached in confidence and sounded regarding Soviet interest in the Papers."

"That's why we have not heard from Leningrad before this, I daresay," said Pons dryly. "The Clubs, looking forward to disposing of the Papers in Russia, withheld activity harmful to Russia for the time being."

"Precisely what I supposed," agreed Hatry.

"Is this the only dispatch?" asked Pons,

"Oh, no. They've got the Seven in Austria, and another in Tokyo."

"Are they more efficient over there?" I put in.

"No," said Hatry. "It's just that the Continental police have ordered general clean-ups, and they've taken these fellows in by a lucky chance. I think it's pretty certain that the headquarters of this gang are in London. for these men taken over there are natives, not especially distinguished for intelligence, I gather."

"So it would seem," commented Pons, who had been reading the reports with great care, now and then taking a note or two.

"What do you say, Mr. Pons, to a general raking of Limehouse and Stepney – all our poor districts, in fact?"

"Not a bad idea, Hatry. But I should suggest that we wait for developments regarding Lord Norton before we make any definite move. Meanwhile, I think it would be well to gather any material you can on an individual known as the Dove, a hunchback. I have reason to believe that he is the hunchback in this mystery; the Knave of Clubs, and incidentally their killer."

"Do you think we will be able to find Lord Norton soon?" asked Hatry nervously.

"Within twenty-four hours, I hope," replied Pons. "I should want the net to be thrown out immediately after he is found – but there is a strong possibility that he will not be found. Let us not overlook that."

Pons rose. "Call me if anything further comes up, as usual," said Pons.

Together Pons and I left the Foreign Office. We had some difficulty in finding a taxicab to convey us to Seven Praed Street, for the fog that had come up that morning had thickened considerably. However, without the loss of any considerable amount of time, we were soon put down before out rooms, and started to ascend the steps of Number Seven.

At the same moment, the door of the house opened slowly, and the slim figure of a woman came from it. She came toward us with some hesitation; it was then that I noticed that her features were concealed by a heavy black veil. At her approach, Pons slackened his pace considerably, and as she passed us going down the steps, he paused and looked after her. She was dressed totally in black, and her cloak reached to her ankles. For a moment Pons looked at her; then he looked vainly into the fog in all directions.

"Has that taxicab gone?" muttered Pons.

"No," I replied.

"Come," he said suddenly. "We are going to follow that woman."

We ran quickly to the cab, and as we got into it, Pons turned and shot a glance upward toward our windows. Then he sat down beside me. "And," he added, "I am going to arrest her."

"Good heavens!" I protested. "For what?"

"For entering my room, turning up the lights, and leaving them on – to shed a green glow."

"Are you mad, Pons?" I started back and looked at him.

"Not quite," he replied grimly.

The cab shot forward, and the lady in black went on, apparently unaware that she was being followed. As we crept along behind her in the fog, there came suddenly into our line of vision, the lights of an oncoming car, going at as slow a pace as our own, and keeping tightly to the curb.

"Quick!" shouted Pons to the cabman, "get to the woman! That car is waiting to pick her up."

A burst of speed brought our cab to the curb alongside the woman, and Pons was out of the car before it came to a full stop. I came after him. "Will Your Majesty step into my car?" said Pons icily.

The woman looked at him from behind her veil, and her hand went up to her throat. Something clattered to the pavement.

"See what that was, Parker," said Pons.

"A skeleton key," I answered, having located it almost at once. As I looked up at Pons, I saw that he held in his hand his revolver.

The woman looked toward the oncoming car, the occupants of which had noticed nothing amiss, but Pons motioned curtly with the weapon in his hand. The woman entered the taxicab, and immediately Pons and I followed.

"Scotland Yard," directed Pons, and sank back in his seat.

The woman made as if to speak, but thought better of it.

"Will you lift your veil, madame?" asked Pons.

The woman made no response for a moment; then her hands went up, and she disclosed a face of remarkable beauty. On her lower lip there had formed a curiously shaped mole, and Pons' eyes fastened on this.

"Ah," said Pons. "Madame Tatiana Markovna, Her Majesty, the Queen of Clubs."

The woman looked at Pons with a curious smile on her dark face. Then her lips parted, and she said, "You have it perfectly, Mr. Pons. Perfectly."

IX

THE GREEN LIGHT

As we stood before Number Seven, looking meditatively up toward the green glow of our windows, Pons chuckled dryly.

"Well," I said, "what are we waiting for?"

Pons shrugged his shoulders carelessly. He drew his revolver from his pocket, looked at it, and, raising it, fired two quick shots, shattering both the windows looking from our rooms upon Praed Street!

"Good God!" I exclaimed, "Pons, have you gone mad!"

"Gas," said Pons. He dropped his revolver back into his pocket, and ran lightly up the steps. "I daresay we can expect Mrs. Johnson to come charging at us!" He chuckled dryly.

But Mrs. Johnson had gone out. "So much the better," said Pons. "Leave the front door open – I'm going up to open our rooms. We'll have the devil of a time getting that gas out of here in this beastly fog, and it's just as well that Mrs. Johnson isn't about. There's no need to frighten her."

Pons mounted the stairs, and, with his handkerchief over his face, threw open the doors to our room. From below I could see a green cloud billow outward, collapse formlessly and trail vaguely down the stairs toward the outer door. In half an hour our rooms were closed once more, and Pons had already sent for a man to repair the damage done to our windows.

"Very deadly," said Pons later, in answer to my questions. "It is what was known in 1915 as the Dunfer Gas. James Dunfer, its discoverer, shortly after announcing its discovery to the government, was mysteriously killed, and all data about the gas had vanished when the government began to look into his death. It was later discovered that he had confided his hopes to a young German who had lived in England for years, and was at the time connected with the Foreign Office; this young German was nowhere to be found, and it is supposed that he made use of his knowledge, engineered the death of Dunfer and the stealing of the formulae and other data, and sold them to the German government, for it is known that the Germans used a small quantity of Dunfer gas in an offensive early in 1918. Since it did not fulfil expectations at that time, it was not used again. Of its composition we know very little; it is thought to be either a chloride or fluoride variation."

"Has the German agent ever been seen again?" I asked.

Pons chuckled. "Not yet," he replied. "But unless I am very much mistaken, he soon will be." Pons now stood up and went rapidly over the books on his shelves, reseating himself presently with what he called his private notebook, containing records of criminals, suspected persons, crimes, solved and unsolved, and all other data that interested him. This he leafed through slowly, and paused at last to read:

> "'Störing, Heinrich von: German spy, independent. Arrived in England early in 1905. Through social connections he worked himself into a position at the Foreign Office. Was known to have great interest in James Dunfer and his work regarding the Dunfer Gas.'

"Here follows the incident of the German's disappearance after the death of Dunfer," said Pons looking up. "We can pass over that."

> "'In personal appearance he is tall, and is said to be very handsome. Clean-shaven, smooth, bloodless face, thin lips, brown eyes, undershot jaw, with a small wen on the left slope of his nose.'

"Why!" I exclaimed, "that might easily fit the mysterious Dr. von Storck."

Pons nodded. "And that, I am now fairly certain, will also fit the man known as the Deuce of Clubs, allowing for the difference the passage of years will make."

"But if it were von Storck," I put in, "how is it that the German government is wiring London to watch for him?"

Pons chuckled. "You forget that this is not wartime, Parker, and that in all probability von Storck knows too many of the German government's private affairs to be allowed liberty. The system of espionage employed by the Clubs seems to be after all an independent one; these people pry into all governments, and emerge with a stock of trade for all of them. At present, it is thought that the British plans for the Ritchie-Carroll super-aeroplane will interest Russia; I need not, of course, make it clear that Russia realizes that these Clubs may turn immediately and sell Russian plans to Britishers. The only way to foil them, is for the governments to unite in fighting them."

I nodded. "And the gas," I ventured.

"Seems a new weapon," Pons replied. "And, needless to say, a decidedly effective one. Perhaps it was because the German government discovered that von Storck had made off with the formulae for this gas that they so quickly communicated with us; it is not unlikely."

"What are you going to do with the Queen of Clubs?" I asked. "You left her quite abruptly at the Yard, it seemed to me."

"Quite so," returned Pons. "I am going to leave her to spend the night. She will be well guarded, and despite the extraordinary activity of the Clubs, I am extremely doubtful of their ability to penetrate the Yard. I have other plans for her tomorrow; since the King has failed us, the Queen remains to be dealt with."

"Surely you are not going to press her?" I protested.

Pons laughed. "You are entirely too sentimental, Parker. But rest assured; I am not going near her."

"The men at the Yard then?"

"Nor they. I am going to send the Lady Ysola Warrender to deal with her. I daresay Ysola can be much more effective than I."

With this, Pons reached for the telephone, and in a few moments, he had the Lady Ysola on the wire. "I want all that you can get about the Clubs, though I'm afraid that won't be much," he said, and as from a great distance, I could hear the sound of her voice. "And there's another thing," he added, after some further instructions, "I want you, the next time you find yourself in Sir Ronald Duveen's company, to ask him in some way – not too openly, you understand – about a mysterious underworld terror who is known to us as the Dove. I shall expect you to gauge his reaction very carefully." After a few more words, Pons turned away from the instrument.

"Why did you do that?" I asked. "Make that suggestion about the Dove's relation to Duveen?"

"There are various reasons," said Pons. "Lady Ysola has suggested that Duveen himself is the hunchback who appears to be the Knave of Clubs, and is known to the underworld as the Dove. But this suggestion, apt as it seems to be, is far from tenable. I have taken the trouble to look up Sir Ronald Duveen, and I'm afraid we must put aside Ysola's suggestion; but that Duveen knows something about the Dove, I am willing to believe – hence, the suggestion to Lady Ysola."

"Well, let us hope it does some good. It seems to me that we're doing entirely too much standing still in this matter."

Pons looked at me over his pipe. "And what else, my dear Parker, can we do?"

X

MR. HOWELLS ONCE MORE

Midnight. The muffled sound of the last stroke from Big Ben came to me dimly as I started from my sleep. What had I heard to disturb me? Then it came again. There was someone in the hall; I sat up quietly.

I listened for the merest sound. The footsteps in the hall halted at our door. For a moment there was silence, and then came the unmistakable sound of someone fitting a key to our door.

"Pons!" I whispered.

"Oh, don't be alarmed, Parker," said Pons in a low voice, and I knew at once that Pons had heard all that I had, and more. "It is very likely Howells."

The door came open and closed again. Now there was a sound of shuffling feet. And almost immediately there came the welcome taps that I had heard only the night before. Yes, our visitor was surely Mr. Bert Howells.

Pons rose and went into the room where Howells was, and I followed close upon his heels.

"Well, Mr. Pons," said Howells, leaning against the table upon which he had beat his taps, "you've got no privacy at all, have you?"

"It seems not," said Pons.

"Well, you'd better take care of that door," said Howells slowly. "The Clubs are after you strong, and we're all provided with skeleton keys – they work, too, you'll have noticed by this time."

Howells reached into his pocket and produced a key, the duplicate of the one we had got from the Queen that afternoon, and placed it in the circle of dim light thrown by the lamp on the table. Beside it he placed a small black medal, resembling a clover leaf.

"I'm initiated, Mr. Pons," said Howells. "Frick got me in."

"You weren't followed here," put in Pons quickly.

"I hope not." Howells grinned. "It's ticklish business, Mr. Pons, but I know my way pretty well in the fog; my best friend, the fog is."

"You know that we have taken the Queen of Clubs," said Pons.

Howells chuckled. "Why, Mr. Pons, not one of us has been allowed to forget that. Orders from the big boy himself. Pons must be put out of the way, and I'm afraid they're even pretty badly-intentioned toward Dr. Parker, harmless as he is."

At this Pons smiled, and I could not help smiling also. Mr. Howells shrugged his shoulders and went on. "Why he sent the Queen, I don't know. What'd she try on you? The Dunfer Gas?...I thought so. He's a tricky old boy, and seems to know every move you make. I think he's got someone in the Foreign Office, too. He knows too much, and he passes it right on to the rest of us. I don't want to suggest anything, of course, but Lord Norton is still pretty much himself. He'd better be rescued tonight, though. It's not too late now, is it?" He looked questioningly at Pons.

"It is never too late for us, Howells. You know that," said Pons. "You know where Norton is, then?"

"He's at Number 21, Limehouse Causeway. Three doors removed from Shen Han's, where you always see Frick. A tea shop. But that's a blind. You go straight through; there's a little passage. You follow that to the end, and there's a false door; get through that. Then there's a brick passage and a trapdoor. You go down. Be careful, and bring plenty of tear bombs with you. They've got a machine gun, and they don't hesitate to use it. The big boy himself won't be there, I'm afraid. He's never around. If you ask me, there's only one of us who knows who he is – that's Albert, the Dove. You'll take the Trey if you're careful enough. You'd better go as soon as possible, I think."

"Anything else?" asked Pons, drawing the telephone toward him.

"Yes. As I said before, they're out to fix you, Mr. Pons. And they've got someone onto you that you're not suspecting, I'm afraid. They know you're wise to Albert, and they're keeping him hidden for the time being. And they know all about the dispatches that you get at the Foreign Office. If I were you, I'd go through that group of clerks handling the news; there's somebody there, I'm thinking. And for yourself – keep out of sight in the daytime; the Deuce has some dirty yellow knife men watching for you, and you might pick up some steel when you don't expect it. Keep away from the windows, too; the old boy likes his men to use air-guns, and he's out for you. He's not afraid of you at all, Mr. Pons, but he's all worked up because the Queen was taken right under his eyes, so to speak."

Howells turned a melancholy eye on Pons, and gazed at the monophone, upon which Pons' right hand rested. "You going to telephone the Yard, Mr. Pons?" he asked.

"Yes," said Pons.

"I wouldn't," said Howells. "Not with that phone, anyway. They've been speaking of putting a tap on your 'phone, and they might have done it already."

"Well, the fellow is certainly thorough," chuckled Pons. "Has he discovered my private phone?"

"Have you got one?" asked Howells.

"Oh, yes," replied Pons. "I'm on a private wire connecting me directly with the Yard. I'm afraid he didn't find that, did he?"

"I don't know," said Howells. "Where do you keep it?"

Pons motioned toward his reference shelves. "Behind those shelves. I don't use it very often, but I don't regret having it now."

Howells nodded disinterestedly. "The Queen left the light on here this afternoon, did she?"

Pons nodded

"And you shot out the panes of your windows. That excited him, I can tell you. Sometimes at night we can hear him; he comes to Number 21, locks himself in a room, and gives directions from behind a closed door. Then Albert sees that there's no one around when he leaves. Anyway, he wears a domino."

"You saw him?" asked Pons eagerly.

"Well, I'm not wasting my time," answered Howells. "I can't help you very much, except that I know he's well dressed, and I'm sure he's the fellow you know as von Storck. But no wen on his nose, as you said. And I suppose you've suspected that before this."

Pons nodded.

"Well," said Howells, "I'm afraid that's all this time."

"You have certainly earned five pounds," said Pons.

"I still have cigarettes," replied Howells, "but I'll not refuse the five pounds." He took the note that Pons thrust at him and put it gravely into his pocket. "And don't forget to be careful, Mr. Pons," he said. "I wouldn't leave this place in the daytime until I was absolutely certain no one was around. With the Deuce behind this, I wouldn't be certain of that anyway. It's like France in 1916; snipers all around the company I was in."

Howells went to the door and stood there listening intently. "I guess I'm hearing things," he said. "Thought the stairs creaked – but I guess they do that once in a while." He shuddered, inexplicably, and pulled his coat close about his shoulders. "I'll try to get to you again soon, Mr. Pons," he said, "but don't worry if you don't hear from me. Bert Howells can take care of himself yet."

He opened the door and slipped quietly out. As the door closed, Pons rose and moved swiftly to the bookshelves, where he was soon busy with Scotland Yard.

XI

NUMBER 21, LIMEHOUSE CAUSEWAY

My attempts to dissuade Pons from accompanying the Scotland Yard men on the raid were futile; I had all I could do to keep him from going rashly to the tea-shop in Limehouse Causeway before the Yard men had assembled and started. Certainly he would have got there earlier, had not our cab blundered in the fog, and lost considerable time in this way.

Two o'clock in the morning found us walking slowly down the Causeway; in pairs on either side of the street were the Scotland Yard men under the direction of our old friend, Inspector Jamison.

Pons dropped into a doorway from which he could keep the tea-shop in sight, and presently Jamison sidled over to us. "Well?" said Jamison.

"All the men here?" asked Pons in an undertone.

Jamison nodded.

"Back of the place looked after? Back of all the buildings nearby?"

"Everything," whispered Jamison. "Shall we go at them, do you think?"

"You have the tear bombs ready?" asked Pons.

"We're not taking any chances," replied Jamison. "We're going to draw their fire; then smother them with the tear bombs. That's the best way, I think."

"Quite so," said Pons. "Let's go, then."

Swiftly Pons crossed the street, produced his elaborately made picklock, and had the door of the tea-shop open in a moment. Silently the Scotland Yard men trooped into the little shop and followed at Pons' heels. Pons quickly located the door of the passage, and likewise the false door at its end. Here there was a slight drop to the brick passage. The trapdoor was clearly evident in the floor of the passage, but Pons made no move toward it. Instead, he motioned the men about him to group themselves anywhere but where they might be expected to stand when the trapdoor was lifted. The purpose of his direction was clear, and when the trapdoor was lifted, the resultant machine gun fire was almost utterly futile.

For no sooner was the trapdoor lifted than there came a furious rat-tat-tat of machine gun fire. Two of the constables fell, seriously wounded, but a deluge of tear bombs temporarily halted the gunfire. Then, carefully prepared against the effect of the tear bombs, we descended into the darkness below the trapdoor. Here there was nothing save the smoke and gas of the short battle. Inspector Jamison produced a flash that soon revealed a stone panel, which slid easily to one side at pressure on a brick jutting from the wall near the panel.

The panel opened on an empty room, which gave every evidence of having been left in great haste. A sliding door at the far wall had been left open in the retreat that had evidently been made. Pons ran quickly through this room and into the adjoining one. There we found Lord Norton; he had been stripped of most of his clothes, and lay in collapse against the wall. He had been tortured, but he was not dead, as a hasty examination immediately showed. Several of the Yard men hastily passed him out to the police cars which had by now collected in the street outside. Then the pursuit continued. More and more passages were disclosed, and more and more confusing the chase. It was evident now that the machine gun fire had been kept up to give the others time to escape, and all signs seemed to justify the belief that the escape had been successful.

"We're coming out at the rear of Shen Han's," said Pons, turning to Jamison and me. "Unless they are outnumbered, our men must surely have taken some of the Clubs!"

At this moment we stepped out into a narrow alley, and found there Constable Mecker, who came forward at once at the sight of us.

"Have you taken any?" asked Jamison eagerly.

"I think we have seven, perhaps eight," replied Meeker. "Quite a number got away, escaping through other buildings."

As he stood talking to us, other Yard men emerged from the shadows and collected around us.

"Where are they?" asked Jamison.

"We've taken them to the cars," said Meeker

"No hunchback among them, I daresay," put in Pons.

"No, Mr. Pons. I watched most carefully, but there was no hunchback in the group that came from the house there."

"Very well," said Jamison. "Let's get on."

The cars bore us as swiftly as the fog would allow to the Yard, and there the prisoners, seven of them, were lined up for inspection. To Pons' intense disappointment, all of the prisoners proved, when searched, to be only more or less unimportant members of the organization, for each of them carried the plain emblem that Howells had shown us a few hours before. Pons readily recognized six of them as underworld characters with whom he had at one time or another come in contact; the seventh was identified as a foreigner, a German. From him, nothing could be got, though both Pons and Jamison drilled at him in German and English; the fellow remained perfectly stolid, refusing so much as a nod of the head to all the questions shot at him. The six Englishmen, however, were perfectly willing to talk, but their knowledge was even more limited than Howells', for they knew only a fraction of what Howells' had told us. Yes, they knew it was Lord Norton they were torturing. How were they torturing him? Oh, they had put him in a wire sack, and were drawing the wire tighter and tighter; not very hard on him, though. And they knew about the Ritchie-Carroll Plans, yes. In the end, the men were unceremoniously bundled off to await further judgment.

Lord Norton proved to be not seriously injured, and the two constables who had been shot were quickly pronounced on the road to recovery. It was to Lord Norton that Pons and Jamison next gave their attention. He was conscious, and was ready and willing to talk.

"Your Lordship is feeling better now, I hope?" asked Pons, bending over him.

"Quite, thank you," said his Lordship.

"Your Lordship will answer some questions?" asked Jamison.

"Yes, Inspector. I am only too willing to answer anything you may ask. I daresay I am rather indebted to you, and if I had obeyed warnings at first, I would not now be here."

Inspector Jamison now proceeded to ask Lord Norton routine questions about his treatment, his observations, and further details which would enable him to identify any of the torturers. It appeared that the man who had questioned him in regard to the Ritchie-Carroll Plans was the hunchback. At this juncture Pons bent forward with a question.

"Did your Lordship notice anything about this hunchback – anything that might have recalled someone you know?"

His Lordship appeared for a moment to think. "No," he said at last. "When I first saw him, I thought of what a good subject he would make for my crippled friend, Sir Ronald Duveen, who is, as you know, keenly interested in physical abnormalities."

Pons nodded, but said nothing. Then Jamison bent again to continue his interrogation. Pons and I stood patiently listening, despite the fact that Jamison uncovered nothing that we did not already know. Presently, however, Jamison finished, and left the room for a moment to deliver his notes to a stenographer.

"Your Lordship is the only one who knows where the Ritchie-Carroll papers are?" asked Pons.

"Yes, Mr. Pons."

"You are certain there is no one else?"

"No one else," answered his Lordship firmly.

"Very well," said Pons. "Then I shall want to know exactly where they are."

"If it is necessary," began his Lordship, but Pons' curt nod satisfied him, and he went on to detail the hiding place of the all-important plans.

"Yes," replied the Foreign Minister.

"When you return, I want you to give out that the plans have been put in a certain definite place – no matter where, for you must put dummy plans there, and let matters come to a head."

"But what of the real papers?" asked his Lordship.

"I shall come to you first thing in the morning and take them away with me to a place where they will be absolutely safe," replied Pons.

"Oh, but I can't allow that, Mr. Pons. No, that would be most irregular," protested his Lordship.

"Undoubtedly most irregular, your Lordship, but believe me it must be done."

"Oh, very well," said his Lordship, "Very well," and sank back among his pillows.

XII

THE ENEMY STRIKES

Two days passed in comparative quiet. Jamison appeared once or twice. He was jubilant, and felt certain that the raid on Number 21, Limehouse Causeway had for the time being, at least, disrupted the organization. But Pons was not so certain. "The calm before the storm," he said.

"But I am very glad that the papers have been removed," he said on the day following the raid. "It will most certainly bring matters to a head; there will be something doing at the Foreign Office before long – you may depend upon it."

"Where have you taken them?" I asked.

"I have put them in the crypt of the chapel on the Earl of Leicester's estate in the suburbs," replied Pons. "There they will be as safe as anywhere else – certainly safer than at the Foreign Office."

I nodded. "Then you alone know where to find them?" I asked.

"Yes. Of course, the Earl of Leicester has been informed that I am secreting something in his crypt, but my venerable old uncle has not enough curiosity to find out what it is. If he knew, he would most probably pass his nights in mortal terror of his life." Pons chuckled.

Later in the same day, the Lady Ysola Warrender called. She had been to Scotland Yard, and had seen the woman known as Tatiana Markovna. "What have you discovered?" asked Pons.

"Not much, I'm afraid," said the Lady Ysola. "The woman has no idea who the Deuce is, for one thing."

"How did she get in with the Clubs?"

"They picked her up in Russia. She claims noble descent, and indeed, carries herself very well. She was destitute, she says, and she was told that the Deuce was quite taken up with her beauty, and thought of using her. Ever since the famous case of Mata Hari, the idea of a woman as a spy seems to have caught on."

"Quite so," chuckled Pons. "Go on."

"She went with them gladly, it seems," continued Lady Ysola, "and soon learned all that she could. She confesses that she was very largely responsible for the Monaco swindle at Monte Carlo."

"Yes, I understand there was a mysterious woman in the matter somewhere," said Pons. "At any rate, the matter was hushed up."

"She has come in contact with the Knave. He is your Albert, the Dove, as you thought."

"Ah, what does she say of him?" put in Pons.

"She dislikes him violently. But she seems to think that he has a great amount of influence in the City, and often appears quite opulent, despite the fact that the man is known not to go in for robbery of any kind. Certainly, she says, he is the killer of the organization, though I understand that all of them are taught to kill. Her mission here this afternoon was the final test for her. She has failed, she says, and only asks that we keep her well hidden from now until you catch the Deuce."

"She has confidence in us, at any rate," murmured Pons.

"Yes," answered Lady Ysola. "She feels that the Deuce will sooner or later over-reach himself. He strikes her as an out and out egotist, with a positive mania for impressing people with his power."

"You told her of the raid last night?"

"Yes. She felt that no good would come of it."

"Nor do I," said Pons moodily.

"Since you took no one important, she says there is no danger of your having caused any sort of interruption in their plans, and she feels that the Deuce will strike back quickly. You knew that you were kept closely under observation, I daresay?"

"Oh, quite," replied Pons.

The Lady Ysola nodded, and was silent for a moment. "She seems to think that your greatest danger now lies in the hunchback. The Deuce will not condescend to you, though according to her story, he is thoroughly familiar with you."

"I fear he flatters himself," I put in.

Pons nodded. "Certainly an egotist," he said. "Very often I am not even familiar with myself." He looked sharply at the Lady Ysola, his cousin. "She made no mention of how the Deuce might strike back?"

"None, beyond saying that he would strike indirectly at you, to break up your organization to catch him and punish him."

Pons nodded thoughtfully.

"Shall I try again?"

"There'll be no need, I fear," said Pons. "She has shown her willingness to talk, and has very probably told you all. And you have done excellent work, Ysola."

The remainder of the day after the Lady Ysola Warrender's departure passed without incident. On the following day there was only one interruption: Jamison called to announce that the seven men taken in the raid were to be kept under heavy guard at the Yard. Meanwhile, they were being questioned and cross-examined daily, though nothing new had been forthcoming.

It was on the third day that the shock Pons had been expecting came. Dawn had hardly streaked the grey sky before Pons was up and about, his nervousness growing on him apace. He started from room to room, muttering to himself, and occasionally sat down to work out some problem on paper. At eight o'clock, the telephone rang sharply. It was the private telephone from Scotland Yard. I had dressed, and I came from my bedroom just in time to see Pons turn away from the instrument, his face set in hard lines, and his dark eyes sharp and clear.

"It has come," he said in a bitter voice.

"What?" I asked, not quite sure of what he spoke.

"The enemy has struck, and indirectly, I have been the cause of it. Oh, I should never have caused Lord Norton to announce that he had hidden the papers in his desk."

"What has happened?" I pressed him.

"Lord Norton was found dead in the Foreign Office this morning. All of the various dummy plans have disappeared, and Undersecretary Hatry cannot be found. Jamison is apoplectic on the telephone, and I can see him having visions of poor Hatry in their infernal wire sack."

Pons slipped quickly out of his dressing gown and put on his street clothes. I followed his example, for the breakfast I had in mind had been driven to remote worlds by this extraordinary and ghastly occurrence. Within a few moments we were seated in a taxicab bearing us swiftly toward the scene of the crime.

Pons had snapped up a paper before entering the cab, and he now went quickly through it. "It is now too late to keep this thing from the press," he muttered. "Let us hope that they will not guess at the immensity of the organization and the intelligence behind it."

I looked over at him. "What is the headline?" I asked.

"'TRAGEDY AT THE FOREIGN OFFICE Foreign Minister Slain at Desk' – "

He crumpled the paper in his hand and threw it in disgust to the floor of the cab. Then suddenly something caught his eye, and he picked it up once more, tearing it across in his haste.

He read the article that had taken his attention, and as he read, I saw his face go white with rage.

"This too," he muttered between clenched teeth, and without a further word, he handed the paper to me. The article he had been reading immediately came to my eye. It read:

"BODY FOUND IN RIVER

"The body of a man was found in the Thames early this morning by several Chinese labourers. The body was so badly mutilated that identification was thought highly impossible, but certain marks tend to show that it is the body of an ex-criminal, Bert Howells, whose record shows that he served a prison term for forgery. It is thought that the unfortunate man was the victim of an argument in a Chinese dive."

XIII

MR. JOHN DEVORE

The Foreign Office teemed with excitement. Newspaper representatives thronged the curb facing the building, pressing as close as the constables on guard would let them. Occasionally someone emerged from the building, shouted something to the reporters immediately dashed off to nearby telephone and telegraph booths to wire the latest developments to the papers. Off to one side two constables were leading away a representative of an American newspaper who had attempted to force his way into the Foreign Office and photograph the body of Lord Norton.

Inspector Jamison met us as we pressed our way past the constables on guard. Not far behind him came High Commissioner Steele.

"This is a terrible business, Pons," said Jamison, coming up to us. There was no mistaking the agitation in his voice.

High Commissioner Steele came up, dolefully nodding his head. "No expenses must be spared," he said. "We have had a visit from the Prime Minister himself; he is, of course, familiar with the activities of the Clubs."

Pons nodded curtly and went on into the building, the three of us following at his heels. He strode into the Foreign Minister's private office. Immediately the body of Lord Norton caught his attention. It lay on the floor next to his desk, partly on one side, partly on its face. Pons bent swiftly and examined the body with precision. The Foreign Minister had been stabbed to the heart, and it had undoubtedly been done from behind. In the midst of a mass of papers scattered all over the floor lay the deuce of clubs; it had been carefully marked off by Jamison's orders. Pons stood looking at this for a moment, and then glanced back at the body.

"Hm," he muttered. "Evidently a second warning was insinuated into his Lordship's papers in some manner. I daresay it is most probable to assume that just as his Lordship found it he was stabbed from behind."

"That is how I look at it," said a voice close by, and at once Pons and I looked up.

A medium-sized, square-jawed blonde gentleman stood at the side of High Commissioner Steele. He was smiling pleasantly in our direction, and the High Commissioner immediately came forward with him.

"I am sorry if I forgot," he apologized, "but in the stress of the occasion I omitted entirely to introduce you to Mr. John Devore of the American State Department. Mr. Devore – Mr. Solar Pons and Dr. Parker."

We shook hands with the American detective, who immediately stepped back to Steele's side to watch Pons. Pons continued his examination of the room, going from case to case, from desk to files all about the room. It was obvious that everything had been rifled, for drawers stood wide open, papers were scattered about, and even supposedly secret drawers had been forced and now were open and empty.

"You say all the papers – the dummy papers, are gone?" asked Pons.

Jamison nodded. "All of them are gone. With Norton gone, we do not even know where the real papers have gone. It is entirely possible that these were taken also."

"No," answered Pons. "The real papers are still quite safe, Jamison. How is it that you know all the dummy papers are gone?" he asked.

"Only yesterday Lord Norton, the Undersecretary, and I saw that they were in their places."

"Hm!" exclaimed Pons. "That's curious. There were only the three of you, then, who knew where all the dummy papers were. Is that right?"

"I think so," said Jamison.

"And now all of them are gone, and Undersecretary Hatry with them."

"It occurs to me, Mr. Pons," put in John Devore, "that the gang might have tortured Mr. Hatry into revealing the hiding places."

"That is quite possible," assented Pons. "Quite possible."

"What impresses me," continued Devore, "is the manner in which this thing was carried out. You have not yet heard, have you, Mr. Pons?"

"No," said Pons, "I haven't." He turned to Jamison. "Where, for instance, were the six guards? What happened to them?"

"They were chloroformed," replied Jamison. "It was done very nicely, according to them. In the first place, Lord Norton and Hatry were working overtime last night; there was an important matter in hand. At half after nine there was some trouble with the lights all along the street; for at least five minutes the entire street was dark. While the guards were trying to ascertain what the matter was, they were chloroformed in the darkness; then we find from the other guards along the street that the lights came on once more. There must have been at least six of the gang here – one to take care of each guard, that is; and I daresay it is not amiss to suppose that there were more. It was the leak in the office that brought them, I think; when Lord Norton announced here that he had hidden the papers in his desk, he literally brought about his own death."

"It is rather curious that they should have taken all the dummy papers, once they found where the supposedly genuine plans had been concealed by Lord Norton."

"Isn't it?" struck in the American.

"They were taking no chances, I should say," said Jamison.

Pons stood in silence, and then abruptly changed the subject. "Has Downing Street intimated who will take Lord Norton's place?" he asked.

High Commissioner Steele nodded. "The Prime Minister said that if all went well, Sir Henry Bishop would become Foreign Minister."

"A very capable man," said Pons. "Let us hope that all goes forward immediately."

Jamison nodded glumly, and looked expectantly at Pons.

"Well, what have you done?" Pons asked at last.

"We've taken fingerprints and photographs, Mr. Pons," said Jamison, "and we've checked up through the general secretary on the papers. Only the papers pertaining to the Ritchie-Carroll plans are missing."

Pons nodded abstractedly, and remained for some moments deep in thought. "And Mr. Devore?" he asked at last. "When did Mr. Devore arrive?"

"Only last night, Mr. Pons," replied Mr. Devore. "About ten days ago our State department was indirectly approached in regard to the Ritchie-Carroll plans, and, of course, we cabled to England at once. We learned about the Clubs, and instructed our Secret Service to be on the lookout. The Ritchie-Carroll suggestion was followed up, and we managed to successfully dupe several members of the organization into our hands. We now hold four members in high positions; their medals read A, 4, 9, and 6. The first three were in Washington; the last one in New York City. Though we tried, we could extort no confession of any kind from them."

"And you were sent over to cooperate with us here?" put in Pons.

"Exactly. The State Department felt that in view of the dispatches from your Foreign Office, it seemed perfectly obvious that the headquarters of this gang are in England; most probably here in London. Naturally, we are just as anxious to stop this espionage business as you are."

Pons nodded. "You say you have taken four of the head Clubs."

"Yes, four – A, 4, 9, and 6. I understand that the King and Queen have already been apprehended together with 7, 10, and 5. That still leaves the Deuce and the Knave, and Trey and 8, doesn't it?"

"Quite so," assented Pons. "And we know that the first three of those left are in London; I think it quite possible that 8 is here also."

Mr. Devore nodded.

"Well, I think there is little else to be done here," said Pons suddenly. He turned to the American agent. "Will you accompany us, Mr. Devore? We can go over the case in detail if you like."

XIV

THE HORROR IN THE FOG

Following the tragedy at the Foreign Office, there came a week of strange silence. The American, Mr. Devore, had penetrated Limehouse in disguise, and had not been heard from since. Jamison flew here and there, unearthing a great many clues, all of which invariably came to nothing. Then, suddenly, came evidence that the Clubs had resumed their activity in London.

Pons and I were walking one night toward our rooms in Praed Street – we had just emerged from Paddington Station. There was a beastly fog, and we walked slowly. It came over me suddenly that Pons and I were not alone; I had that horrible feeling of fear that comes with the presence of the supernatural.

"Pons," I whispered. "I am sure there is someone following us."

"I am afraid there is," said Pons.

His calm voice reassured me for a moment. "Don't let us forget the warning we received not long ago," I muttered.

Then, before Pons could answer, a voice came out of the fog. A hoarse, guttural voice that seemed to come from the fog itself, a voice that might have whispered directly into my ears.

"In three days you die," it said.

At once Pons turned about and ran; I followed close at his heels. We had not gone ten steps before we ran into a constable.

"Here, here," he said, "What is this?" He caught Pons in his arms, and recognizing him, said, "Oh, it's Mr. Pons, is it? Is something the matter, Mr. Pons?"

"Did you see a man running this way, constable?" asked Pons.

"Not a soul, sir."

Pons paused. "Well," he said at last, "there is no use trying to catch him in this fog. He might well have run the other way, anticipating us, or he might even have dashed into the street and boarded a car."

"Is there anything I can do, Mr. Pons?" asked the constable.

"Nothing, I am afraid. Keep a close eye on Number Seven, that's all," replied Pons.

"Very well, sir," said the constable, and saluted Pons.

We retraced our steps rapidly, and soon left the constable far behind in the fog. We continued on our way in silence, and were mounting the steps of Number Seven before Pons spoke.

"I daresay we shall find something here," he said.

"What do you mean?" I asked.

"Oh, another official warning," said Pons.

We passed into the house, up the stairs, and entered our rooms. As Pons put on the light we saw on the floor of our rooms an envelope that had evidently been slipped beneath the door. Pons merely held it up to the light, and threw it to the table without opening it.

"Another deuce," he said dryly. "At least, they seem to have plenty of them. Jamison is, by the way, collecting them; he seems to think that they may be traced in some manner."

"Well, we can be grateful that our door held this time," I put in. "There's no telling what we might have found here if it hadn't."

"Oh, I think we were in no great danger," said Pons. "We have three days, you remember."

The following morning came an unexpected visitor. Sir Henry Bishop, now Foreign Minister, a tall black-bearded, pince-nez individual, condescended to call upon us. That he was labouring under extreme agitation was manifest.

"Mr. Pons," he murmured, "Mr. Pons. I have got their death warning, and they've been haunting me ever since."

He threw the inevitable deuce of clubs upon the table. Pons did not even glance at it.

"Haunting you?" repeated Pons.

"Yes. Last night in the fog. Everywhere, Mr. Pons. I can hear those ghastly voices even now – 'You have three days to live. Prepare to die in three days.' I tell you it is devilish, Mr. Pons. Devilish!"

"Voices in the fog, eh?" said Pons. "Well calculated to frighten, at any rate. Is that all; was there no provision for your escape made?"

"Oh, yes, Mr. Pons, yes, indeed. 'The papers or your life,' they said. And I do not know where the papers are."

"Do you want to know?" asked Pons quietly.

For a moment the Foreign Minister stared at him. Then, "No, no, Mr. Pons. It is utterly shameful, but I do not think I could trust myself with the knowledge. If I had to think of those ghastly voices night after night, I don't know what I should do. I think I should go mad."

"You saw nothing, of course?"

"Nothing, Mr. Pons. But then, there was a fog."

"Were you walking?" asked Pons.

"Twice, but not after that," said Sir Henry. "I thought I could avoid the voices that way, but I heard them in my car just the same."

"Surely not while you were driving?" put in Pons.

"Three times while I was driving, Mr. Pons. Every time my car stopped for traffic signals I heard them. Twice I looked to both sides; once there was an elderly lady fast asleep on my right, a constable in a taxicab to my left; the second time there was no one to my right, and a group of newsboys on a truck to my left. At first I did not know what to think, but I became more and more alarmed. I've heard them in my home even, and that is too much. I summoned a guard, and even then I heard the voices; I think I must have imagined them. Do you think there is anything I can do? I refuse to be frightened into a resignation, and I am determined to stay; but these ghastly voices wear and wear and..."

"Scare," said Pons. "But at least you have an alternative, Sir Henry. Dr. Parker and I have heard the voice once tonight; we have no alternative, it seems. Three days is our limit."

"What! You, too?" exclaimed the Foreign Minister, and half rose out of his chair.

At that moment the Scotland Yard telephone rang, and Pons went quickly to answer it. There was a few minutes of conversation, and Pons turned away from the instrument. I had recognized the voice on the other end of the wire as that of Jamison.

"Well, Sir Henry, our company is fast increasing, it seems."

"What do you mean?"

"Both High Commissioner Steele and Inspector Jamison heard similar voices in the fog last night. Once more, and the matter will have become farcical, though I do not for one minute overlook the horror of it. I have no doubt whatever but that these people will try at least to carry out whatever plans they have made for our disposal."

The Foreign Minister coughed dryly. "You are certainly not very enthusiastic, Mr. Pons."

"I daresay I am not," replied Pons.

"Is there nothing we can do to combat this persecution?" asked Sir Henry.

"In three days we may be able to do a good many things," said Pons.

"Very well. I will say no more," said the Foreign Minister and stood up to go. "By the way, have you any news of Hatry?"

"None," replied Pons. "The man has vanished into thin air. I understand he has no connections."

"That is quite true. I knew him quite well some years ago, but after his long illness somewhat under a year ago, his attitude seemed somehow to have changed. A good and capable man, though getting along in years."

Pons stood silently looking at the swirling grey-yellow fog massing against the window panes. "That is very curious," he said suddenly. He turned to the Foreign Minister. "Would you mind sending off an official wire for me?"

"Not at all, Mr. Pons," answered Sir Henry. "Where does it go?"

"To Germany."

"It is about the Clubs?"

"Yes."

"Write it out. I shall be only too glad to push forward anything leading to the heart of this affair," said the Foreign Minister.

Pons retired to his writing desk and swiftly wrote his message. He read it over once, marked a correction, and handed it to Sir Henry.

"Send it in code, of course," he said.

Sir Henry looked at the paper and read it aloud. 'Can you inform this office regarding last date von Storck definitely known to have been in Germany?' Is that correct?"

"Quite, Sir Henry. Cable that immediately, and call me through Scotland Yard the moment the reply comes in. Scotland Yard will relay all calls to me since my telephone has been tapped."

"Very well, Mr. Pons."

The door slammed behind the Foreign Minister, and Pons and I sat to wait for the answer to the cablegram. Two hours later, the telephone skirled harshly.

"That cannot be an answer already," I said.

"We shall see," said Pons. He went to the instrument, and there was a short interval of conversation. When he returned to his seat, he wore a look of satisfaction which I had not seen on his face for many days.

"What is it?" I asked.

"Lady Ysola reporting through Scotland Yard. She saw Sir Ronald Duveen last night, and broached the subject of Albert, the Dove. The old man almost had an apoplectic fit, according to Ysola; though I have no doubt she exaggerates. At all events, his agitation was unmistakable."

"Surely you do not suspect him of being the Dove?" I protested. "You dismissed that only a few days ago."

"Quite so," said Pons. "No, he cannot be the Dove! But there is a connection. And that I must discover as soon as I can."

Later in the day came the answer to the wire to Germany. It came through Scotland Yard exactly as it had been received: "Von Storck last known to have been in Berlin ten months ago, April 27."

XV

THE HALTING FOOTSTEPS

Solar Pons stood at the window looking vainly into the fog clouds beyond. He turned as I entered the room, and came over to the breakfast table.

"Well," he said, as he sat down, "if this fog keeps up, the Clubs will have little difficulty in disposing of us, I daresay."

"How can you take it so coolly?" I asked. "It makes me shudder just to think of it."

Pons shrugged his shoulders. "Because I look upon these so-called voices in the fog as idle threats, designed to scare us into giving up the papers they want. I have no doubt whatsoever that our persecution is getting too strong for them, and they are as willing to leave England for the time being as we are to trap them."

"And what if we do not surrender the papers – as we are certainly not going to do?" I asked.

"Then we may expect some action on their part," returned Pons.

"Today is the third day, is it not?" I said, as calmly as I could.

Pons nodded. "Quite so. This fog, as I said, will make it convenient for them to come into action. Sir Henry Bishop is quite thoroughly frightened, and I have advised him to retire to his country place for the present; he has gone, leaving the impression that he is still at work in the Foreign Office. It is just as well, I fancy, for Sir Henry is entirely too nervous to be of any use to us in a crisis."

"And Jamison?"

"At his wits' end – as usual," added Pons dryly. "He is chasing all over London with squads of constables; he has even ordered the Thames patrolled, all of which would be very well if by any chance we knew for whom we were looking. I daresay this fog makes patrolling the Thames a very delectable occupation, especially at night." He chuckled.

"What has Steele done?" I asked.

"Surrounded himself with guards," said Pons, "which is quite excusable. He means to take no chances, but I suppose it is needless to say that if the Clubs want him very badly, they will find some way to get them. The organization is large, but it will collapse once its leaders are taken."

"Have you heard yet from Devore?"

Pons shook his head. "No. It is very curious. He seems a capable fellow, and comes with a very high recommendation; of course, I verified his connections at once. It is quite possible that the Clubs will send someone into our midst to spy on us while we least expect it, though somewhat improbable. I hope that the Clubs have not got hold of him. I protested his going into Limehouse, you remember, but he assured me he was familiar with every corner of it.

"Then, too," he continued, "we have not heard from Frick, though I have no doubt he will turn up when he has something of value to report. I should hate to lose so good a man as Frick. The loss of Howells is sharp enough."

"The body was positively identified, then?" I asked.

Pons nodded. "So it seems. Two of his underworld friends identified Howells. I myself did not get to see the body, because, as you know, it was interred immediately after identification."

At this moment the telephone rang sharply; to my surprise it was not the Scotland Yard instrument, but our own telephone on the table. Pons reached quickly to answer it.

"Are you there?" he said. From where I was sitting I could distinguish a rapid flow of sound, but I could not identify any words. Then there came a sudden click, and I knew that the person at the other end of the wire had left far the instrument.

"Who was it?" I asked.

Pons shrugged his shoulders. "I couldn't definitely say, but from the voice, I should say it was Frick. Warned us not to leave the house today, and abrupt especially not tonight."

"Well," I said, "we are getting warm."

"Decidedly," agreed Pons. "And I intend to go out to draw their fire; I am quite certain they will not use firearms, and an attack with a knife I will surely be able to prevent, even in the fog."

I looked at him in amazement. "Well, then," I said with decision, "if you are going out, I shall go with you!"

Pons chuckled. "I am flattered to see that your decision mounts with mine, Parker."

But my decision was considerably cooled later in the afternoon, and more than once I half-hoped Pons would change his mind. For shortly after five o'clock, there came a call from Scotland Yard. An attack had been made on Inspector Jamison, and in the fog the Clubs had made a mistake, killing one of his constables instead. Inspector Jamison had seen no one; one of the constables thought he saw a hunchback, but he could not be sure. So far, nothing else had occurred.

Pons and I left the house shortly after eight o'clock that evening. I ventured one feeble protest before leaving.

"Has it occurred to you," I asked, "that this warning might have been a deliberate ruse to get us out of the house?"

"Yes, certainly," said Pons. "Again, it might have been designed to keep us in the house. You see, that works both ways. I am content to believe that the voice I heard was Frick's. Come, let us go."

The fog was very dense. The street lamps were visible only as we came up to them; then, abruptly, they were lost in the fog. Pons had stated his intention of not going far, and for this I was indeed grateful. The night was certainly not one in which I cared to exercise a fondness for walking; leaving entirely out of consideration the warning which we had received, and which was being steadily magnified as we went along. We walked toward Edgware Road, and turned once more along the street to venture as far as Paddington Station in the other direction.

We had got almost to Paddington when we received the first intimation of danger. Pons suddenly put his hand on my arm and cautioned me to listen intently. We stopped suddenly, and I was immediately conscious of the stopping of padding footsteps following behind us. Pons made a tentative motion with his feet, and at once there came a curious shuffling walk, and, as Pons stopped, so did these footsteps halt also. I grasped Pons' arm nervously. "What shall we do?" I whispered.

"Wait until he comes close enough, and go for him," said Pons calmly.

"Who is it, do you think?"

"I think they have put the hunchback on us. He shuffles along very oddly; you will hear it if you listen. Come, let us be on our way; we must not give him the impression that we know."

We walked forward as quietly as we could, and at once came the sound of the halting footsteps; they shuffled along a little way and stopped. Then they began again and stopped; they halted all independent of our own walking. Certainly the shuffling footsteps were those of the hunchback. I conquered a strong desire to run, to run blindly ahead into the fog – seek the shelter of Paddington Station, hide myself there in the crowds.

Then suddenly I was conscious that the footsteps had halted and had not started up again.

"Pons," I whispered, "they've stopped."

"Watch out," warned Pons. "he's coming for us, I think. In a moment we'll go for him."

But suddenly there came to our ears an unprecedented sound; a totally unexpected sound – that of some blunt thing striking a yielding substance. A dull thud, and immediately after a low moan, and the sound of someone crumpling to the wet pavement. With an exclamation, Pons began to run rapidly into the fog. I came close at his heels. We were not many doors removed from Number Seven when we had stopped, and as we ran rapidly back toward our rooms, it came to me suddenly that there was some design in all this.

At the same moment Pons stopped and bent to the pavement. I glanced hastily around me; we were one door removed form Number Seven. Then I looked down at the crumpled form on the pavement.

"He is not dead," said Pons, "though he has been struck a terrific blow. Bleeding, you see. I think we had better take him into our rooms."

On the pavement at our feet, lay the unconscious form of the hunchback, Albert, the Dove!

XVI

A DEAD MAN COMES TO LIFE

We dragged the unconscious hunchback up the stairs with great difficulty, and Pons threw open the door to our rooms. Then Pons and I exclaimed simultaneously. For, sitting comfortable at our table, looking over Pons' notes, was Mr. Bert Howells!

"Bashed him pretty bad, did I?" asked Howells, rising and coming over to help us with the hunchback.

"Good Heavens!" I exclaimed. "I thought you were dead, Howells."

"So did the Clubs. Funny, eh?"

He helped us put the hunchback on a low couch against the farther wall, and stood there looking moodily from the unconscious form to Pons and I, and back again. "You're altogether too careless, Mr. Pons," he said. "They'd have got you tonight, only I sort of figured you'd not listen to Frick and come out anyway."

"It was Frick who called, then?" asked Pons.

Howells nodded.

"He's all right?"

"Leave that to Frick," said Howells with a wide grin. "He's not only all right, but if he gets what he's after, we'll have enough evidence to hang the entire gang, and that," he added reflectively, "would be very nice, indeed." He chuckled. "After the way they handled what they thought was me, I'm wasting no love for that gang. Ugh!"

"You escaped them on a substitution, then?" asked Pons.

"Yes. It was either one of them, or me, I thought that I was worth a good deal more to both myself and the country at large; so I thought nothing of swapping clothes with one of them when he was asleep. I'd overheard them talking about me, you see, and I decided I'd better be on the move. That would have been a bad move, if I hadn't hit on the plan of changing my belongings for someone else's. They don't know me by sight; they don't know very many of their men by sight, but quite a few of us bunk in an empty house on Brockwell Road. They came there one night, and, sure enough, began to look through the clothes. Then they got the dope I'd changed with, and slashed him up something terrible; lesson to the rest of us, I suppose. Next thing I heard they'd found him in the Thames, and were blaming the poor Chinese for the whole thing. I suppose those clothes of mine, and my watch, did the trick of fooling the morgue people."

"Two men identified you," I broke in, looking over to him from my position beside the hunchback, whose wound I was doctoring.

"Yes," said Howells slowly, "I hoped they would. You see, I sent them to do it." He smiled affably.

"You're not going back there, I hope?" asked Pons.

"I don't think so," said Howells. "I think Frick can manage things all right from now on. The Clubs are thinning out; most of the small fellows are pretty scared, and even the big boys aren't sitting so easy. But they're going to get those plans if it's the last thing they do."

"It will be," said Pons grimly.

"And there's one more thing the big boy would like to do," continued Howells, grinning, "and that's get their hands on you, Pons. He'd like to draw and quarter you, put you together, and do it all over again. What he's got against you, I can't see; he seems to be afraid you know who he is and all about him."

Pons chuckled. "I'm afraid he's right," he said. "I'm afraid that I know who he is and all about him, and I'm afraid that I can put my finger on him when I'm ready to."

"Good Heavens!" I exclaimed. "Surely you don't mean that, Pons?"

"Just like Mr. Pons, eh?" said Howells, grinning. "He's going to wait for Frick to collect the evidence, isn't that right Mr. Pons?"

"Quite so," said Pons, and turned away without any intention of revealing the information my curiosity demanded.

"What will you do with the Dove?" asked Howells.

"Try to question him, I suppose," said Pons. "There'll not be much use of that, however, since he can tell us little we won't know from Frick when he comes."

"How is he coming?" asked Howells, looking over at me.

"He'll come to in a little while," I answered. "Though you did bash him pretty hard."

Howells chuckled. "He was getting all ready to sink his knife into Mr. Pons, and it would have hurt me to see him do that; so I bashed him. That's a sort of self-defense, isn't it, Mr. Pons; you see, you're the source of my income, and I couldn't live without that – you work it inversely."

Pons laughed. He moved away to the telephone connecting with Scotland Yard, and in a few moments had Jamison on the wire. "We've got the hunchback, Jamison," he said. "If you come right over you'll be in time to help question him. He's pretty badly bashed – "

"Skull's fractured," I put in.

" – Parker just says his skull's fractured... Send Meeker out to bring old Sir Ronald Duveen here. I think he'd like to see the Dove before we send him away."

"I wonder if this Duveen fellow is the old boy who came to see the Dove once in a while," said Howells, when Pons had turned from the telephone. "I told you I'd have him trailed, and it did work for a while."

"Comes to see him, you say?" put in Pons.

"Big car, chauffeur, and all the rest. The Dove meets him outside of Shen Han's; the old fellow won't come in. The Dove gets money from him; I know that."

Pons nodded. "It is very probably Duveen," he said.

"The fellow I fixed on the Dove never saw him," continued Howells, "and I couldn't identify Duveen as the man you want. It didn't seem as if Duveen – if it is he – had any connection with the Clubs."

"No, I don't think he has," said Pons.

"He's coming out of it," I put in.

Pons and Howells approached the couch and stood looking down at the crippled murderer. He was breathing jerkily, and his eyelids fluttered feebly. In a moment, I knew, he would be conscious once more.

"I've gone through his pockets," I said, looking up at Pons. "The black medal was there."

I indicated my find, and Pons bent to take it up. "Well, he is certainly the Knave of Clubs," said Pons. "T – I daresay that stands for Jack."

"It docs," said Howells.

The hunchback began to move his arms about now, and Pons bent closer.

At the same time, the outer bell jangled sharply, and in a few moments, Inspector Jamison strode into the room; beyond the door in the hall he posted two constables. He made his way quickly to the couch and looked down upon the prostrate hunchback.

"Just coming to, is he?" he asked.

"Quite so," said Pons.

Jamison looked up, and his eyes fastened on Bert Howells. "And who is this?" he asked.

"One of my most valued and trusted men," said Pons. "Mr. Bert Howells, Inspector Jamison."

The two men shook hands.

"I was just about to propose," continued Pons, "that you put Mr. Bert Howells permanently with Scotland Yard; thus far, he and Frick have done the best work in this case."

"But I thought Mr. Howells was dead," said Jamison.

"Isn't that strange?" said Howells blandly. "Now I wonder how that got about?"

Pons chuckled. "He arranged that himself, Jamison; and an excellent piece of work it was."

"Well, we can take you on, Mr. Howells," said Jamison.

"Special investigator, eh?" said Howells. "I am interested chiefly in the salary; always a vital factor, you know. And I would have to be free for Mr. Pons here."

Jamison laughed good-naturedly, and at the same moment the hunchback groaned and opened his eyes.

XVII

ALBERT, THE DOVE

Pons stepped quickly to the hunchback's side. "Well, Albert," he said. "We've got you at last."

The hunchback groaned once more, but did not condescend to answer.

He glared from one to the other of us, and grunted once or twice; then he looked away to the wall.

Howells grinned. "That's that," he said.

The outer bell jangled once more, and we could hear someone coming slowly and laboriously up the stairs.

"Sir Ronald Duveen," said Pons. "A cripple, as you know," he added to Jamison.

At the mention of this name, the hunchback turned his head and looked at us painfully. "What?" he stammered. "What was that?"

The door opened, and on the threshold stood Constable Meeker, leading Sir Ronald Duveen. Instantly Sir Ronald's eyes were fastened on the figure on the couch. The hunchback looked at the man on the threshold for one moment; then he relaxed and sank back, giving vent to a low moan.

"Will you come in, Sir Ronald?" said Pons. "You see, we have taken your brother."

Brother, I thought. So that was the connection! Sir Ronald came slowly over toward the couch.

"I knew it would come at last," he said. "Albert!" he exclaimed hoarsely. "Albert!"

The hunchback mumbled something; he opened his eyes and rested them on Sir Ronald's face.

"How do you feel, Albert?"

"All right. But don't bother me, now. Don't let them bother me – not now. Something's wrong, Ronald. Don't look at me like that. I think I'm going – going to die."

"No!" said Sir Ronald sharply. "No, you're not!" He turned away and sought a chair. "My youngest brother," he murmured.

Pons nodded. "How does it happen that a brother of Sir Ronald Duveen spends his days in Limehouse?" he asked.

Sir Ronald shook his head sorrowfully. "We were not both born cripples," he said. "Though I was. When Albert was small, he used to make fun of me – all the time. Sometimes I couldn't stand it any more; I used to try to get at him. I think I hated him more than I've ever hated anyone since. – Then, one day, Albert was struck by an automobile, and that growth came up on his back; the accident injured his mind. He stole things; that's common, isn't it, doctor?"

"Very common," I answered at once. "There are many cases on record where even a slight mental shock, a small skull fracture or injury, has caused mental derangement of this kind."

Sir Ronald nodded. "then – he ran away. We never found him, and gave him up as lost. Four years ago he came back one night, and told me who he was. Albert, the Dove – one of the worst murderers in all England. He demanded money; said he would stop his thievery and murder if I would support him. I was only too glad to do that, and I did it. But he never left off his ways, and now it's too late to save him."

"It was he who murdered Lord Cantlemere, and Sir Harry Mackenzie," put in Jamison.

"I know," said Sir Ronald wearily. "And Lord Norton and one of your constables. He told me; he took a fiendish joy in telling me, and I lived in fear of him. He was very fleet-footed, and with a fog to help him, he was most daring. But I am glad to see that he is caught at last; I shall not know what I will do now without him and his exposure to worry about."

"Well, he will most certainly end on the gallows," said Jamison curtly.

"On the contrary," I put in. "He will not live long enough; I think that he had best be removed to a hospital at once if his life is to be preserved long enough to permit any questioning."

"Thank heaven," breathed Sir Ronald. "Then the matter can be kept from the papers."

"Certainly," said Jamison.

Albert, the Dove, looked over at his brother and grinned feebly. "Well, Ronald, this will make it easy for you. Easy...I'm going to die."

"It would be best if you wouldn't talk," I said.

The hunchback grinned once more. "Best? I should live – to confess. You don't think I'm going to tell on the chief, do you? I'm not...I tell you, I'm not. My head hurts, doctor. It hurts like hell. Can't you do something?" Sir Ronald rose and went over to the couch as best he could. Pons had gone to the telephone and called for an ambulance to come from Scotland Yard.

"Albert," murmured Sir Ronald. "Albert, the doctor is going to let your head hurt like that until you tell them everything."

Albert, the Dove, glared at his brother. "It hurts," he said. "It hurts."

"Albert," continued Sir Ronald. "Have you been to church, Albert? You are going to die, Albert, and you know what they told us when we were boys. If you die like that, Albert, it's going to hurt you all the time where you'll go."

The hunchback turned a terrified gaze on his brother. "Do you think so, Ronald?" he muttered. "All the time...hurting, like this?"

"All the time, Albert," continued Sir Ronald inexorably. "It will not be so little as this. And you are going to die!" he said hoarsely. "To die!"

"Not yet," said Albert with difficulty. "Not yet, Ronald. Don't let it come now."

"It's coming," said Sir Ronald. "It's coming, and no one of us can stop it. Will you tell them what they want to know? Will you tell them?"

For a moment the hunchback hesitated. Then he put one hand out and clung feebly to his brother. "I will," he murmured gutturally. "Yes, I will."

"All right, Albert," said Sir Ronald. "I'll have them call a priest for you, and then, when they've taken you away from here, you can tell them what they want to know."

Sir Ronald stood up and went with bent head back to his chair. "If you see to it, gentlemen, that there is a priest present – a Catholic priest – I think you can persuade him to tell you what he knows. Both of us were brought up in the Roman Catholic faith; I am still deeply religious, because of my rigid early training. This Albert had, too, and to recall it now will be most helpful. Let him, at least, die a Catholic."

I came away from the patient. "He'll not last long," I said.

"Will it be all right to move him?" asked Jamison.

"Quite all right."

"How long will it take, doctor?" asked Sir Ronald.

"It is difficult to say," I replied. "He seems to have great vitality, and may live for two or even three days. But I should not be surprised to find him dead by tomorrow night at this time."

The hunchback had sunk into a coma, and this was just as well, for the police ambulance came shortly after. Jamison and Sir Ronald left together in Sir Ronald's car, following the ambulance.

"Well, that's the last of Albert, the Dove," said Howells philosophically. "I think I'll send the old boy a pack of cards; he'll feel more natural holding a deuce or jack of clubs than a crucifix!"

XVIII

FRICK IS HEARD FROM

If we thought that our adventures for that evening were over with the removal of Albert, the Dove, we erred. Not half an hour after the ambulance had departed, there was a short ring at the outer door, and then silence. Pons half rose to go to the door, but Howells looked up and said "I wouldn't," and Pons thought better of it.

A few moments passed. Then we could hear Mrs. Johnson mounting the stairs to our rooms, and in a moment she tapped on the door, opened it slightly, and stuck her hand into the room extending in our direction a dirty envelope. Pons took it at once, and Mrs. Johnson retired hastily.

Much to my curiosity, Pons spent some time over the message that had come in the dirty envelope. When he did finally pass it to me, neither Howells, who looked over my shoulder, nor I, could make anything out of it. We read:

> "efbs ns qpot j ibwf gpvme uif nbo zpv xbou boe j bn hpjoh up usz boe csjoh ijn bxbz upojhiu j ibwf tffo ns efwpsf boe mfbsofe if jt bo bnfsjdbo efufdujwf ifmqjoh vt if jt hpjoh up ifmq nf upojhiu xjmm zpv ibwf b hvbse po zpvs sppn cfdbvtf xf uijol xf njhiu cf gpmmpxfe boe uibu xpvmeou cf wfsz hppe jn bgsbje g"

Pons chuckled at the amazement which our faces must have shown. "Can't make it out, eh?" he asked.

"Not a word," I replied.

"Does it mean something?" asked Howells.

"Give it to me," instructed Pons, "and I will write it out for you. This code is one of Frick's pets; wherever he picked it up, I don't know."

Pons took the code message, and wrote rapidly. Finishing at last he returned it to me. "By merely carrying the letters of the alphabet forward one – that is, *a* equals *b*, *b* equals *c*, and ending with *z* equals *a* – Frick constructs that weird code. It is very elementary, and almost anyone could work it out with just a little study. I have written the correct letters beneath Frick's code letters."

Certainly the message was now clear enough. It read:

> "Dear Mr. Pons, I have found the man you want and I am going to try and bring him away tonight. I have seen Mr. Devore and learned he is an American detective helping us. He is going to help me tonight. Will you have a guard on your room, because we think we might be followed and that wouldn't be very good I'm afraid. F."

I looked up. "Who is this man Frick refers to?" I asked.

"That is the man whose evidence will clinch the case against the Clubs. Once he is brought here, and we hear what he has to say, then we can move definitely against the Clubs."

"Who is he?" I asked.

"He is a man who has been kept prisoner by the Clubs for many months; I did not suspect his existence until just shortly ago, and then I got word to Frick at once."

Pons called the Yard at this point, and asked for three constables to be stationed before the house. He requested particularly for Meeker, and suggested that Jamison hold himself in readiness for whatever might come from Pons.

Pons returned to his easy chair and sat in silence for some considerable time.

"You'll have to wait a good time, yet, Mr. Pons," said Howells suddenly. "The boys aren't left off until after midnight; then they can go their own way."

Pons nodded.

"And you'd better get everything ready for a fight. When the big boy finds out you've got him, he's going to run for it, plans or no plans."

"I have instructed Jamison," said Pons.

"He's got an aeroplane," continued Howells, imperturbably, "so you'd better see to it that you get that way blocked, too."

"Good Heavens!" I put in, "If you know where he is, why don't you go and get him at once. You can depend on Frick's coming, can't you?"

"Dear me," said Howells naively, "when you're fighting the Deuce of Clubs, you don't go at it that way, Dr. Parker. You never can tell whether Frick will get here or not. He's dependable, no doubt of it; but he's not as sharp as he ought to be. I wouldn't be surprised if we got Frick's body shipped to us instead."

"Do you mean to say that if Frick succeeds tonight, the organization known to us as the Clubs will be wiped out of existence tonight?" I asked in amazement.

"Practically," returned Pons. "With the heads gathered in our net, the small fry cannot function. And tonight, if Frick succeeds, we shall take the heads."

"And there's good luck in sight for us, too, Mr. Pons," said Howells from his position at the window. "The fog's beginning to lift."

"Excellent!" exclaimed Pons. "Let it take its time, and serve an excellent purpose in covering Frick and his manoeuvres tonight."

"Then, for heaven's sake, tell me, who is this all important man you are expecting Frick to bring?"

"It is a man who knows every secret of the Clubs. He has been their prisoner for ten months, and has during that time been consulted on nearly every project that the Clubs have pushed forward. His evidence is absolutely vital to us, and his rescue is even more so. From the moment he received my message, Frick's activities were centered on this rescue, and Devore went into Limehouse with the suspicion of his existence.

"It was seven months ago, when the Foreign Office first became alarmed over the number of so-called secrets that had in some way managed to get out to the public; from that time on, no state secret of importance seemed to be safe. It was to their prisoner in Limehouse that the agent of the Clubs in the Foreign Office went with the scraps he gathered so persistently, and it was this prisoner who was forced to interpret their significance. And this man, Frick brings to me tonight."

Pons sat back moodily and looked toward the window, where the grey-yellow of the fog was already lessening in its intensity. For some time he sat thus; then he relaxed, and I saw that he did not want his thoughts disturbed and turned to my book, though reading was out of the question entirely.

It was shortly after midnight when one of the constables outside blew two brief blasts on his whistle, and Pons leaped to his feet in considerable agitation. He went to the door leading into the hall and threw it open. From where I sat I could hear a fumbling at the outer door, and then suddenly I heard it thrown open, and immediately there came a quick rush of feet up the stairs. There were rapid footsteps along the hall, and Pons re-entered the room, followed by Frick, whom I knew by sight, and the man Devore in underworld disguise, holding between them a cowering wretch, who had gone long unshaven and uncared for in any way. He stood there shuddering, and as

I looked at him, he seemed to me the embodiment of all the wretchedness of the Limehouse lounger.

"Parker," said Pons, closing the door behind this odd group, "Allow me to present to you the Foreign Undersecretary, Sir Landon Hatry."

For a moment I stared as if shot. Then I started out of my chair and went toward the figure held by Frick and Devore, and peered intently at him.

"Surely," I began, "Surely this is not Undersecretary Hatry, who disappeared only a few days ago?"

"No," said Pons, motioning the group to be seated, "not at all, Parker. This is Undersecretary Hatry – the Undersecretary who disappeared ten months ago!"

"Then what of the man in the Foreign Office – the man we have known as Hatry?" I asked wildly.

Pons smiled. "Before I answer that, Parker, let me ask you a question. Is it possible for anyone to remove a wen from any place on the body?"

"Why, yes, yes – but," and then I saw it. "The man at the Foreign Office was a Club!" I exclaimed.

"More, Parker, more," said Pons. "The man at the Foreign Office was the man von Storck, the man who is known to us as the Deuce of Clubs!"

XIX

THE END IN SIGHT

"What danger can we expect from the big boy, Frick?" asked Howells.

"Not much just now," said Frick. "He'll not miss Hatry for at least two hours yet, and there's that much time to get ready to go for him."

"Capital!" exclaimed Pons.

"You had better watch out," said Hatry weakly. "The man has both my town house and country house at his disposal. I'm sure he has an aeroplane at my country house over at Windsor." He coughed. "May I ask how you guessed, Mr. Pons?"

Pons nodded. "I suppose the man masquerading in your position at the Foreign Office when I found that he had disappeared with all the dummy papers ten days ago. There were only three people who knew where all the dummy papers were hidden; Lord Norton, the false Hatry, and Inspector Jamison. Only Lord Norton and I knew where the real papers were, and now only I know where they are. Immediately I wondered why Hatry was not also disposed of, together with Lord Norton; the answer was inevitable. Hatry was the leak in the Foreign Office; we had neglected him entirely, and given our attention to the clerks in charge of the news department, together with others in less important positions. It is now clear that Hatry was the cause for the first leak to the press which plunged all of us into a frenzy.

"It came to me at once that von Storck, under the name of Störing, had held a position in the Foreign Office at the time he had tried to get the Dunfer Gas in 1914 and 1915. He would be well qualified to take Hatry's place after the time of Hatry's illness ten months ago. Of this illness I became suspicious at once, and so confirmed my suspicions by having Sir Henry Bishop wire to Germany; the time of Hatry's illness coincided with the time von Storck was known to have been last seen in Germany.

"What happened was simply that the Clubs invaded Sir Landon Hatry's house, carried him off, and substituted in his stead, von Storck – the Deuce of Clubs. Then, I daresay the old servants were slowly discharged, and the Clubs substituted. An operation was performed on von Storck's nose, the wen was removed, and when this was accomplished, von Storck, whose appearance is generally like that of Hatry's, took his place in the Foreign Office. Hatry's return after his illness marked the beginning of the loss of state secrets."

"They kidnapped me, yes," said Sir Landon Hatry. "And I know that all of this is true, because I have heard it from the Deuce himself. I was forced by torture to interpret all state papers they had copied or made off with, and in the last days they have put before me all the dummy plans for the Ritchie-Carroll aeroplane, which were to assist me in constructing the plane substantially as it should be."

"Well, you shall rest now," said Pons. "We shall make after von Storck at once. Frick, Howells, and Devore, I want to stay here until our return. Parker and I will help with the raids on Sir Landon's town house, and, if necessary, on the country house near Windsor."

Pons now went swiftly to the telephone, and in a moment had Jamison on the wire. "Are you there?...Take all the men you can find, Jamison, and surround Sir Landon Hatry's town house. Ask no questions; do as I tell you... Yes, and have the Thames boats in readiness. I shall want also an aeroplane; call Sir Henry Bishop and have him arrange the matter with the war office. Or better, Jamison, get Sir Henry on the wire and call back here... Very well."

Pons turned from the telephone and looked once more toward Sir Landon Hatry. "Do you know anything of their plans?" he asked.

Hatry nodded wearily. "Most of the papers of the Clubs are kept in my town house, in my secretaire. Look for them there. If they anticipate a raid, as they undoubtedly do, they will attempt to carry the papers with them. They use my country house merely as a place of refuge, that is, when they are hard pressed. The Trey and another man high in the organization are located at my country house. To the best of my knowledge, the members of the organization, with a single exception of the man known as the Knave of Clubs, who is the brother of my good friend Sir Ronald Duveen, do not know the Deuce of Clubs. Even those people who serve him in my town house are led to believe that the Deuce is some enigmatic individual higher up."

Pons nodded. "That is all we need know, I think," he said. "We can go for them as soon as our preparations are made."

The telephone jangled harshly, and Pons went quickly to the instrument. "Ah, Sir Henry... Yes, we are about to proceed against the Clubs. We have located the Deuce, and identified him. I haven't time to explain the situation to you, but first I want you to call the War Office and see that two aeroplanes are placed at my disposal – or better, make one amphibian... Yes, they are to be waiting for me at Croydon. I want machine guns attached... Yes. But we may not need to use them... Then I should like to have you come up to London immediately and arrange to send dispatches to Germany and France to enlist their aid. It is practically certain that the Deuce will make a dash for the Continent by air, and he may get too strong a lead on us. Therefore, it is necessary that you wire Germany and France to detail an air squadron to be on the lookout for any passenger plane making for the Continent...Yes, that will be all. Inform Germany and France that our planes will send out rockets when we are hailed by them. Goodbye."

Pons waited a moment, and then called Jamison once more, telling him to call for us at once, and to send the C.I.D. men on ahead to surround the house of Sir Landon Hatry.

"I'd like to go with you, Mr. Pons," said Howells.

"And I," put in Frick.

Pons shook his head. "No, you had better stay here. Above all, guard Sir Landon Hatry. It might be well to have a physician here to look him over."

"Not at all, Mr. Pons, not at all," said Sir Landon in some haste. "It is not necessary, let me assure you; the mere fact of my being free of that horrible prison is enough to give me heart."

Despite Sir Landon's opposition, Pons signified to Devore that a physician should be called in, and Devore nodded that he understood. We sat in silence for some moments, and then at last we heard the blaring of horns that told us of Jamison's arrival, and we left to join him.

As we got into the car, Jamison greeted us with a further announcement.

"The hunchback's dead," he said.

"Did you get anything from him?" asked Pons quickly.

Jamison nodded. "Everything. I know all about the matter, from the beginning to the end. We've a signed deposition."

"Does he say how he happened to run into von Storck?" asked Pons.

"Met him the first time he was in London under the name of 'Störing,' and got mixed up with him then already. He left the country with him after the death of Dunfer, which it seems Störing or von Storck engineered."

Pons nodded. "So I thought," he said. "I have Hatry up at the rooms," continued Pons. "Frick and Devore managed to bring him in, and we'll get a statement from him. The aeroplanes we will need, he thinks, to pursue von Storck, who will probably fly from Hatry's country place. They will be waiting for us at Croydon, though I hope it will not be necessary. You will instruct your men to search through Hatry's secretaire, where the Clubs kept all their papers."

We rode for a time in silence, and then the constable at the wheel turned and spoke. "We're getting there, sir," he said, addressing Jamison. "Shall I go on, or stop before the place is reached."

"Best leave us off a street or so before," instructed Jamison.

XX

THE LAST OF THE CLUBS

The town house of Sir Landon Hatry was set well away from the street in the center of a plot of well kept ground, overgrown with bushes and flowers. The small estate afforded an excellent hiding place for Jamison's men, for, as we passed into the grounds and made for the front door, more than half of Jamison's men rose up from behind shadowy bushes to show themselves. The house was well lighted, and Pons interpreted this as a bad sign.

"This means that von Storck has not even been here," he whispered.

"Either he does not know of Hatry's disappearance, or he has gone direct to Hatry's country house and taken flight."

"Surely he must know of it by this time," said Jamison.

"I am afraid he does, and that means that we will have to pursue him by air, where our chances of ever seeing him again are very small."

Pons rang the bell, and in a moment footsteps echoed along the hall. The door was thrown open by an elderly man in butler's outfit, who started back in alarm when he perceived the constables who had suddenly risen up behind us. We stepped quickly into the house, and despite the protests of the butler, we passed him out to the waiting constables. At the same instant there was a loud shouting coming from the rear of the house, and we knew that the C.I.D. men had got in.

A door in one wall flew open, and a tall dark gentleman in evening clothes burst into the corridor. Jamison immediately leaped forward and flung himself upon him. A brief scuffle followed, but with Pons' help, Jamison easily subdued the man in evening clothes. From the floor Pons picked up a metal club which he handed to me with a smile. On the black metal was engraved a gold 3.

Pons now made his way into the different rooms on the first floor, and soon he found what he sought. The secretaire in the library had not been touched; it was jammed full to the top with papers and plans, government secrets that it had taken years to gather.

But it was only too obvious that the Deuce of Clubs was not there, that he had not been there.

"You'd best put Mecker in charge," said Pons, "and come with us. You'll take the aeroplane; Parker and I will take the amphibian. Come on."

We raced wildly to Croydon Aerodrome, and ran swiftly across the great field to the planes which were all in readiness for us.

"I have little hope," said Pons, as we ran, "for the man has too great a start on us. He must surely have reached the Continent by now."

"Still," I put in, "if he had to take flight so quickly that he could not even save his papers, then certainly he cannot have so great a lead on us."

"That is so," said Jamison.

"Have you sent men to Hatry's country place?" asked Pons.

Jamison jerked his head up and down as he ran, and Pons appeared satisfied.

We zoomed away into the night and headed toward the Channel. To our left, and a little in the lead, flew Jamison.

Our spotlights swung in great arcs, stabbing into the black all around us. In a few moments the swing of one of the lights brought into view the coast of England, fast receding into the blackness behind us.

"We'll never get him," shouted Pons above the roar of the motor.

But even as he shouted, there came a sudden flare of light from ahead, and up from the sea below there mounted a rocket! I shouted and leaned forward. Then suddenly came five more rockets, and once more six together. Jamison, too, must have seen them, for his machine began to circle downward toward the surface of the Channel, though he could not land in the water. Already our amphibian began the descent, and as we came rapidly down, we saw in the air before us four aeroplanes, two from France and two from Germany, as our lights revealed them to us. Jamison came to rest with his plane in line with these four. In a moment, our amphibian was gliding smoothly over the waves. Our spotlight shot forward, and immediately six spotlights came from the resting amphibians and focused on the object floating tranquilly on the water before them.

It was a shattered aeroplane; it had been wrecked by machine gun fire, and now lay, a battered mass, in the waves. But what drew my eyes at once was the figure in the cockpit; he lay there, his dead white face turned upward toward the stars – the last of the Clubs!

As the sound of our motor died away, there arose from the seaplanes a great cry – "Hoch!" from the German and Austrian ships to our right, and a loud "Vive!" from the French ships to our left. Pons rose in his seat and shouted in answer. And there, in the middle of the English Channel, the secret agents of four European nations saw the last of Heinrich Störing, alias Heinrich von Storck, alias Sir Landon Hatry, super-spy of the decade, the Deuce of Clubs. His cold, bullet-riddled body sank beneath the waves as the first grey streaks of light on the horizon heralded the dawn.

Mr. Fairlie's Final Journey

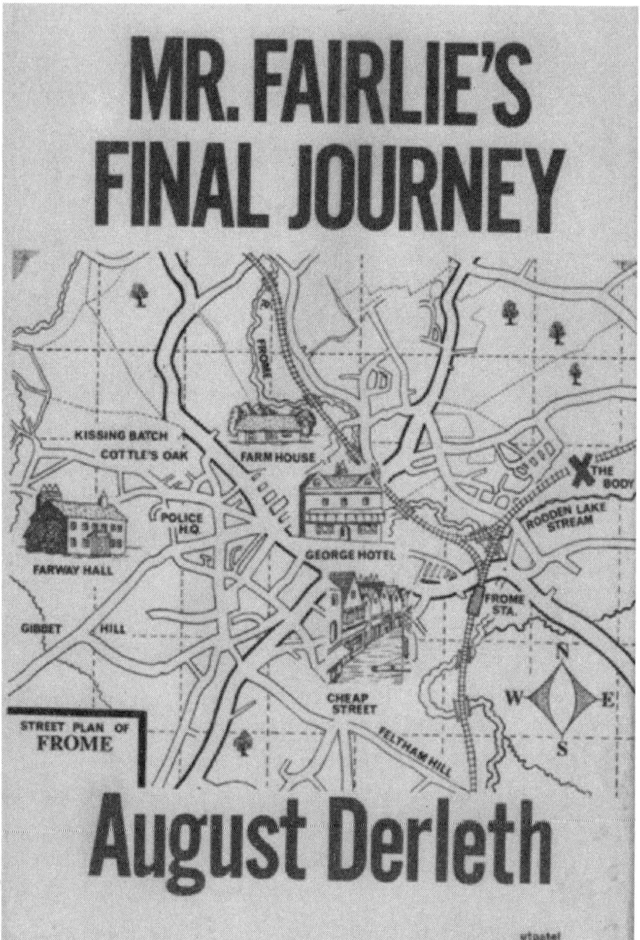
MR. FAIRLIE'S
FINAL JOURNEY
KISSING BATCH
COTTLE'S OAK
FARM HOUSE
FROME
THE BODY
POLICE H.Q.
RODDEN LAKE STREAM
FARWAY HALL
GEORGE HOTEL
FROME STA.
GIBBET HILL
N
W
E
S
CHEAP STREET
STREET PLAN OF
FROME
FELTHAM HILL
August Derleth
utpatel

I

THE LAST OF JONAS FAIRLIE

It was on a blustery night in September that my friend, Solar Pons, the private enquiry agent, was called into one of the most puzzling adventures of his career. He had completed the curious matter of the Cathedral Ghost but two days before, and had put away his notes and clippings about it. The hour was late, and now he paced the floor, restless and preoccupied. Outside, a chill wind blew, making wintry sighs at the windows. Our good landlady, Mrs. Johnson, had built a cheery fire, and the flames danced high on the hearth, adding their voice to the wind's up the chimney.

I made some comment about Pons's restlessness, and he had just replied, "I am always restless when I have no problem before me," when the telephone rang.

"At this hour!" I cried. "Why, it is almost eleven."

"Time waits on no one," said Pons, and picked up the telephone with an eagerness he made no attempt to conceal. I heard him say only, "Pons here," and then no more, though I could hear distantly a rapid monologue at the other end of the line.

When at last, with a brief assurance that "we" would be ready, he put down the telephone, his eyes were alight. He stood rubbing his hands together, all his restlessness gone out of him before a rising anticipation, and faced me.

"Are you free for a little venture into Somerset?" he asked.

"Mrs. Bassett's baby isn't due for a month," I answered, "and Mrs. Parker won't be back from Australia short of a fortnight."

"Capital! Capital!" cried Pons. "A little problem has just come up at Frome."

"The last train from Paddington has gone."

"Too slow, in any event. The Chief Constable is on his way for us. That was he, telephoning en route."

"What is it?"

"We shall hear," said Pons, "Apparently it is murder. Just hand me that *ABC Railway Guide*, will you?"

I did as he asked, and watched him look up Frome.

"We can take quarters at the George, facing the market square, if it is necessary for us to stay. Frome still holds a cattle market – and, if I am not mistaken, an annual cheese show. It is a city where old customs prevail and thus one with character."

"I had better arrange for a locum, then," I said.

It was just past midnight when Sir Hugh Parrington, Chief Constable of Somerset, came for us. Within minutes we were on our way southwest of London, bound for Frome. Sir Hugh was a tall, lean man, florid of countenance, with a grey moustache and intense blue eyes under shaggy white brows. He began to talk from the moment we got into his Rolls-Royce.

"A senseless thing," he said. "Jonas Fairlie hadn't an enemy in the world. Got into the train for Paddington at 9:13 – the last train out of Frome – and turned up dead at the next station. Sitting there as if he slept. Might never have suspected anything but heart failure if it hadn't been for the smell of chloroform. Fairlie used to be Charlie Farway's batman. Charlie died two years ago, but Fairlie kept his old place at the manor along the Nunney Road on the southwest edge of Frome. Kept to himself and made no trouble. Mrs. Farway wouldn't have him disturbed, but in any case there was some kind of arrangement with Charlie. He was sixty-two. He had something on his mind – no doubt of that. Funny thing. We searched him – we're holding the body and the carriage at Frome." He pawed at a pocket of his waistcoat and came out with a slip of paper. "Found this in the lining of his hat."

He took a pen-flashlight from his pocket and turned it on to the paper he had handed to Pons.

I leaned over and read, in a thin, spidery script:

Solar Pons
7B Praed Street
W. 2 – Ambassador 10,000

"You knew him?" asked Sir Hugh.

"No," answered Pons.

"You had some communication with him?"

"None."

"Did you know Charlie Farway?

"Not to my knowledge."

"A queer business. Nothing else on Fairlie. All dressed up for his journey to London. His ticket was to Paddington – that's near your place, Pons. So he must have been coming to see you."

"That would seem to be the elementary deduction," said Pons dryly.

Sir Hugh grunted impatiently. "Fairlie came back from the war with Farway. Been with him ever since. Managed the estate and made some show in the business. The Farways have been in printing for some time – books for London publishers, that sort of thing. Fairlie kept his hand in, and I suppose he would have done so until he passed on. Normally, that is. She's fading away, they tell me. Never see her about anymore. Confined to the house – in bed most of the time."

"Had Farway known Fairlie before the war?" asked Pons. Sir Hugh looked at him in dim astonishment. "Would that matter? That's almost twenty years done, Pons."

"One never knows at this stage what matters and what doesn't," said Pons mildly. "The picture you've given me is of two strangers fallen together who come out of the war inseparable. Had Fairlie saved his life, perhaps?"

"If he had, you'd never have got it out of Fairlie. It was all he could do to give you the time of day."

"Uncommonly secretive?"

"Say he was 'quiet.' He went about like a shadow. He went off on journeys, but there wasn't much secret about most of them, for he had a daughter in Cheltenham and a grandson, and he went to visit them from time to time. She's been sent for."

"Farway's family?"

"Oh, you'll meet them, no doubt," said Sir Hugh. "No children though. They had a son, but he lost his life in a shooting accident seven years ago. Grouse-hunting in Scotland."

Pons sat for a few moments in thoughtful silence before he spoke again. "Mr. Fairlie's journeys – I take it he went to places other than Cheltenham?"

"Twice to Scotland. Now and then to some cottage he owned on the coast of Wales. But it's his final journey we ought to be concerned about. Why was he coming to see you?"

"Granted that he was, we can only conclude that he had some reason imperative to himself, some troubling problem he wished to lay before someone. Other than that, we have no way of knowing at this point what it might be. But surely it is idle to speculate; we need to have certain facts before we can do so."

"If we can get them," said Sir Hugh with gruff skepticism.

The third-class carriage containing the body of the dead man had been shunted to a siding not far from the station at Frome.

It stood under guard of four constables and Police Sergeant Arthur Bates, a grim-faced young man, who led us to the small compartment and stood at the door, making a succinct report, while Pons began an examination of the carriage. Sir Hugh, too, remained outside. I joined him presently, so that Pons might have the carriage to himself while he heard the sergeant's account of how the dead man had been seen by a guard before the train had quite come into the next station, as a result of which the carriage had been detached there, and by order of the Chief Constable, brought back to Frome, since indications were that the death of Mr. Fairlie had taken place in Somerset rather than in Wiltshire.

The dead man himself might have been sleeping. He sat with his head back, his eyes closed, his mouth slightly open. The skin on the left cheek showed the kind of burn that might be expected from the pressure of a chloroform-saturated pad, which had evidently been carefully covered to prevent maximum burning; some similar discoloration was visible also about the dead man's nostrils.

"Mr. Aston, the guard," explained the sergeant, "said that as he had known Mr. Fairlie well, and that he had traveled many times in the same train with Mr. Fairlie, and that he had never known him to sleep on the train, he became suspicious when he saw him in this position, and thereupon entered the compartment to make sure he was all right. Mr. Fairlie was dead, and Mr. Aston smelled chloroform – though the window was open. There is still that smell about."

The dead man wore a look of austerity; his clothing was conservative, save for a small-plaid waistcoat, across the front of which a thin gold watch chain could be seen; his bowler hat lay on the seat beside him; his luggage – a small overnight bag – stood under the seat. Mr. Fairlie was thin-faced, and his grey hair was cut close to his head. Even in death he looked very much like a civil servant.

Pons made a cursory examination of the body, paying closest attention to the dead man's hands; then he dropped to his knees to scrutinize the compartment itself.

"Nothing's been disturbed, Pons," boomed Sir Hugh.

"I assumed as much," answered Pons.

"Insofar as Mr. Fairlie's appearance indicates," the sergeant carried on, "he was evidently taken by surprise."

"And suddenly attacked," said Pons. "Let me call your attention to the middle fingernail of the right hand."

The sergeant worried forward like an aroused bulldog. He bent over the dead man.

"A touch of blood and what is certainly some skin, however small a fragment," said Pons. "He evidently had time to make some slight resistance. There is, too, a tuft of what appears to be hair in that hand – and, if I may, I will just borrow that for a day or so."

"By all means," decided Sir Hugh before the sergeant could protest.

Pons pried it from the dead man's hand and placed it in one of the small envelopes he habitually carried for such purposes.

"There would also seem to be the suggestion that he was searched by someone other than the police," Pons went on. "There is a slight tear along the edge of the inner pocket of his coat, as if someone were in haste to see what he carried there."

"His spectacles in their case," said the sergeant.

"Mr. Fairlie's very appearance suggests that he would repair a tear before he wore the coat," said Pons.

"That he would," said Sir Hugh, crowding forward. "What did he have that someone else was looking for?"

"If we knew that, we might have the solution to his murder."

He got up off his knees. He looked out into the corridor, and back at the dead man. The yellow light of the carriage – the body of Jonas Fairlie – the voice of the wind and the dark night pressing in from all sides made for an eerie scene, one that held while Pons stood silently, his eyes dwelling on the dead man, his gaze thoughtful, one hand toying with the lobe of his left ear, and dissolved when he turned abruptly and stepped outside the carriage.

"Now then?" said Sir Hugh inquiringly, looking hopefully at Pons, as if he expected a miracle to be performed on the instant.

"Who knew he was coming to London?" asked Pons.

"We don't know. We've not questioned anyone at the house. We'll do that in the morning," said the Chief Constable.

"Of course, Mr. Pons, the booking-clerk knew," said Sergeant Bates.

"Very probably not before he bought his ticket," said Pons. "Yet someone must have known he was going on a journey – or waited upon his doing so."

"Oh, Fairlie was always going on journeys," said Sir Hugh. "Fact. He went off on the average once a fortnight."

"Curious. Had he always done so?"

"Well, now," said Sir Hugh. "Well, now – I can't say."

"Only in the last year or so, Mr. Pons," put in Sergeant Bates. "He began to go off a little oftener when Mr. Farway died – once every six weeks, then – that was to see his daughter in Cheltenham. We've made inquiries at the booking-office. Then, after that, he must have grown more restless and perhaps more lonesome – and he went oftener."

"To Cheltenham?"

"No. To Scotland first. Then to Wales. Once to London. And then he increased his visits to his daughter and grandson."

"Did they not visit him here?"

Sir Hugh cut in. "There was some stiffness at the Hall, Pons. Farway wouldn't have it. He could be a hard man in some ways."

"Yet Fairlie and Farway were evidently inseparable, to judge by your account," said Pons.

"Well, there was some trouble about the girl," said Sir Hugh.

"Or Fairlie's wife?"

"I think not. They liked her. She was a town girl – Lucy Freeman. Died about ten years ago."

"They lived at the Hall?"

"On the grounds. There are tenant houses," explained Sir Hugh. "Diana was born there – his daughter. Grew up there. Since she left, Fairlie gave up the house. He now has quarters in the Hall." He shrugged impatiently. "But all this has nothing to do with the fact of Fairlie's murder."

"You must bear with me, Sir Hugh," said Pons imperturbably. "But I think we are done here. Let us repair to the George and resume in the morning."

"Very good. I'll come around then and take you over to the Hall – or wherever you want to go."

It was now dawn, but Pons showed no inclination to retire. Once in our quarters on the second floor of the George – a handsome, dignified hotel that faced the marketplace – he began to pace the floor restlessly, to and fro, out to the balcony overlooking the street, and back, his grey eyes keen, his mind evidently turning over what little we knew of the crime. I flung myself down on a bed and watched him go up and down, waiting upon him to speak of Mr. Fairlie's death.

But he was not inclined to do so. He came back in from the balcony at one point to say, "There is a carnival moving through the town. I should not be surprised if the Cheese Show is imminent. In any case, this must be market day, for the stalls are being got ready across the way. I am delighted at the maintenance of these old customs."

"I have heard you say so," I said. "But what do you make of the case?"

He paused in mid-stride, and gave me a reflective look. "I should not be surprised to learn that these waters are deeper than it would now appear."

"Why do you say so?"

"The little matter of Fairlie's journeys, for one thing," he said. "Does a man of his stamp chase off to Scotland and Wales because he is restless or lonesome? I doubt it."

"Oh, come, Pons, it is entirely possible," I protested.

"Possible, yes. Probable, no. I am inclined to think that his frequent journeys were not matters of pleasure."

"Apart from his visits to his daughter."

"Oh, that is elementary," said Pons brusquely. "So, if not pleasure-bent, what then? Mr. Fairlie had access to a cottage on the coast of Wales – he owned such a cottage, Sir Hugh has said. One would have supposed that if he sought rest or pleasure, he would go there. But the evidence is that he went there least of all. Scotland and London. Now, surely, that is ambiguous. We must inquire a little further to learn just where he went in Scotland. At his age, not tramping in the highlands, certainly. And London! His cut is not that of a man who would haunt the music-halls. Indeed, it might not be amiss to look into the entire pattern of Mr. Fairlie's journeys; perhaps in them lies the answer to the importance of this final journey he did not live to make."

"I believe, with Sir Hugh, that he was certainly coming to see you."

"It is reasonable to think so. He had made a note of our telephone number. He meant to call, once he reached London, and make an appointment."

"Someone suspected and killed him to prevent his doing so."

"Gently, gently, Parker. That is a *non sequitur*. It may have been only coincidence that he was killed at this point. Someone clearly meant him to make no more journeys. Why?"

"Because he felt that something about Mr. Fairlie's journeys threatened him?" I ventured.

"Perhaps," said Pons enigmatically.

"If you ask me," I said stubbornly, "somebody didn't want him to reach you. It's as simple as that."

"Ah, you have an unhappy tendency to see all things as simple, Parker," he said. "Would matters were so! I should think it highly unlikely, on the basis of what we know about Fairlie, that he told anyone of his plans. He has been described as a quiet, secretive man, little given to speech. Does it seem probable to you that such a man would announce his intention of consulting me?"

"Well, no," I admitted reluctantly. "But then something else suggests itself – Fairlie was being watched."

"I am always gratified to observe the felicitous effect of exposure to my little feats of ratiocination," said Pons dryly. "Then you think me right?"

"Never more so. Fairlie was indeed under some kind of surveillance, for his murderer had to strike at just the right time. He evidently hoped that Fairlie's death would be laid to heart trouble of some kind, and he did not count on the discovery of his body quite so soon. Only the guard's familiarity with Fairlie's habits, perhaps, prevented his plan from being fulfilled. The chloroform was detected – despite the carriage window the murderer opened – and suspicion was aroused. We are dealing with no mean opponent."

"Fairlie obviously underestimated him."

"He may not have known his identity."

"He could hardly have been unaware of being under surveillance," I said. "Surely, in a city like Frome, and for a man who has lived here so long, he would have been aware of someone – stranger or one familiar to him – too frequently nearby."

"He may never have suspected it," countered Pons. "He seems to have been a man involved with matters that concerned him exclusive of all else. Then, too, I suspect that we are dealing with someone who, if he undertook to keep Fairlie in view, would not always present the same appearance."

"But the fact that he was coming to consult you," I put in, "surely suggests that Fairlie knew or suspected something beyond his power to handle."

"That is a possibility – even a probability," conceded Pons. "We have, however, no knowledge that it is so. We can only conjecture. Clearly, it was not at this point sufficient to warrant involving the police. But there are one or two little things that may have escaped your notice, Parker."

"I would be happy to hear of them."

"It did not strike you as curious that Mr. Fairlie's journeys should have so markedly increased in the past two years?"

"Not at all," I answered. "His companion had died. What more natural but that he should attempt to fill the vacuum left at Farway's death in some such manner?"

"Ah, that is cogently put. It may be. In time of stress or emotional difficulty, there is a normal tendency on the part of many human beings to take flight. But I submit that there may very well have been some other reason for Mr. Fairlie's absence from the estate he was obliged to manage, as Sir Hugh put it."

"What else?"

"There is the curious lack of obvious motive. Mr. Fairlie could not have been a wealthy man; in any event, his daughter is – as far as we know – his only legal heir. One could hardly suspect Mr. Fairlie of being involved in a crime of passion – though it is not impossible. We are left then with the clear suggestion that for some reason – which is certainly dark as of now – Mr. Fairlie alive was dangerous to someone.

"No mention has been made of robbery as motive, for all that Mr. Fairlie was searched. What then was the object of that search? I submit that something Mr. Fairlie knew or suspected, or something he possessed was so dangerous to someone else that only Mr. Fairlie's death could diminish that danger.

"But we are not yet in possession of enough facts to warrant any but the most elementary conclusions. Let us just sleep on it."

II

FARWAY HALL

In mid-morning Sir Hugh Parrington made his appearance. We had had less than five hours' sleep, and I suspected that Pons had slept little of that time, for I had heard him about now and then as I was drifting off in the early hours. The Chief Constable, however, was fresh and in high spirits, as if he expected Pons to present the constabulary with a solution to Mr. Fairlie's death in a matter of hours.

As we drove toward Farway House, Sir Hugh kept up a constant stream of talk with a bluff heartiness clearly integral to him. Was it not possible, he now wondered, that Fairlie's killer had not meant to kill him, but only to render him unconscious so that he could be searched? Unless one accepted the premise of a professional robber equipped with chloroform, which was admittedly far-fetched – one could only conclude that a considerable premeditation was involved.

Pons smiled, with visible patience. He dismissed the Chief Constable's theory with a mere shake of his head. "I take it," he said, "you've interviewed the booking-clerk. I believe the sergeant said something to that effect."

"Done right away," said Sir Hugh.

"There could not have been many travelers who looked forward to reaching London in the early hours."

"Four. But who's to say the fellow who did Fairlie in got on at Frome? Perhaps he was on the train."

"Unlikely," said Pons brusquely. "Who got on here?"

"Well, seven people got on here – four for London. Fairlie and Gerald Farway, the old man's nephew, who spends most of his time at the Hall. They were known to the booking-clerk. They got on independently, apparently – neither knew the other was traveling, and Farway's presumably off in London at this moment. Farway went first-class, Fairlie third. One fellow, a Mr. Max Stubbs, a salesman, frequented the line; he was bound for Westbury. He'd come into Frome yesterday morning on his route from Exeter. He made it regularly. One was a woman no one knew, but I should think it unlikely a woman could have done it. Besides, she traveled first class, too. The other three Mr. Nichols didn't know. He'll come on again at five if you want to talk to him."

"The others," prompted Pons.

Sir Hugh shrugged. "Oh, men – two of them – between thirty and fifty, Nichols judged. The one was bearded. The third was an old fellow. Nichols guessed him to be in his seventies. All bundled up against the wind. Walked with a cane and a little unsteady on his feet. That's the lot."

"What of fingerprints in the compartment?" I put in.

The chief Constable shook his head. "Oh, Doctor – dozens of fingerprints. You may be sure whoever killed Jonas Fairlie came prepared. We won't find his. We're doing all this routine work, of course – there's no need for Pons to spend his energies at it."

Pons sat in reflective silence.

"Surely, there were other travelers in that carriage," I said.

"Only two people. A woman traveling from Exeter to London, and a clergyman who had got on at Castle Cary."

"Have they been reached?"

"Oh, yes. Our men are efficient, Doctor, believe me – even to the point of resenting Solar Pons a little. They'll get over that."

"Could they have heard anything in their compartments?" I asked.

"Nothing. The train's hardly quiet, but then, in all likelihood, the way it was done wouldn't allow for much noise, would it now?" Sir Hugh looked at me earnestly as he spoke, his eyes intent. "He was got hold of and the chloroform pressed over his face, all in a moment. He'd hardly have time to cry out. He had time only to scratch the fellow. It must have been done just out of Frome – when he was found his body was still warm. No sign of rigor."

"And whoever did it could have slipped off the train as it slowed down along the line."

"Or stayed on to mingle with the rest of the passengers," said Sir Hugh. "We can't detain a trainload of people."

Pons came to sudden life. "They are examining the line?"

"They're at it now, Pons, looking to see if anyone jumped off. But here we are at the Hall."

As the Chief Constable spoke, the car turned off the road and into a driveway through a gate flanked by stone pillars crowned with Georgian vases. The driveway led between banks of rhododendron that presently gave way and disclosed a handsome, ivied late Georgian house of dark red brick. The house was of two floors, with an attic storey above the cornice. The entrance was framed by attached Doric columns and crowned by a curved pediment, and the whole doorway was cased in wood painted white.

I observed, as we got out of the car, that we were on a pronounced rise, and said so.

"Yes, this is Gibbet Hill," said the chief Constable.

"Ah," said Pons. "This is then the place where the unhappy ringleaders of the local inhabitants who took part in Monmouth's rebellion were hanged."

"Yes, that is so," said Sir Hugh. "Two hundred fifty years ago."

The view from the front of the house was impressively beautiful. In the west rose the limestone of the Mendips, all combes and caves among the rocks. The Frome River could be seen winding northwards toward the Avon through meadows, and to the east were more hills reaching to the edge of Salisbury plain. Hills and downland stretched away in all directions save to the northeast, where the country lay in flat green meadows.

The front door was opened to us before Sir Hugh could apply himself to the bronze knocker. A butler held the door wide.

"Mrs. Farway is expecting you, sir," he said as Sir Hugh announced himself. "Please follow me. She is waiting in the upstairs sitting-room."

He led us down the hall to a quasi-spiral staircase, rather more of the mid-Georgian period than the late, with slender turned balusters standing on the treads, columnar newels and a ramped handrail. As we were mounting the stairs, a door below opened a little way and someone looked up at us – a dark-faced woman of thirty or more, with her black hair drawn straight back away from her forehead and down across her ears, startling me, for I thought at first that she was coloured, rather than only very dark of skin. Her face was cold and expressionless, and she looked at us only briefly before she withdrew and closed the door once more. Pons, I saw, had also noticed, but the Chief Constable apparently had not.

Lady Farway reclined on a chaise lounge near one wall of a conservatively but expensively appointed room. Her hair, for all that she was in her early seventies, was still dark and only streaked with grey. She had very dark eyes and a fine, sensitive mouth under a sharply defined nose. Her skin was remarkably free of signs of age, but it was evident that she was not in good health, for there was a marked, almost febrile fragility about her, and her colour was unnaturally high. She smiled at sight of the Chief Constable, but it was only a tremulous, troubled smile that vanished almost at once.

"A dreadful thing, Hugh," she said. "Who would have harmed Jonas?"

"We have brought in the best assistance," said the Chief Constable, and introduced us.

Lady Farway acknowledged us graciously. "I do remember your name, Mr. Pons, in connection with that dreadful tragedy at Yeovil. I hope you can help us to learn why anyone should want to kill Mr. Fairlie." She shuddered a little and raised one thin-fingered hand to her lips, as if to brush away her words.

"I will try," said Pons with unbecoming modesty. "But we need to know more about Mr. Fairlie, to begin with."

"Anything we can do, Mr. Pons, we will do."

"Did you know that he was going to London, Lady Farway?"

"No, Mr. Pons."

"Might anyone in this house have known it?"

"I should be very much surprised if anyone knew," she replied. "Mr. Fairlie was a very reticent man. He came and went as he pleased. Once a month he came to me with the reports. I seldom saw more of him. I had every confidence in him, just as my husband had. They were – well, I suppose one might say, inseparable. Charles depended on him – and Jonas in turn on Charles. You must understand that Mr. Farway saved Mr. Fairlie's life in the war."

"Ah," said Pons.

"But, of course, they had known each other casually before. They belonged to some sort of club – they were sportsmen of some kind, though Mr. Fairlie was not originally from Frome."

"Indeed," said Pons.

"No, he came from Swindon."

"What was the nature of Mr. Fairlie's reports, Lady Farway?"

"He took care of the estate and of Farway Printers – our small business. He was a most exact – and exacting manager.

I suppose you might say that he was so exact that he might have been created for his position. He was precise and very honest, scrupulously honest – and he expected the same kind of honesty from everyone else."

Pons sat quite still, his fingers tented before him. "Looking back now, Lady Farway," he said presently, "can you say that Mr. Fairlie's attitude differed in any particular since Sir Charles's death?"

A small wrinkle grew and deepened on Lady Farway's forehead. For a few moments she sat in silence, visibly trying to assess importance against unimportance in what she recalled. "Of course," she said finally, "he was upset by Charles's death."

"Beyond that."

"He did seem preoccupied. He took to going off more frequently, I was told by members of the household. But I hardly noticed, to tell the truth. There have been so many sad events in our family, ever since our son's death. My brother-in-law – Austin – fallen to his death – our nephew Ronald drowned – now Jonas. Mr. Pons, one of the tragedies of growing old is seeing one's world pass away before one's eyes. All we have left now are our niece Rebecca, and Gerald, our nephew, Austin's son, and Robert, Henry's son, whom we see all too seldom since he began his studies at Edinburgh years ago. He means to become a doctor, and there is no end to their work in preparation. Gerald is with us here from time to time, and Rebecca keeps me company constantly."

"Harumph," trumpeted Sir Hugh. "You've forgotten Jill."

"Oh, yes, Jill – but we seldom see her and we don't often speak of her."

"Wild," added the Chief Constable.

"She lives in London or Paris – or both," said Lady Farway. "For some strange reason, she's become an artist. One of these – what do you call them? – impressionists? After Cezanne or Van Gogh or somebody like that."

Plainly, an artist's life was thought somewhat *gauche* and Lady Farway preferred not to talk of her niece Jill.

"Let us return for the moment to the late Mr. Fairlie," said Pons. "Can you think of any motive for his murder?"

"None, Mr. Pons."

"He had no enemies? I should think someone who demanded strict honesty of all his associates might be resented in some quarters."

"I knew of no one. But how can one say? What you suggest is very possible, true. A man discharged at the shop at his instruction might have hated him for it. Like so many strictly honest people, Jonas was unyielding. Transgressions must be punished – so he believed, and he couldn't abide slovenly work either here or at the plant. Perhaps you should inquire there. Ask for Mr. Bramshaw."

"Thank you," said Pons. "Do you know – who are Mr. Fairlie's heirs?"

"I believe his daughter Diana is his only heir."

"We don't want to tire you," put in Sir Hugh. "If this is wearing – we can return at another time."

She brushed this aside with a languid gesture, and nodded to Pons, inviting him to carry on.

"Can you recall any circumstances in recent years that altered or in any marked way affected Mr. Fairlie's character or way of life?" asked Pons then.

"None. Oh, the frequency of his recent journeys, yes. But we all thought that was natural after my husband died." She paused thoughtfully and looked briefly away, a troubled shadow briefly in her eyes. "If it had been Charles . . ." She left her sentence unfinished.

"Do go on, Lady Farway."

"There was that occasion a month before Charles died. He and Mr. Fairlie went away together. No one knows where. Neither of them said – either at that time or afterward. But when he came back, Charles was beside himself. I never knew him to be so agitated. There were long conferences with his lawyer – there were discharges from the staff and from the plant. We assumed that something had gone wrong with the business, which Mr. Farway was not in the habit of discussing with me. And, of course, he died within a month of that time – so if he had meant to speak to me about it, he never had the opportunity."

"How did he die, Lady Farway?"

"My husband suffered a cerebral thrombosis. He tried desperately to tell me something, but he couldn't speak. Our doctor, however, said that this was an entirely natural reaction, and what Charles may have wanted to say may have been totally inconsequential. He died within a day of his attack, and was comatose for most of that time."

"None of your husband's brothers survives?"

"None, Mr. Pons. Henry died many years ago – Robert and Rebecca are his children. Austin passed away four years ago. – Gerald and Jill are his. Ronald was also his son. That is our entire family."

"And your heirs?"

"I wish I knew, Mr. Pons," she answered with a wan smile. "My husband's will left me the living and to share the control and administration with Mr. Fairlie, but until my death no one knows who will inherit our estate. Though I suppose Mr. Abercrombie does."

"His solicitor?"

"Yes."

"A Frome man," put in Sir Hugh.

"You would appear to be a closely-knit family," observed Pons.

"I think we are. Particularly since my husband's brothers died. Perhaps it was only natural that our nieces and nephews should come to us. Mr. Farway made it possible for Jill to become an artist – gave employment to Gerald – saw to it that Robert could leave the study of law for medicine. Rebecca became my own companion."

"And Ronald?"

Lady Farway smiled. "Ronald was always the independent one."

"I take it, Lady Farway," said Pons bluntly, "that neither Austin nor Henry was a man of means."

"That was unhappily true, Mr. Pons. They were all at one time in the business. Farway Printers, Ltd. is widely-known, and has been established for some time. My father-in-law started it on a small scale, but it expanded very rapidly. The three Farway sons inherited it, but Charles finally won control. There was some disagreement, though it was unpleasant only in Henry's case, and in my opinion Henry's wife was the cause of that. Charles bought out his brothers as long as fifteen years ago. Neither of them seems to have been provident, and neither much suited to success in any other venture."

The door of the room opened suddenly, and the dark-haired young lady I had observed watching us while we mounted the stairs stood there. She gazed darkly at us, but her look was unfathomable. Then she came softly into the room, her expression all solicitous, her eyes only for Lady Farway.

"Don't you think you may be tiring yourself, Aunt Ellen?" she asked.

Lady Farway smiled. "Never fear," she said to her and, turning again to us, added, "This is our niece, Rebecca."

The young woman looked toward us. Her gaze was a challenge – not unfriendly, but decidedly reserved. She acknowledged the introduction with a wintry smile, excused herself, and drew away from the lounge.

"They are all as attentive as if I were their own mother," said Lady Farway. "Our nephews as well as our nieces. When I was taken ill a year ago, Robert sent down a specialist from Harley Street."

"Miss Rebecca may be right," said Pons. "There is no need to impose on you further at this time, Lady Farway."

Miss Rebecca flashed Pons an appreciative glance. It was surprising to see how that dark face lit up when she smiled.

"We should like now to examine Mr. Fairlie's quarters," said Pons.

"Rebecca will show you there, sir," said Lady Farway.

"Certainly," said Rebecca, and turned at once to the door.

Mr. Fairlie's quarters consisted of an apartment at the southwest corner of the second storey. The apartment was little more than one rather large room, with a bathroom adjoining it. The room was sparsely furnished, containing but a minimum of furniture, and that austere. A crowded desk occupied one corner, and what was manifestly a lounge was certainly also used as a bed by night, whatever its disguise by day. Though it had not been used – since Mr. Fairlie had departed early in the previous evening – it was in some disarray. Indeed, the entire room presented an appearance of disorder, minimal, to be sure, as if Mr. Fairlie's departure had been so hasty that he had not had time to set it right.

Having shown us to the room, Miss Rebecca excused herself and withdrew. I thought, judging by the somewhat startled expression she wore, that the appearance of the room surprised her.

Pons glanced at the Chief Constable. "The police have not been here?"

"Not yet," said Sir Hugh.

Pons took a turn around the room, peered into the bathroom, bent over the lounge, pulling at the covers that concealed its real nature as a bed, lingered at the desk.

"I fear we are a trifle late," he said. "This room has almost certainly been searched."

"Then it must have been by a member of the household."

"I submit that a member of the household would have had time to put the room to rights. You must have observed Miss Rebecca's surprise at sight of it. No, it was searched in haste and – if I am not in error – after Fairlie was killed."

Sir Hugh's florid face betrayed his astonishment. "You are surely not suggesting that the fellow killed Fairlie and then came here to search his quarters?" he cried.

"If he failed to find on Fairlie's person what he sought – and we have reason to believe he did so fail – it would be only logical that he search here."

"Preposterous!"

"Let us not be hasty, Sir Hugh. It had to be done last night or not at all. Once Fairlie's body was discovered, his quarters would come under the attention of the police."

"But no one has reported any evidence of breaking and entering."

Pons shrugged. "A window left open – a door unlatched. I put it to you that gaining entrance was perhaps the least of the difficulties such an enterprising man as our murderer might encounter."

"But what could he have wanted that he took such desperate measures?"

"We have already asked ourselves that," said Pons dryly.

"We can be certain that its importance cannot be overestimated."

The Chief Constable said soberly, "Well, now, Pons, you open up some interesting possibilities – very interesting. It must have been someone who knew Fairlie well, if not intimately."

"Elementary."

"Who was familiar with his quarters."

"Oh, with his habits, his reputation, his person," finished Pons. "It was evident that when he entered the railway coach where Fairlie sat that Fairlie was not alarmed or believed he had no reason for alarm. He was quite clearly taken by surprise, gripped firmly by the back of the neck while chloroform was pressed upon his face. It could have been done only immediately out of Frome. He was then searched and his effects were searched. It was certainly not done by anyone Fairlie distrusted, unless his murderer was in disguise."

"The scrap of paper with your address on it was not discovered."

"Or ignored as meaningless. I submit, however, that what Fairlie's murderer sought was something of more bulk. He had, in any case, too little time to be more thorough. He had to open a window – go through Fairlie's bag – and, having failed to find what he was after, he had to get off the train, and make his way to this house. There was only a minimum of time before the guard might look in on his passengers."

"Why, he must have been at it even while the body was being discovered and we were at work."

"It is possible."

"Highly likely!" exclaimed the Chief Constable. "What a bold fellow! But did he find here what he was looking for?"

"I doubt it."

"Why do you say so?"

"Consider. Not a square inch of this room has been left untouched. Even the pictures on the walls have been moved and the rugs taken up. The desk and the bed did not yield it, and these were the likeliest places. So all else was looked into. We may find that even the mattress has been opened."

The Chief Constable crossed the room to the lounge, pulled up the covering, and scrutinized the mattress. He turned and looked over his shoulder.

"By Gad, Pons. You're right. There are slits here – made recently."

Pons crossed to his side and palpated the mattress near the slits indicated by Sir. Hugh.

"This was poorly made. It has the feel of being stuffed with paper at these points," he said. "Is that not suggestive?"

"It must be an old mattress."

"Oh, that is inconsequential," said Pons impatiently. "We can now reasonably conclude that what is being sought is paper of some kind. The mattress has been slit only where its packing on palpation suggests paper. And something bulkier, obviously, than could be carried in the lining of a hat."

"So Fairlie had a document of some kind. Is that what you are suggesting, Pons?"

"It would seem so."

"But what?"

"Ah, that we are not yet in position to say. It may have been something pertaining to the business – stocks or bonds – it may have been a signed paper which placed someone in jeopardy. We may be certain that whatever it was did endanger the murderer."

"Evidence of some criminal act, for example."

"Perhaps."

"But that suggests he knew Fairlie had it."

Pons shook his head. "Not necessarily. He may only have guessed. Not having found it now, he may conclude that he was in error, that someone else has it, or that Fairlie hid it so well that he will have to look elsewhere for it."

"We're going too fast," said the Chief Constable. "If that were the case, what need would Fairlie have to call on you?"

"He may not have been coming to consult me about whatever it was he had in hiding," Pons pointed out.

"Improbable."

"Not at all. I should think, however, that these matters are related. If Fairlie had possession of an important document for some time – there is nothing to show how long he may have had it, though," he added cryptically, "I should be inclined to believe it was not more than seven years nor less than two – it would hardly have sent him to 7B now. But that his purpose in coming to see me might be in some way related to whatever he had kept secret is neither impossible nor too improbable. He was clearly involved – and deeply – in the affairs of the Farways, particularly the printing business. Indeed, he seems to have been involved considerably more deeply than Lady Farway herself."

"Charlie always believed that business is no place for a woman," said Sir Hugh. "He never brought his troubles home. You heard her say as much."

"I did, indeed. So that, in a sense, Lady Farway has for these past two years been at Mr. Fairlie's mercy."

"You put it strangely."

"I meant to do so."

The Chief Constable shook his head wonderingly. "This whole matter – as Alice said – is becoming curiouser and curiouser."

"Is it not!" cried Pons enthusiastically. "I should like to have known Mr. Fairlie. A pity he was not permitted to complete his final journey."

He now went back to the desk and began a most methodical examination of its contents – envelopes, notepaper, and the accoutrements of a man of business affairs: account books, ledgers, and the like; but there were, I saw, only a few papers that interested Pons – a letter or two, a blank pad, a page or two of random notes. The blank pad especially intrigued Pons; from it he turned to the wicker wastebasket under the desk and went through its contents with some care, though he did not evidently find what he sought – plainly, I inferred, the page or pages torn from the pad of notepaper.

Next he pulled open the drawers of the desk, one by one, and examined their contents; but there was nothing in them that gave him much pause. Then came the surface of the desk, from which he moved to other surfaces in the room, and the jambs of door and windows.

"Wiped clean of fingerprints?" guessed Sir Hugh.

"No, no. But I should say, as with the compartment on the train, that whoever searched this room wore gloves." He held fast still to the papers he had collected from Fairlie's desk. "I shall want these for a little while."

"By all means," said the Chief Constable.

"I have no doubt your men will put everyone in the house through it," said Pons then. "I may wish to speak to some of them later. For the time being, however, I think we are done here. If you will be so kind as to drive us back to the George, I will pursue my inquiry from that post."

III

THE POOR COUSINS

Once back at the George, I felt my lack of sleep. Though Pons himself, as always when he was pressing an investigation, was alert and untired, he urged me to rest for a few hours. I lost no time in stretching out on the bed and fell asleep immediately.

I awoke in mid-afternoon with a hearty sneeze.

"Ah, Parker," said Pons, "I'm sorry that my examination of Mr. Fairlie's papers woke you."

"The room is filled with pepper!" I cried.

"A capital deduction," he replied with a thin smile. "I needed something with which to dust this pad. Pepper was the handiest substance. Unfortunately, since this is certainly the second sheet – perhaps even the third – under that written upon, it is of little help."

I was now on my feet and walked over to the table at which Pons was at work. The pad, still covered with a coating of pepper, to which Pons seemed to be impervious, though I sneezed yet again, lay before him. The pepper outlined but a few markings, which I saw at a glance could have conveyed no meaning to Pons. The top line was one of indistinct figures which could only have signified a date; the second line consisted of letters – "G. A.", and the third of more of the same: "R. H.", with a fourth of two more letters – "J. H." The rest of it was simply too blurred to be read. I sneezed again.

"You can hardly make anything out of that," I said.

"Yet someone thought it of sufficient importance to remove the sheet Fairlie had written, as well as one or two of the sheets below," retorted Pons. "These sheets were not in the wastebasket at Fairlie's desk; furthermore, material in the basket dated as far as a week back; so it is reasonable to assume that it was not Fairlie who tore away the sheets from his pad.

"Perhaps it is a cryptogram of some sort," I ventured.

Pons merely shook his head impatiently. "These notes – and we may be certain that only their beginning shows here – were important to Fairlie and they were of equal importance to whomever took his life."

"Is there anything else?" I asked.

"Only this," said Pons, and handed me a brief letter addressed to the dead man.

"Dear Sir:

In the matter about which you make inquiry, Mr. Gerald was not at his desk on August 16 and 17, 1937.

Respectfully
Ralph Bramshaw."

"You will note that it is on the stationery of Farway Printers. Evidently Gerald Farway is employed there."

"Ah, and Fairlie was checking up on him," I said.

"It would seem so."

"A martinet."

"Sir Hugh spoke of him as a good manager," said Pons. "But observe the date of Bramshaw's letter. Does not this suggest something other to you?"

The date on the letter was April 7, 1938. "It is certainly late to make an inquiry," I said.

"Is it not! And what could it matter to the efficiency of the printing plant so many months after the event?"

"Unless Gerald Farway was in the habit of absenting himself from his post," I ventured.

"I am inclined to think, rather, that Fairlie's inquiry had nothing to do with Gerald Farway's usefulness to the plant," said Pons thoughtfully.

I took issue with Pons. "Surely it isn't impossible that Fairlie, in his capacity as general manager of the business and the estate, might be preparing a bill of particulars against Gerald Farway?"

"The possibility exists," said Pons with such an enigmatic air that I could not help but feel that his meaning was not the same as mine.

"And he may just have learned of Gerald's absence from work on those days," I continued, "and only now got around to inquiring about it."

"It is not improbable," agreed Pons amiably. "But it remains a curious instance. Would it not be more likely to have confirmation from Bramshaw of a series of delinquencies all at once? But here we have a single, isolated date – eight months before the date of this letter to Fairlie. And why a letter? Surely Fairlie could have telephoned for this information."

"It may not have been at Bramshaw's fingertips. He may have had to institute an inquiry. Fairlie may simply have asked him to send the information around when he had turned it up."

"True."

So saying, Pons returned to the letters outlined in pepper on Fairlie's pad. He had now copied them, but he scrutinized the pad once again, trying – in vain – to read more of what had been written on it. At last, however, he abandoned his scrutiny and tipped the pad into the wastebasket, loosing a cloud of pepper into the room. We were both set to sneezing.

We had hardly done when there was a tap on the door. Pons sprang at once to open it.

A young man in his thirties stood there – blonde, blue-eyed, scowling. An air of truculence was unmistakable in his attitude.

"Mr. Solar Pons?" he asked.

At Pons's nod, he walked into the room.

"Mr. Gerald Farway, I presume," said Pons.

Our visitor neither bothered to affirm nor deny Pons' assumption, which had clearly been based, prosaically, on an initialed scarf around his neck. He said only, "I learned that you were acting for the Chief Constable in making inquiries into the death of Jonas Fairlie. Since I must be out of Frome today, I felt I had better come around to talk with you. I looked first for Sir Hugh, but couldn't find him. I'm sure you know I was on the 9:13 last night."

"Pray sit down, Mr. Farway."

"I'd rather stand, if you don't mind," said Farway. He took his stance somewhat belligerently before the now closed door. "They tell me Fairlie was murdered. I consider that preposterous."

"Ah, small wonder! The facts, however, are clear enough."

"Outside of the plant, he didn't have an enemy."

"But he had some at the plant?"

Farway shrugged impatiently. "Fairlie was forever poking his nose into the affairs of the business, demanding greater efficiency, and that lot. This hardly makes for popularity."

"And rarely for murder," put in Pons. "I understand there had been firings."

"Certainly of no importance. The biggest changes took place a month or so before my uncle died – but they were in the making a long time. They'd been building up, you might say, and my uncle just got around at that time to ordering them carried out."

Pons nodded and seemed to dismiss the firings at the plant from his thoughts. "Mr. Farway, I assume you saw and heard nothing untoward on the train to London last night."

"Nothing," replied Farway. "I was in first – he in third class. We were separated by several carriages. I wasn't even aware that he was on the train. You must know by this time that Fairlie was a very independent man. He came and went as he pleased. He didn't have to report to anyone, though he did see my aunt as least once a month. Few of us at the house were ever aware of his comings and goings."

"You live at the Hall?"

"Ever since I took a place in the business. At least, I am there most of the time."

"And your position in the business?"

"I am the assistant manager."

"Under Mr. Bramshaw?"

Farway nodded, flashing Pons a quick glance of surprise at Pons's knowledge of his superior's name.

"Mr. Farway, you were absent from the plant on August 16 and 17, last year," said Pons then.

Our visitor's face darkened. He stared hard at Pons before answering. "How can you know that, sir?"

Without a word, Pons handed him Bramshaw's letter to Jonas Fairlie.

Farway read it at a glance. His brow was knitted with suspicion now, and he was a trifle reluctant to return it to Pons.

"How did you come by this, Mr. Pons?"

"It was found on Mr. Fairlie's desk."

"Ah, you searched his room."

"Under the Chief Constable's supervision," said Pons. "Can you now remember where you were on those dates?"

Farway's scowl deepened; his face grew darker with colour.

"That is my private affair."

"As you wish," said Pons amiably. "Mr. Fairlie evidently did not think so. Are you frequently absent from the plant, Mr. Farway?"

"Other than on the business of the firm, I have been absent only once before," answered Farway without hesitation. "I can assure you that my absence had nothing – I repeat, *nothing* – whatever to do with Mr. Fairlie's death."

Pons smiled. "It is only that he had been inquiring into it," he said.

"And I can't explain that, either," Farway put in. "It may have been his right to do so."

"He did not speak to you about it?"

"No."

"Nor make any reference, however indirect, to it?" pressed Pons. "Some time has elapsed since this information came into his hands. Yet he did not once bring the matter up to you?"

"He did not."

"Curious! Curious!" murmured Pons. "Tell me, what was Mr. Fairlie's precise position in relation to the printing business? Mr. Bramshaw here signs himself as in authority."

"Mr. Bramshaw *is* the manager," said Farway, an edge of resentment showing in his voice. "It's only that my uncle – that is, Sir Charles – left specific instructions that Fairlie was to continue in control. By 'control' he meant that Fairlie was to exercise the same kind of ultimate authority that my uncle himself exercised. He doesn't – and didn't – have any official position in the business, but the plant is part of my uncle's estate, and Mr. Fairlie is the administrator and does exercise final control."

"He never occupied an office at the plant? Not even prior to your uncle's death?"

"Not Fairlie. He was my uncle's liaison man, and we all understood that he spoke for my uncle, who never came to the plant when he could send Fairlie in his place."

"So that, in fact, Mr. Fairlie never discharged anyone?"

"In most cases, no. My uncle ordered any discharges that took place during his lifetime. And there have been only two since he died. I suppose Mr. Fairlie may have had a hand in those, yes, but I wouldn't be prepared to say that he did. I'd say those two men had asked for it – careless in their work, cheating on time, and all that. But whether it was Mr. Bramshaw put it up to Fairlie or the other way round I couldn't say."

Pons took a turn around the room, while Farway followed him with his eyes. He came back to our visitor. "Thinking back now, Mr. Farway, can you hit upon any reason anyone would want to kill Mr. Fairlie?"

"None," replied Farway emphatically and without hesitation. "I still think the idea preposterous. The only solution that occurs to me is that he may have been mistaken for someone else."

"Not likely. Mr. Fairlie was murdered with deliberate intent. His effects and his quarters were searched."

Our visitor's eyes widened. "His quarters?" he repeated, amazed. "But when?"

"Evidently immediately after his murder."

"Incredible!"

"But inescapable."

"Why, old Fairlie didn't have a thing anybody else'd want," scoffed Farway. "He was tight-fisted enough – he had money in the banks and he wasn't what I'd call poor – but there certainly wasn't anything on his person or in his rooms to tempt anyone."

Pons appeared to meditate briefly. "And in the household, Mr. Farway – was Mr. Fairlie obtrusive, demanding?"

"Quite the contrary. He was like a ghost – and of late he acted as if he were haunted himself."

"Indeed!" cried Pons sharply. "Preoccupied?"

"Haunted!" said Farway again, emphatically.

"In fear?"

"No, sir. It wasn't fear. It was more like the attitude of a man who had a very disagreeable task – a hateful obligation – to perform, and who knew he must do it no matter how much he bucked at it."

Pons's eyes positively glowed now. He began to stroke and tug at the lobe of his left ear. "And all the more a task for one so customarily reticent, I daresay."

"Yes, you might put it so. To be honest about him, Fairlie wasn't one who liked to use his authority. Not that he ever backed away from what he had to do, but just that it troubled him too much. I remember once, long ago, Rebecca did some little thing – oh, I no longer remember what it was – but Fairlie thought it important and brought it to my uncle's attention. Rebecca was reprimanded – and it bothered Fairlie for weeks – weeks! Some little thing of no significance, really, except to someone with Fairlie's Victorian outlook."

"An old-fashioned gentlemen?"

"Rather!"

"So that if Mr. Fairlie had a highly disagreeable task, its importance might have seemed exaggerated."

"Exactly."

Pons nodded in some satisfaction. "Now, then," he went on, "do the initials G. A., R. H., and J. H. mean anything to you?"

Farway, a little surprised at Pons's change of subject, repeated the initials aloud, twice. He stood in deep thought for a few moments, teetering on his toes, but at last shook his head, his eyes clouded with perplexity. "I can't say that they do," he said finally. "I suppose if I think long enough, I might come up with one or another name to fit them."

"In connection with Mr. Fairlie?"

Our visitor shook his head anew. "You're asking too much, sir. I knew less of Fairlie's business than he seems to have known of mine."

Suddenly Pons was all brisk activity. "Thank you, Mr. Farway," he said crisply. "We may take the liberty of making some further inquiries later on – after you return to Frome." Farway bowed a little formally and bade us goodbye.

"Well, that has certainly not added very much to our store of knowledge," I said when Farway's footsteps had ceased to sound.

"You think not?"

"Surely you cannot think otherwise?"

"I submit that Mr. Farway's intelligence was informative," said Pons with an annoyingly patient smile. "He confirms us in our estimate of Mr. Fairlie as a most estimable and conscientious retainer. He underscores my conclusion that Mr. Fairlie was not murdered by someone who hated him. It now seems inescapable that he was about a task so disagreeable to him, and of such significance, that he was planning to lay it before me and escape the obligation he could not otherwise avoid when he was murdered. He was killed then because someone did not want him to discharge that obligation."

"You have an odd way of putting it, Pons," I said. "It takes hatred to kill with such deliberation."

"Nonsense, Parker! It takes necessity. Mr. Fairlie had no wealth to stimulate someone's greed – he was patently not involved in a crime of passion – but he was certainly in somebody's way and had to be removed."

"Why?"

"We are on the way to determining that, my dear fellow. Be patient. This is not, I regret to say, one of those little matters that can be solved from an armchair. There are crimes in which the motivation is so clear, and the opportunity so limited, that only a little ratiocination is necessary to solve them. In Mr. Fairlie's case, the motivation is anything but clear – granted that he was in somebody's way, we have as yet no way of knowing for what reason he had to be eliminated."

He might have gone on, had not someone's rapping on the door interrupted him.

"Not another one, surely," muttered Pons, as he opened the door.

One of the hotel page-boys stood there. He had a note on a salver. "Sir," he said to Pons, "a gentleman left this for you."

"Thank you," said Pons, and took the note.

He opened it, read it and stood for a thoughtful few moments gazing at it. Then he handed it to me.

It was from our erstwhile visitor. "It has just occurred to me," Farway wrote, "that those initials you asked about, must be those of our cousins – Gareth Ainslie, Russell Hattray and Jennifer Hattray – though I'm blessed as to how they relate to Fairlie."

"We are making some cautious progress," said Pons.

"I don't recall any previous mention of these people. 'Our cousins' – perhaps they are the poor relations of the Farway clan."

Pons took a turn or two about the room, hands clasped behind his back. He had lit a pipe of his abominable shag and was puffing away like an express train. I could more readily have tolerated another dose of pepper. His eyes were narrowed, his lips pursed; he ignored what I said for some moments while his thoughts were elsewhere. But presently his gaze met mine once more.

"I think we may have time enough before Sir Hugh joins us for dinner to run around to the station and ask the booking-clerk some questions. It may be we can prod him to some further memory of last night before time dims the details. Let us just walk over to the station; the booking-clerk should have come on duty by the time we reach there."

Jock Nichols proved to be a wiry man in his fifties. He was short, thin-faced, with a stubby moustache and bushy eyebrows.

He had a no-nonsense look about him that said plainly he would not stand still for anybody wasting his time. When Pons introduced himself and brought up the subject of Mr. Fairlie's death, he reacted instantly.

"I gave all my evidence to the police last night," he said primly, as if that were an end to it.

"Ah, there are one or two little points on which I am not clear," said Pons. He took from his pocket the tuft of hair he had pried from the hand of the dead man. "You've told the police that an elderly, bearded gentleman traveled third-class from Frome last night. Did the colour of his beard match that?"

He laid the tuft down before the booking-clerk.

Nichols stared at it.

Someone pushed up for a ticket. We stepped aside. The ticket sold, we moved in again. Nichols was still examining the tuft of hair.

"How'd you come by it?" he asked finally.

"Found it in Mr. Fairlie's hand," replied Pons.

"Have the police seen it?" He regarded Pons suspiciously.

"Sir Hugh Parrington was with us."

"Oh-ah," said Nichols, mollified. "It could have been that colour. I'm not in the habit of looking over the travelers close. My job's to book 'em. If I knew I'd be called upon to remember, I'd do it. I say only it might have been."

"You need say no more, Mr. Nichols." Pons pocketed the tuft of hair, while the booking-clerk looked at him gravely. All around us now people were stirring in the station, waiting upon the arrival of the 6:50 from the west. Free briefly again, Nichols beckoned Pons closer to his window.

"That old fellow couldn't have done it," he said earnestly. "From what I hear, that is. He *tottered*."

"Indeed," said Pons.

"Must have been one of the younger men."

"You mentioned, I believe, that a woman you didn't know also took the train last night?"

"First class, first class," said Nichols peevishly. "As for my not knowing her – she wore a veil; I couldn't see her face."

"So she, too, might have been deliberately concealing her identity?" asked Pons.

Nichols looked at him sharply. "What do you mean by that?"

Pons took the tuft of hair out again and held it between thumb and forefinger. "This is commercial hair, Mr. Nichols, We might wonder how much else was false about the passengers on the 9:13 last night."

"As to that, I'm not qualified to say, sir," Nichols shot back. "And I don't know your qualifications, if it comes to it. All I know is Sir Hugh trusts you and I've told all I know."

"One more thing, Mr. Nichols," pursued Pons.

The booking-clerk was all attention now.

"You knew Mr. Fairlie. And the other clerks knew him, too. When was the last time – before last night – you sold him a ticket?"

"I thought that'd come up sooner or later," said Nichols, indulging in a frosty smile. "Three weeks ago."

"Where to?"

"Scotland."

"What station?"

"Glasgow."

"Thank you, Mr. Nichols," said Pons.

We walked back to the George in silence. Pons was not disposed to talk, but went along at a casual gait, turning over in mind the unrelated facts we now had had put before us. He had come to no conclusions about them, and therefore would not speak.

Sir Hugh Parrington waited for us in the lobby of the George. He looked as fresh as if he had slept all day.

"Thought you'd forgotten I was coming to get you for dinner," he said. "Made reservations at the Somerset. You must be famished."

"Now that I think of it, I am," said Pons.

"We can ride or walk, as you like," said Sir Hugh. Pons chose to walk.

We had hardly set foot on the pavement before Sir Hugh began to talk animatedly, summarizing the police reports that had come in during the day, the result of the routine investigations that had to be made. He recounted the finding of a place almost four miles outside Frome where someone had evidently jumped from the moving train.

"Footprints?" asked Pons.

"The prints were all but obliterated – the ground torn up, that sort of thing. It would be impossible to obtain any sort of cast."

"Then he had to travel back across or around Frome and to the Hall," said Pons. "How much time would that take?"

"Oh, the fellow must have had a motor somewhere. Certainly not far from the railway, and surely not any farther than the eastern edge of Frome. He'd not want it to be conspicuous. Nor would he make himself conspicuous by running. He might reach the Hall in less than an hour – not more than an hour and a half, taking everything into consideration and allowing him the maximum distance to travel on foot. He'd probably avoid Christchurch Street. He'd likely go by way of Lock's Hill and Somerset Road to Nunney – less chance of being seen at that hour. And that would be between ten and eleven."

"The search wouldn't have taken him long – either in the carriage or in the Hall," mused Pons. "He could have been away from the Hall well before any alarm about Fairlie went out."

"He could, indeed. A man of some resource and daring."

"Do not eliminate the ladies, Sir Hugh," said Pons dryly. "Some of them are remarkably resourceful."

"I am surprised to hear you say so," said the Chief Constable.

We reached the Somerset and were shown to our table. Once seated, Pons ordered sparingly, as always when he was occupied with some problem. He did not speak until our orders had been taken, and the waiter had left us. Then he leaned toward Sir Hugh.

"Tell us what you can about the Hattrays – Russell and Jennifer, and Gareth Ainslie."

The Chief Constable's jaw fell. He sat for a moment, mouth agape; then he shook his head, as if to emphasize his surprise.

"They're cousins of the Farways – the poor cousins, you might say."

"How do they come into the family?"

"Oh, Charlie's father had a sister. Married Fred Hattray. Had two children, who'd be Charlie's first cousins. Esther had one son – that would be Gareth Ainslie, and John had Russell and Jennifer. Esther and John are dead. So is Russell's wife. The other two never married. They live together here."

"Where?"

"North near the river. In Dyer's Close Lane."

Pons cogitated. "If I am not mistaken, that would be rather near to the railway."

"To Radstock, yes."

"Would they be mentioned among the heirs of Charles Farway's estate?"

"Not likely."

"Perhaps they have money invested in the printing business?"

"That's possible. After all, the business goes back a generation beyond Charlie. It was a family venture, and came into Charlie's hands only when he bought control – though he was the one of the three Farway men who ran it in his generation, and the one prepared to do so by the old men."

"Have you any idea of the size of the estate?"

"Counting the business, of course," said Sir Hugh thoughtfully, "I should say it would run into well over a million pounds."

"No small sum," observed Pons.

"But it's all tied up in land, buildings, stock, investments," the Chief Constable went on. "Most of the rich couldn't liquidate in any short time and put that much money down."

"Hattrays and Ainslies now," said Pons. "Are they moneyed people?"

"I should say they're moderately well-off."

"Wealthy?"

"Sir Hugh shrugged. "What is wealthy, Pons? They don't seem to do much work. They live in a country house – used to be a farm, but there's little farming done there now. Russell once raised cattle, but I don't know whether he still floes." He paused suddenly and lowered his voice a little. "There he is now. That's Russell Hattray."

He pointed out a burly man, dark of skin, with thick black hair and very black eyes. He wore a short, carefully trimmed beard.

"He had the look of an Italian," said Pons. "His mother?"

"Italian, yes."

"In his forties, clearly. He was once in service."

"Oh, yes, wounded in action. That's why he wears the beard – to conceal the scar."

"A brute of a man."

"Strong as an ox."

Russell Hattray passed out of sight.

"Would you like to meet them?" asked Sir Hugh then.

"Not now."

"I should think it quite unlikely that they were even very well known to Jonas Fairlie, or he to them," the Chief Constable went on.

"In retrospect, Mr. Fairlie impresses me as a man who would know every investor in the business," said Pons. "He appears to have been a thoroughgoing caretaker of the Farway holdings."

"He was that," replied Sir Hugh with equanimity. "He could very probably have told you the amount of every investor's holding, but I doubt that he would have known the colour of Russell Hattray's eyes or the cut of his coat. He was not a man to clutter his mind with inconsequential details."

"I should not have thought so," agreed Pons. "But when I examined that pad we took from his desk – dusted it – "

"With pepper!" I put in bitterly.

The Chief Constable laughed heartily.

Pons waited upon his laughter to subside, then resumed. "I found that Fairlie had jotted down what appeared to be the initials of Ainslee and the Hattrays."

"Incredible!" exclaimed Sir Hugh, his face reflecting his astonishment.

"So that there may well be some connection to which we have no clue."

"I am at a loss to understand what it might be. To tell the truth, there was very little mixing of the families. Charlie had his circle – a very small one, to be sure – and those cousins of his weren't his kind of people. For instance, they were always at hand for the market days – you'd see them there, all three of them – but as for Charlie, never. Why, they are even out of the line of inheritance."

"How many other relatives are there, then?"

"None to my knowledge. And if there were, they'd be even more distantly connected."

"Let us assume that Lady Farway dies."

Sir Hugh knit his brows. His strong blue eyes clouded. In a few moments he spoke thoughtfully. "I didn't know Charlie's intentions, of course, but I knew him, and if I had to predict what he'd be likely to do, I'd say that the estate would be divided among his nieces and nephews, with one of them left in charge of the printing business."

"That would be Gerald," said Pons.

"In all likelihood."

"But supposing there were no nieces or nephews?"

Sir Hugh looked at him blankly for a moment. Then he smiled. "Aha! I see what you're getting at, Pons. But that's pretty far-fetched, you know. There are nieces and nephews – healthy, too."

The waiter began to bring our food. For a while then all was silence. Pons ate rapidly, as was his custom; food, much as he appreciated it, was invariably secondary to the problem in hand, and he treated it as a necessity and nothing more. The Chief Constable and I took our time. Sir Hugh's brow, I noticed, remained furrowed; he was obviously turning over what Pons had inferred and not looking favorably upon it.

"There is one little factor we must not overlook," said Pons, when he had finished. "It may be more important than we think. It may have no bearing at all on Mr. Fairlie's death."

"What's that?" demanded Sir Hugh.

"That journey Farway took with Fairlie a month before Farway's death. Lady Farway said that on his return her husband consulted his lawyer. Perhaps it had some bearing on the distribution of the estate."

"Possibly," conceded the Chief Constable grudgingly.

"I mean to talk to Mr. Abercrombie tomorrow."

"A cold fish. You'll get nothing out of him. He's a stickler for the rules."

"We shall see."

"I know him."

"Evidently Farway did, too. Abercrombie may have been his lawyer, but Mr. Fairlie was left as administrator," said Pons.

"Precisely."

"By the way," said Pons then, "there is one other little thing. In addition to those initials, Fairlie had written a date on that pad. Presumably there were other dates – I suspect there were – but only the one showed up. It had been jotted down just above the initials. August 16-17, 1937. Does that have any family significance?"

Sir Hugh's white brows contracted, then shot up. "August 17, 1937, was the day Ronald Farway drowned."

IV

MR. ABERCROMBIE'S RETICENCE

When I awoke next morning, Pons had gone out. He had spent the evening in deep thought, saying not a word; and it was evident to me that he had opened up some deeper vein in the problem in which we were involved, and was pursuing it. He was still lost in thought when I fell asleep.

At his return in late morning, he offered no word of explanation.

"Ah, you are up," he said. "We have an appointment with Mr. Abercrombie at eleven, and we have just time to walk over to his office in Cheap Street."

"You telephoned?"

"I thought it best. He seemed to me remarkably lacking in enthusiasm," he said dryly. "Come, let us be off."

Cheap Street was only across Market Place from the George – a narrow, old world street with a stream flowing along its gutter. It was an old corner of Frome, a street of great charm, filled principally with shops, restaurants, chemists, hairdressers – and a few offices. In this setting Mr. Douglas Abercrombie fitted quite satisfactorily.

He proved to be a tall, bony man, with a dour expression on his lantern-jawed face, framed in grey sideboards; and his eyes, looking out under unkempt and shaggy brows, were wary.

"I cannot imagine why you have come to see me, Mr. Pons," he said, directly upon his introduction to me. "I had very little to do with Fairlie – very little. But do sit down, gentlemen."

He sat down cautiously himself, behind a desk that must have been a valuable antique.

"Ah, it was not about Mr. Fairlie that I came," said Pons, "but about the affairs of the late Sir Charles Farway."

Mr. Abercrombie visibly tightened up.

"I understand you were his solicitor, Mr. Abercrombie," Pons went on.

"Yes, sir."

"It is specifically about his will that I wished to ask," said Pons.

"A delicate matter, Mr. Pons," said Abercrombie. "Very delicate. I cannot be expected to violate the ethics of my profession.

"Indeed not," agreed Pons.

"What is it then?" asked Abercrombie.

"You may recall that about a month before Sir Charles Farway's sudden death he came to you in the company of the late Mr. Fairlie. Presumably at that time he drew up a new will."

A fox-like expression took over the lawyer's face. "That he did, Mr. Pons. I remember it well."

"Can you recall any specific points about that new will, Mr. Abercrombie?"

Mr. Abercrombie smiled. He looked relieved. "Mr. Pons, I have not the slightest idea of the contents of that will."

Now it was Pons's turn to be surprised.

"I remember that day very well," Mr. Abercrombie went on. "Sir Charles came in with Mr. Fairlie. Sir Charles was very agitated – very agitated; indeed, I have never seen a man more upset. Mr. Fairlie, on the other hand, was very calm, very grave yes, but very much in control of himself. 'Abercrombie,' Sir

Charles said, 'I am about to draw up a new will – I will set it down myself. Jonas will witness it, and so will one of your clerks. You will be able to testify that I wrote it out.' He sat down then and there to this desk. He knew the forms, and he wrote out a new will – his last will, to be opened only at his wife's death. There was another document drawn up that day settling the matter of Lady Farway's succession to the property, and Mr. Fairlie's administration of it – that is public knowledge, and I am not violating my trust in admitting it. But the new will, Mr. Pons, was not read by me. It was not read by Mr. Fairlie. It was certainly not read by my clerk. For when he finished writing it out, Sir Charles folded the page to the place left for signature, and we all signed it without seeing a line of it. We could testify that it was his last will and testament on his word that it was, and on seeing him indite it."

Pon's eyes danced. "A page, Mr. Abercrombie?" he asked. "A single page?"

The lawyer nodded. "Legal size, of course."

"You did, however, see previous wills?"

"Yes, of course."

"They have been destroyed?"

"Yes, Mr. Pons – at Sir Charles's direction. That day."

"And none of them but one page in length, I daresay."

"Indeed not."

"Sir Charles had not indicated at any time immediately prior to making his last will that he contemplated such a change?"

"He had not."

"A man of impulse?"

"On the contrary." Judging that Pons had now finished, he added, "I am sorry I am not able to help you, Mr. Pons."

"Ah, you have already helped me, Mr. Abercrombie," returned Pons. "It is possible that you may be able to add something more."

Mr. Abercrombie's relief faded from his face, which became more dour than ever.

"Since Sir Charles's earlier wills were destroyed, there can hardly be any point in keeping their contents secret," Pons went on. "Can you outline for us briefly the distribution of the estate as set forth in the second-last will Sir Charles signed and subsequently destroyed?"

"I fear, sir, that would be unethical, highly unethical."

"Let me then hazard a guess. I submit that Sir Charles left his estate to be divided among his nieces and nephews with Mr. Gerald Farway in control of the plant." Pons smiled. "You need say nothing, Mr. Abercrombie. I see by the expression on your face that I have hit it. It would have surprised me were it not so. But now let us look a little further. Can you conceive of the direction his last will might have taken?"

"I have tried to think. I cannot do so."

"Was it your impression that Mr. Fairlie knew what changes Sir Charles made?"

"It would surprise me if he did not."

"So that, Mr. Abercrombie, no one alive now knows what is in that will. I trust, sir, you have it in perfect safekeeping."

"Bless my soul!" cried Mr. Abercrombie, startled from his dour reserve. "You are surely not suggesting that some attempt to destroy it might be made?"

"Since no one save your clerk and yourself knows about its existence, I should not think that likely," said Pons dryly.

Mr. Abercrombie swallowed, hard. "Mr. Devins – my clerk at that time – was killed in a motor accident at Devizes a year ago."

"Ah," said Pons. "Then only you remain to testify to the authenticity of that will, Mr. Abercrombie."

The lawyer lost a little colour. His face became very grave, his mouth drew down. "You put matters strangely, Mr. Pons," he said.

"I assure you, I have no intention of doing so. But there is matter for some thought here. It does not hang together clearly to the eye, Mr. Abercrombie, I put it to you. What do you suppose put Sir Charles in such a flurry and agitation as to make him change his will?" He did not wait upon the lawyer's reply, but pressed on. "Did he do anything more on that day? Or do you not wish to say?"

"I will speak of it; it is no secret," said Mr. Abercrombie in some haste. "He increased the stipend paid Mr. Robert – to hasten his study of medicine. He settled a small sum on Mr. Fairlie's daughter – to be paid immediately; and it was paid. He arranged for a sum to be paid into the account of his niece, Jill, in Paris."

Pons waited upon more to come, but there was no more. "Did he make any explanation of all this?"

"It was not Sir Charles's habit to do so."

"Did he say nothing at all? I put it to you, Mr. Abercrombie – surely he could not be so secretive with his lawyer."

"He could. He was. He said nothing, nothing...but..." Mr. Abercrombie slowed to a pause.

"Out with it, Mr. Abercrombie. Let us not forget that we are inquiring into a murder."

"Why, he did say something – no more than muttered it. I discounted it. He was distraught."

"Yes, yes. But what was it."

"Let me see. 'Injustice compounds injustice.' That was it. Just that." He shook his head. "A fairer man never existed. Oh, he was conservative, now and then a trifle self-righteous – but fair, Mr. Pons, very fair. I did not understand his talk of injustice."

"We make progress," said Pons. "How was he unjust to Jill, for example?"

"He disliked her inclination to an artist's life."

"And to Miss Fairlie?"

Abercrombie grimaced. "Young Farway and the girl were in love. They planned to be married. But Sir Charles broke it up, and the boy went to Scotland – was sent, I assumed – for the shooting."

"And died in an accident."

"Yes."

"And to Robert?"

"Well, this was a matter of impatience. Robert chose to go into law – and, well into his studies, changed to medicine. It kept him in school, all at the expense of Sir Charles. I suppose he felt that his niggardliness with money for Robert was unjust."

The telephone rang suddenly.

Abercrombie turned to it and spoke. The sound that came back at him was certainly Sir Hugh Parrington's booming voice. Abercrombie held the telephone toward Pons. "For you, sir."

"Thank you." Pons took it, identified himself with "Pons here," and stood listening.

When he put down the telephone, he turned again to Abercrombie.

"Can you tell us how much Sir Charles settled on Miss Fairlie?"

"I rather think that is not within my province to do, Mr. Pons," said the lawyer.

"I will not press it, sir. A 'small sum' is ambiguous and relative."

Abercrombie made a silencing gesture with his right hand. "Let us say that it was a small sum for Sir Charles."

"Good enough," said Pons. "Do you also serve the plant as lawyer, Mr. Abercrombie?"

"Indeed I do."

"Is there or has there been recently any cause for concern about the financial status of the business?"

"None. I may say that it is flourishing. Farway Printers, Ltd. has all the business it can handle."

"Thank you, Mr. Abercrombie. I think that is all."

The lawyer was plainly relieved. "I'm sorry I couldn't be of more assistance. Fairlie's death is a dreadful thing. But in our profession a certain reticence is not only essential but mandatory."

Outside once again, Pons lost no time striding away toward the George. "Sir Hugh is waiting there for us," he explained. "We have been invited to luncheon at Farway Hall. Evidently two other members of the family have made an appearance, and Lady Farway made the decision to have them meet us."

The Chief Constable was walking up and down in front of the George when we came within sight of the hotel. His limousine was parked at the kerb. Marking our approach, he strode out into the street to meet us.

"An impatient man," observed Pons.

"I have seen you fully as impatient," I said.

"If you're ready, we'll go right over," boomed Sir Hugh, coming up. "The newspapers have sent accounts of the murder about. Jill flew over from Paris, and Robert has come down from Scotland. They are rare visitors, and Lady Farway wanted you to meet them."

"We'll go directly," said Pons.

Once in the car, the Chief Constable asked, "Did you get anything out of Abercrombie?"

"Let us just say that I was not disappointed."

"Ah, you found him unwilling to talk."

"Reticent."

"I told you so."

"I learned a few trifles," Pons went on. "For example, no one thought to tell me that Mr. Fairlie's daughter and young Farway intended to marry."

"Fact. They were engaged. Charlie was sticky about it. Can't understand why. Diana was a very fine girl. A looker, too.

Maybe Charlie thought that was it. Anyway, he succeeded in breaking it up..."

"The engagement was broken?" put in Pons.

Sir Hugh shook his head. "No – just abated, you might say. They got him to go away for a while. Scotland. And, of course, then there was the accident. Diana was at the services. Right after that she gave up her position – she worked as a secretary at the plant, as you might guess, and went to Cheltenham to live. She was too bitter to stay here. Can't say I blame her."

"Did Sir Charles regret his interference?"

"Hum! If he did, he wouldn't admit it. She did, though – she felt very strongly about it. For a while there was a rift between them. But that was healed, of course. She's a sensible woman, make no mistake about that – and perhaps stronger than they think."

"I am curious to know how often Miss Fairlie visited her father."

"Odd you should ask. Diana's not come back to Frome since she left. He did the visiting, not she. Nothing was ever said about it. Of course, Fairlie wouldn't say anything anyway. But I took it it was she wouldn't come back. I don't doubt we'll see her tomorrow, though, at the inquest."

"I take it she resented Sir Charles's interference very much."

"She did. She did, indeed! Not so much the interference, I believe, as their sending him away. You know how women reason, Pons. If they hadn't sent him off to think things over, he'd be alive today, they'd have been married, and all that."

"She never married?"

The Chief Constable paused reflectively. "Come to think of it, I don't know. I don't believe she did. But we can learn that tomorrow, if it's important. She's likely to be here all day – the inquest's tomorrow afternoon, and the funeral next morning. Private services."

A baffling expression shone in Pons's eyes before he closed them and sat back, saying nothing more.

We reached the Hall within minutes.

Lady Farway, clad in deep purple, had come downstairs. She dominated the living-room into which we were shown. The entire Farway family appeared to be there – Gerald, Rebecca, and the two we had not yet met and to whom we were now introduced – Jill, a dark-skinned girl whose wild black hair cascaded over her shoulders, and Robert, a moustached young man who constantly hovered about his aunt, as if he meant to protect her even against his cousins and sister. The girl, Jill, had a high colour and an easy manner that was in direct contrast to Robert's formality.

"I know you are busy, Sir Hugh," said Lady Farway. "We shall go in to lunch at once."

"Ha! Must take time to eat," said the Chief Constable. "No hurry."

But Robert was already helping Lady Farway to her feet. Leaning heavily on his arm, she led the way into the dining-room across the hall – a pleasant, sunny room with a faint glow of green in it from the sunshot ivy leaves across the windows.

It was Jill who introduced the subject which had brought them to Farway Hall. "Who did Fairlie in?" she asked Sir Hugh.

"We don't know yet," he answered. "But we will."

"I suppose, as the police always say, you have some promising leads." She laughed.

"We've asked Mr. Pons to look into the matter," continued Sir Hugh. "We can do the routine work. He will look beyond that."

"I don't have much faith in the police," said Jill frankly.

"Nor in any other institution," said Robert coldly.

She threw up her hands in a carefree manner. "Poor Mr. Fairlie! He couldn't have lived much longer anyway. Is it really true – that he was murdered?"

"No doubt of it," said the Chief Constable.

Lady Farway bit her lip. Robert's colour rose.

Now Jill turned directly toward Pons. "I do believe I've read about your assisting the police now and then," she said. "And producing those startling solutions or amazing deductions or whatever they are. I suppose you've uncovered all kinds of things already."

"Some few matters have come to my attention," said Pons, smiling.

"Such as, for instance?"

"Such as why Mr. Fairlie was killed," replied Pons.

"Hear! Hear!" cried Sir Hugh approvingly.

"I think we'd all like to know that," said Gerald, speaking for the first time.

"Mr. Fairlie was killed because he had discovered something that would gravely affect every member of this family," said Pons. "He was killed to prevent his disclosure of that discovery."

For a few moments after Pons's announcement not a sound was to be heard. Then the clink of glasses and utensils resumed.

Once again, it was Gerald who spoke. His plainly apprehensive gaze was fixed on Pons. "And do you know what that discovery was, Mr. Pons?"

"Not yet. I am beginning to see a certain pattern, however, and I fancy it will not be long before I learn Mr. Fairlie's secret."

Gerald's relief was almost impossible to miss.

Jill's wild laughter, completely uncontained, shattered the tension around the table. "Oh, that's the way all policemen talk!" she cried. "They do it in Paris as well as in England. At least half the time you never hear another thing!"

"True," said Pons with perfect equanimity. "But I am not the police."

"Mr. Pons has been at work for only a short time," said Lady Farway with the manifest intention of putting an end to Jill's baiting.

"I'm sure our lives are an open book," said Robert.

Once again Jill burst into laughter. "Mine's not," she said. "Is yours, Gerald? And how about you, Robert?"

"You've forgotten me," said Rebecca with cold disdain.

"Give me time," said Jill.

"Whatever must Mr. Pons think of us!" cried Lady Farway.

Pons only smiled, saying nothing.

"I should think," said Robert then with icy scorn, "on the few occasions on which we meet, we ought to show the most possible consideration to Aunt Ellen – even if we cannot bring ourselves under control for the sake of our guests."

A hush fell on the room and was not broken until Pons turned to Jill and asked, "Do you come back to England very often?"

"Rather more often than I used to," she answered. "There are some interesting things being done in painting over here now. Stanley Spencer's *Resurrection*, for instance – quite the most remarkable modern religious painting we have seen come out of England – or and of the Continental countries, for that matter. And the work of Paul Nash continues to intrigue me, as well as some of the things Wyndham Lewis is doing – I think especially of his portrait of Edith Sitwell. Though no one so far can touch Augustus John."

"Oh, watch Sutherland and Bacon," said Rebecca. "Sutherland has a most marvelous fantastic landscape called *Entrance to a Lane*."

"We seem to have another budding artist in the family," said Robert to his sister.

"Not really," she answered. "I like to keep up with things."

"They *are* most promising," agreed Jill.

Now the conversation became innocuous and more animated, and presently the initial impression I had of a family taut with inner tensions faded before one more favorable – of an interesting group of people whose concerns were not by any means limited to the printing business. Indeed, only once was the business mentioned at all – when Robert asked Gerald about it, and Gerald mentioned a very large printing that had to be done for one of the oldest and most respected British publishers.

After her one enthusiastic comment about young British painters, Rebecca fell silent; she sat dark and brooding over her food. Nor did Lady Farway take any significant part, though she was alert and remained interested. Pons, I saw, contented himself for the most part with a minimum of talk, preferring instead to observe the members of the Farway family, while Sir Hugh entered almost boisterously into the talk, obviously at home among friends. They talked of many things – of the success of the recent Cheese Show and, the quality of the cheeses – of a lad who had been injured at the carnival – of Virginia Woolf's novel, *The Years* and an announced omnibus edition of Dorothy Richardson's *Pilgrimage* – of Dorset and Thomas Hardy – of new plays in London – of everything, in fact, except the late Jonas Fairlie.

I followed Pons' gaze as much as possible, without being obtrusive. Clearly he was studying one after another of the Farways; his eyes ranged from Gerald, who seemed to have a tendency toward pomposity, to Robert, who was more reserved and in his dress looked a little more the dandy, for he wore a handsome scarf around his neck, loosely knotted at his throat, instead of the conventional collar and tie, and his clothes, though plain, were expensive and tailored. Jill's every attitude, every word, every gesture bespoke her independence and the freedom she had sought, while Rebecca's air was far more that of a domestic than of a member of the family, as if she were aware that her role of companion to Lady Farway was far less exciting and offered fewer opportunities for an appreciation of the world and life outside Frome than did the roles of her cousins – Jill in Paris, painting – Gerald occupied with the affairs of Farway Printers, Ltd., and frequently off to London – Robert, completing his studies during his internship in Edinburgh. Yet no hint of resentment could be seen either in her manner or in her words; she was withdrawn but self-assured; indeed, self-assurance seemed to be a distinctive family trait.

The luncheon came to an end. Lady Farway excused herself and retired to her quarters, Rebecca at her side. Gerald in turn left for his office. Jill and Robert were left, and it was immediately apparent that Robert had something to say and meant to say it, for as soon as his aunt was out of earshot, he bore down on Sir Hugh.

"I hope, sir, that you are aware of the delicate condition of Aunt Ellen's health, and that you are not harassing her."

The Chief Constable was somewhat taken aback. "We are not in the habit of harassing people – certainly not ladies."

"I mean no offense," said Robert.

"Of course he does," said Jill, laughing.

Robert flashed her a glance of irritation, but went on. "It's only that I am professionally aware of her condition."

"Harrumph!" boomed Sir Hugh. "Lady Farway has weathered many a storm, Doctor. And I suspect she'll live to weather more. I've known a good many of these frail, ailing women – and I never knew a one who didn't last a good long time."

"With care," agreed Robert.

"Of course, it's good care. They take care of themselves. And everyone around them helps." He chuckled. "But you needn't worry, my boy – we've visited Lady Farway only the once – apart from today – and we don't intend to trouble her unless we must. We've put the servants through it. There's little more we can do."

"Thank you, sir. I'm much relieved. I expect to take the night train back and I can do so easier in mind."

"Can't you wait until morning?" asked Jill. "I could give you a lift. I rented that little runabout in London and drove down."

"No thanks, Jill. I know how you drive," said Robert.

"I don't suppose there's anything either of you wants to say about Fairlie," said the Chief Constable.

"I haven't been in his world for a long time," said Jill, tossing her heavy hair back. "And he was never in mine."

"Did you know his daughter?" asked Pons quietly.

Jill looked at him cautiously. "Yes. Yes, I did."

"A strong-minded girl," said Robert. "And a beauty."

"Beauty is in the eye of the beholder," said Jill airily.

"We'll be on our way," said Sir Hugh, glancing at Pons to see whether he had any objection.

Pons gave no sign.

Once again in the Chief Constable's limousine, Pons said reflectively, "The family is tense with matters to be kept hidden."

Sir Hugh laughed immoderately. "It's all perspective, Pons. It's all in how you look at it. Old families like these are strong on keeping scandal under cover – and they do, they do."

"Such as, for example?"

Sir Hugh shrugged. "Well, take that affair of Ronald's. You'd have to drag it out of them, word for word. But the fact is he was drowned off the coast of Wales – the Merioneth coast, when he was on a holiday. But it was whom he was off with that made the scandal. Gerald's girl – that's who. Everybody thought it was all settled between Harriet and Gerald – and she ran off to spend a week with Ronald at old Fairlie's place in Wales." He chuckled. "Seems to me they were more upset by that than at Ronald's death. So you see it's a matter of values. They look at these things from a different perspective."

"Tell us more of this."

"Little more to tell. Ronald was fond of night swimming and there was a moon that night. He went in. She didn't. He never came back. It was a long time before the body was found – and then it was only by a chain around his neck they identified what was left of him."

Pons listened with manifest interest. When Sir Hugh had finished, he continued to sit in an attitude of deep thought, until the Chief Constable could tolerate his silence no longer.

"What d'you make of that, eh, Pons?"

"A pattern is beginning to emerge," said Pons.

The limousine drew up before the George.

"One thing more," said Pons. "You mentioned your men examining the servants at Farway Hall. The entrances, too, I assume."

"They went over everything. I'm afraid we can't satisfy what you'll want to know. There wasn't a shred of evidence of any tampering with the doors or windows anywhere. We didn't leave a single opening we failed to examine. Even to the chimneys!"

Pons smiled. "Were there any windows open?"

"One in Lady Farway's room – another in Miss Rebecca's. Neither wide enough to permit passage of so much as a hand."

"That leaves us with a door left unlocked. Or a key."

"Well, no one could be certain that all the doors were locked – but everyone believes they were. Rebecca was outside last; she thinks she 'may' have left a door unlocked. After all, it was still before midnight, and the house wasn't generally locked up until the last of them went to bed." He shrugged. "Moreover, as I'm sure you know, a good many houses just don't lock up tight."

"The fact remains that whoever searched Mr. Fairlie's room knew precisely how to get to it, and how to slip away without being seen. That suggests a member of the household."

"I'm not so sure of that. Fairlie had his cronies, too. He came and went as he pleased. We don't know who he might have had up there."

"We have so far heard nothing of his friends," observed Pons. "It has been all family, all business."

"We can get on to that," said Sir. Hugh.

"I doubt it would add much to this inquiry," replied Pons dryly. "But one can never tell to whom Mr. Fairlie may have confided something."

"Right!" cried the Chief Constable enthusiastically. He leaned forward to open the door for us. "I'll see you in the morning."

Back in our quarters in the George, I turned on Pons.

"How could you tell them over at Farway Hall – and so positively – that Fairlie had been killed to prevent his disclosing a discovery he had made about the family?"

"Why, because it is true. It is elementary, my dear fellow. Anything that concerned him would have been handled by him. But something that concerned the family – something unpleasant – put the wind up him. He couldn't bring himself to act. Perhaps he had reached an impasse – a paralysis of action or a point beyond which he feared to go because of whatever else he might find out."

"You did not speak then simply to stir them up?"

"That is a method dear to certain current writers of detective fiction," he said impatiently.

"Come, come," I said, "nothing is beyond you when the interests of justice are to be served."

"I meant it, I assure you. I can say that I am reasonably certain what one of Mr. Fairlie's secrets was."

"One?"

"Yes, yes – there were two, of course. Their relationship was but peripheral. It is the second that is of greater concern to me now. I am finding my way to the identity of Fairlie's murderer, and I already suspect very strongly the nature of the discovery he made and which he was ready to disclose at last – and, unless I am very much mistaken, to me."

"You cannot mean it!" I cried.

"I was never more serious."

"Why, I am completely bewildered. This case has offered us, surely, nothing at all in the way of tangible fact – save that of murder. It is quite one thing to have a problem laid before you – but another indeed to try to learn the problem without help."

"Is it not!" cried Pons, delightedly.

"I find it baffling."

"Come, come, say not so, Parker. I fancy there have been too many attractive young women about. You have always had an eye for the ladies, and you are not thinking through."

"My wife would not like to hear that."

"I am not so sure of that. It has been my experience – "

"Limited!" I cried. "Very limited!"

" – that ladies have a preference for men who take pleasure in their sex. It reassures them, for after all, as in this case, it is the wife who has been chosen – not the other ladies." He sprang to his feet. "And now, if you will excuse me, I have a few routine matters to look into."

V

AN ATTEMPT AT MURDER

A pounding on the door of our quarters at midnight brought Pons out of bed in a bound. He paused only long enough to make sure I was awake and to say, "Come, Parker, the game's afoot!" Then he crossed the room with cat-like rapidity and threw open the door as I turned on the light.

The Chief Constable stood there, obviously in a state of excitement.

"Can you come at once, Pons?" he cried. "There's been an attempt at another murder – and again on the London train!"

"Come in," urged Pons, taking hold of Sir Hugh's arm and drawing him into the room. "You'll have everyone on this floor awake."

"He fought him off – got nothing more than a few scratches. But he's shaken up – badly."

"Which one of them?" asked Pons. "It would have to be one of the Farways."

"It was Robert." He paused, then asked, "But how did you know it had to be one of them?"

"It is their riddle," said Pons impatiently. "How was it done?"

"In the same pattern as the murder of old Fairlie," said the Chief Constable. "Chloroform – a tottering, bearded old man.

But you'll want to talk to Robert. We have him over at the station."

The Chief Constable continued to talk while we dressed. The attack, he said, had taken place beyond Westbury. Robert Farway had managed to fight off his attacker and had reported the attack as soon as he had collected himself. The train, however, had not been stopped. Robert had got off at Edington and been returned to Frome by a local officer.

The police station was not far down Bath Street on Christchurch Street West. A considerably subdued Robert Farway waited there. His clothes were disheveled, though he had obviously made some attempt to put them right. There were scratches on his face and a gouging scratch on his neck. The scarf he had worn knotted at his throat was torn. There was still an almost nauseatingly strong odor of choloroform about him, and, indeed, he seemed not insensible of it, for he was anything but alert.

"I rather think I have done the police an injustice," said Robert at once. "I had not really thought..."

Sir Hugh cut him off. "Don't tire yourself with regrets, my boy. just tell us what happened."

Robert looked at him reproachfully. "You have already taken it all down, sir."

"Yes, yes, but Mr. Pons will want to hear you tell it." Robert transferred his reproach to Pons.

"Perhaps you would prefer me to ask questions Mr. Farway," said Pons.

"Indeed, I would."

"Sir Hugh has outlined your story. We are not clear as to where your attacker entered the train."

"Nor am I, Mr. Pons. He could have got on at Frome or at Westbury. He could have got on looking very much different. He entered my compartment just out of Westbury – perhaps because another passenger shared my compartment to Westbury. He came in from the corridor."

"You say he might have looked 'much different'."

"Mr. Pons," said Robert impatiently, "no one as strong as he was could possibly have been as old as he looked. I tried to tear the beard off his face, but I was fighting for my life, holding my breath to keep from inhaling the chloroform. I couldn't do it. But he was young and strong. Fortunately, I've always kept up my exercises – and he had just so much time. He finally gave up and retreated to the corridor. I was too shaken – and, I confess, too weak, to pursue. I had all I could do to throw up the window and take fresh air."

"You say 'he' with such confidence, Mr. Farway," said Pons. "You are positive it couldn't have been a woman?"

Farway looked startled. "Oh, I should hardly think so. Still – but it would have to be a very strong and masculine woman."

"There are such, my boy," put in Sir Hugh.

"He came in and attacked at once?" asked Pons.

"Yes, but I was on my guard."

"Why?"

"Because, a moment or two before he came at me, I detected the odor of chloroform. In a sense, I was ready for him."

"Just how did he attack, Mr. Farway?"

"He took me by the hair with his right hand, bending my head back, and tried to clap a chloroform soaked pad over my face. I was able to turn my face just enough to avoid it – my scalp still hurts, and there is some skin burn – as you can see – along the jaw and neck where the pad made contact. I fought back at once."

"You were clearly the stronger," put in Sir Hugh.

"I believe so. Still, the surprise of the attack, sir – and the effect of what little chloroform I inhaled, combined to put me off balance. He did recognize, however, that he could not achieve his goal, whatever that was."

"Any idea who might want to kill you, my boy?" asked the Chief Constable.

"None."

"Like the case of Jonas Fairlie, you might know something dangerous to someone," ventured Sir Hugh.

"I could not imagine what it might be," said Farway. "I can't believe it."

"Or you might have something he wanted."

"Whatever could that be?" Farway scoffed. "He could hardly cash a cheque from Aunt Ellen."

"Mr. Fairlie's money was untouched," observed Pons quietly. "Nothing of obvious value was removed from his person. Indeed, we are inclined to think that nothing whatever was taken from him, that his killer, failing to find what he sought, left the train and went directly to Farway Hall to search Mr. Fairlie's quarters."

"You should know, Robert," added the Chief Constable, "we have every reason to believe the same man who killed Jonas Fairlie made the attempt on you tonight. A man, that is, wearing a long coat, a false beard, and looking like a very old man – tottering – with a cane."

"I saw no cane," said Robert.

"Such a man got on to the train at Frome the night Fairlie was murdered," Sir Hugh went on. "We've eliminated everyone else."

"Let us say rather we have *tentatively* eliminated everyone else," put in Pons. "There were on that train some unidentified passengers – including a woman."

"I don't know, Pons," said Sir Hugh gruffly, "I don't see this as a woman's crime."

"Women have committed crimes far worse," said Pons. He turned to Farway once more. "Of course, there was no secret about your leaving for London on the last train."

"None, Mr. Pons." He gazed toward Sir Hugh. "I don't suppose there is any reason for my staying now, is there? I'd like to take the next train."

"By all means," said the Chief Constable. "But why not ride in with Jill when she goes?"

Farway smiled weakly. "I've ridden with her before. I'd rather not do so again."

Sir Hugh guffawed. "I've seen her driving by! But we may send for you to make an identification if you can."

"I will come at once."

Sir Hugh turned to a police sergeant standing in the background. "We'll get in touch with the police along the line and have a search made for the place that fellow left the train."

"While they're about it," put in Pons, "have them keep an eye open for a discarded coat and beard – and perhaps an old hat." He turned to Farway. "He did wear a hat, Mr. Farway?"

"Yes, sir. A rather beaten-up hat – of felt, I believe."

"Colour?" barked Sir Hugh.

"Brown."

"And the coat?"

"Very light brown. The hat was darker in color. And the beard was a kind of iron grey." He turned to Pons. "You think then he may have simply discarded these things and remained on the train?"

"I think it eminently possible, even probable," said Pons.

"What more can I tell you?" asked Farway in the brief silence that fell.

"Only such details of description as you have not yet mentioned," answered Pons. "Was he tall – short – of medium height?"

"Not six feet. Probably five ten."

"And his hands?"

"Oh, Mr. Pons, he wore gloves."

"Of course. So did Mr. Fairlie's killer. The colour of his eyes?"

"I'm not sure. But I believe they were blue."

"His hair?"

Farway shook his head. "I saw nothing but his beard. His cheeks, though, I remember had a high colour. I suppose, Doctor," he added, turning to me, "one becomes accustomed to making such impressions the longer one is in practise."

"Indeed, one does," I replied.

"Go on, Mr. Farway," said Pons.

"Well, sir," Farway continued, "if I had to say, I'd guess that he was accustomed to rough work – his whole manner was rough."

"That may have been assumed."

"But he was quick, very quick."

"He had to be. He had very little time."

"He seems to have taken a great chance – and I cannot think what his reason might have been."

"We shall hope to disclose it in time," said Pons.

Farway looked at him with frank doubt in his grey-blue eyes, his forehead slightly wrinkled by his raised eyebrows.

Then his gaze swung away, back to the Chief Constable.

"I put myself in your hands, Sir Hugh. But I must get back to Edinburgh as soon as I may."

Sir Hugh glanced toward Pons as if he expected Pons to say him aye or nay. Pons, however, made no sign.

"Very well, my boy," said the Chief Constable. "We may send for you for purposes of identification, as I said before. But that's all for now. If you like, I'll send you to London by car."

"I would appreciate that very much, sir."

The Chief Constable walked out of the station with us and stood in the glow of the lights at the doorway to talk. "What do you make of this, Pons?" he asked.

"One factor, I daresay, is immediately apparent," said Pons.

"We've rattled the killer."

"Why do you say so?"

"He has just made a bad mistake."

"How?"

"My dear fellow, he has given his game away," replied Pons. "He may wish to show his contempt for our poor efforts, but he has chosen a poor way in which to do so. He insults us."

"By Gad, Pons! He almost got away with it. If Robert hadn't been as strong as he is, he'd have done him in."

"One or two little points occur to me," Pons went on. "The chloroform, for a beginning."

"I expect to have a report on that in the morning."

"Capital! Then I should lose no time getting on to a search of the line. That fellow can have little more use for his disguise and I should think it most likely that he discarded it: resumed his real identity, and calmly remained on the train. We'll want those things before some rustic appropriates them."

"We'll get right on to it, never fear – the moment light breaks."

We bade him good night and walked away, Pons preferring not to ride. The night was dark, the sky having clouded over, and at this hour no one was abroad.

"I must say, Pons, I failed to follow you," I said.

"Ah, that is not unusual at this stage," returned Pons. "Tell me, did you have opportunity to look at the scratches and bruises Robert sustained?"

"I saw them, yes."

"They suggested nothing to you?"

"Nothing but that young Farway appears to have acquitted himself well against a brute of a fellow who meant to take his life as he did that of Jonas Fairlie."

Pons clucked.

"And what can you have meant by saying the murderer had given his game away?"

"Ah, that is elementary. You need only ask yourself why this attempt had to be made at this point."

"Why was Fairlie murdered?" I countered. "There is clearly a relationship between them."

"There is indeed," said Pons grimly.

"I incline to the theory that Robert must know something – however unwitting he may be – that jeopardizes the murderer," I said boldly.

"You could not be more correct," agreed Pons. "I wish you knew what it is, since Robert is positive he does not."

"We are bound to learn it," I said, "With you on the scent."

"I appreciate your confidence in my slight powers," said Pons, chuckling. "But now let us move a little faster – I smell rain on the wind."

Back at our quarters at the George, I went to bed again immediately. Pons, however, spent some time pacing the floor, his hands clasped behind his back. For a while the vile smell of the abominable shag he smoked kept me awake, and I saw him pause and look again at the notes he had copied from the pad in Jonas Fairlie's rooms, staring at and pondering the initials written there.

I was not therefore surprised when he proposed at breakfast next morning that we pay a call on the poor cousins of the Farways. Rain had fallen in the early hours, but it had now halted, though clouds still held to the sky. Nevertheless, the air was stimulating – fresh and rainwashed, and the wind that rode in out of the north bore the fragrance of the meadows.

Our course – by Pons's preference again on foot – took us past some of the loveliest old houses in Somerset, some of them quaint with age, as well as three churches and a school before we neared the edge of the village in Dyer's Close Lane, off which presently we found the property on which the two Hattrays lived with their cousin, Gareth Ainslie.

The house was of stone, and old. The outbuildings some distance from it clearly suggested that the place had at one time been the home of a sheep farmer who had certainly contributed to the woollen industry at Frome; but a considerable number of years ago Frome had begun to push out toward the farm, and though the buildings were still kept up, and a few sheep could be seen off in pasture, it was evident that no appreciable farming was now being carried on. A copse of beeches that rose just beyond the outbuildings lent the scene a harmonious balance.

As we came in through the gate in the blackthorn hedge that separated the property from the lane, the heavy door of the house opened and I recognized the burly form of Russell Hattray standing on the threshold. He had evidently observed our approach and had not chosen to wait upon our knock.

"Good morning," he said gruffly.

His gaze was fixed on Pons, however, and as soon as Pons had returned his greeting, he said, "What can we do for you, Mr. Solar Pons?"

"Answer a few questions," said Pons.

"Come in."

He turned abruptly, leaving me to close the door, and led the way to a sitting room. There sat a woman – one of medium height, almost as burly and strong-looking as her brother, as dark as he – and a tall, almost slender man whose left eyelid drooped half way down over his eye, giving him a sinister appearance. These two were Jennifer Hattray and Gareth Ainslie; though he did so, Russell Hattray need not have introduced them.

And, having done so, Hattray turned on Pons. "We know you're here to look into Jonas Fairlie's death. Parrington called you in. Can't keep these little matters secret. I saw you with him at the Somerset."

"You knew Mr. Fairlie?" asked Pons.

"Aye."

"How well?"

"Say on sight. Hardly more. We have some investments in Farway Printers – and Fairlie made it his business to know all the investors – that is, all the local ones. So we knew him."

"He was forever prying around," said Ainslie, with some resentment.

"Trying to buy up our stock," put in Miss Jennifer Hattray. "We weren't selling."

Russell Hattray flashed each of them a warning glance. They subsided, looking away.

"I take it the stock paid decent dividends," said Pons.

"Aye," said Hattray.

"Fairlie owned some of it himself," Pons went on.

Hattray made an impatient gesture. "If it comes to it, we don't know any more about Fairlie than most everyone else around here. No need asking us. He worked for them – Farways."

"Your cousins."

"Aye. Distant."

"And kept their distance, too," put in Miss Jennifer Hattray with a bitter smile.

"As we liked it," added Ainslie.

"We're not a friendly family, as you see," said Russell Hattray then. "Mind our own affairs. Expect others to mind theirs. They always did. And we try to do the same."

There was plainly not much to be discovered here – or not much any of them intended to say. They sat like self-enclosed statues, walled in by suspicion and distrust. Yet there was that about them that suggested they had anticipated Pons's coming around to see them, and it was not entirely consistent with their affected indifference. Mr. Fairlie dead, they implied, meant no more to them than Mr. Fairlie living. Plainly, he belonged to "that lot" – that is, their cousins, and his death affected them not at all. They waited upon Pons's every word.

"So you had no social contact with your cousins?" said Pons.

"None," said Hattray roughly.

"For how long?"

"Ever since..." began Jennifer, and quailed before her brother's swift, dark look.

"Go on, Miss Hattray," urged Pons.

Hattray took a deep breath and growled. "Seven years," he said. "That's what you want to know, is it?"

"Let us hear about it, Mr. Hattray," said Pons with an air of already having heard about it and now wanting only Hattray's version.

"You'll have been told, then," said Hattray. "I don't see it has aught to do with old Fairlie's death. Charlie's boy used to meet his girl here now and then – that was it."

"Miss Diana Fairlie."

"Aye." A brusque nod of his dark head. "Charlie carried on about the two of them seeing each other. They met here. When Charlie found it out – why, that was the end of it."

"And the end of what you call 'social contact'," said Ainslie. "He stood between them. Sent the boy to Scotland for the hunting. He never came back. You'll know all that."

"Nothing to do with Fairlie's death," repeated Hattray stubbornly.

"We never know what has to do with murder, Mr. Hattray," said Pons, "until we have examined into it as thoroughly as possible."

"What's *he* think asking you to come down here to look into it?" asked Hattray then, belligerently. "Our local police could handle it."

"We are working together," said Pons. "There was good reason, which you may not know."

Hattray gazed at us with even deeper suspicion.

"So that," Pons went on, as if Hattray had not broken into his train of thought, "Sir Charles cut off all contact as a result of learning that his son had met Miss Diana here?"

"Aye." He shrugged. "And the others never did come here. Not that Charlie came very much. It was just that our relations were more amiable. We liked that boy. A fine lad. He'd have been a credit to the business, too. But in view of what happened, there was a lot of bitterness. Charlie blamed himself – and well he might – for the boy's death. And Fairlie was more on his side than his own daughter's if it comes to that. Sent her off to live elsewhere."

"But not until after the boy's death."

"True. But as she was the living reminder of what had brought it all about, she had to go where Charlie and his wife wouldn't chance to see her. Everything was done for them."

"When did you last see Jonas Fairlie?" asked Pons.

Hattray had the answer to that sudden question in a flash. "The day after Charlie was buried."

"He came here."

"Aye. We didn't attend the services. If we had he might have spared himself coming here and talked to us in the cemetery. Tried to buy our stock in Farway Printers."

"For himself?"

"He didn't say."

"Well, thank you all," said Pons. "I think there is nothing more I wish to know – at this time."

Relief showed all around, and a little thawing. Whatever they had expected Pons to probe into, he had not done so. Russell Hattray walked us to the gate, explaining in answer to a casual inquiry from Pons that at one time sheep in great numbers had been raised here – "Before my time!" – and supplied to local markets, for Frome had always been agricultural, a notable market town, and the center of a great woollen industry – "Not what it was once, but still important to the town." – but the three of them were now more or less retired, and living on a fixed income – "comfortable". He shook hands with Pons at the gate and stood watching us walk away, his hands stuck into his waist.

"We have surely learned little from them," I said when we were well away.

"I should not be inclined to dismiss our visit as fruitless," said Pons. "There is something of value even in the negative."

"That fellow Hattray must have the strength of a bull," I said.

"I daresay he has."

"Were they not waiting for us?"

"I rather believe they were. We were seen approaching, and they were called together."

"To prevent your questioning them separately," I cried.

"Perhaps," said Pons tranquilly. "These people are plainly aggrieved at what they fancy is their slighting treatment by their cousins. At the same time they do not wish to say anything that might be carried back to their cousins and be taken amiss."

It was evident that Pons was not inclined to talk. I fell silent. It was soon also manifest that Pons was not headed toward the George, for he turned off abruptly into Selwood Road, walking a little faster now, for the clouds were thickening and rain again impended.

"Where to?" I asked.

"There is still time to have a word with Mr. Bramshaw at the printing plant," said Pons.

Farway Printers, Ltd. soon loomed ahead. It was an imposing, recently modernized building, divided into three wings, of which the central wing was devoted to offices for the management, while the plant itself occupied the larger right wing, and storage was maintained in the other.

We were shown to the office of the manager with a minimum of delay, for Mr. Bramshaw was conferring with the head of the manufacturing department and one of the designers. He proved to be a rather austere man of middle age and middle height, though his pince-nez made him look somewhat more icily detached than he was in fact. He was conservatively dressed and wore a small rose in his lapel. His cold blue eyes looked at us with more than ordinary interest. He did not wait for Pons to begin a conversation, for, immediately upon our introducing ourselves, he opened with,

"I thought we should see you sooner or later. May I say how impressed I was to learn from friends in the Foreign Office about the splendid feat in which you were both engaged for our government on your recent journey from Prague?"

His reference to the adventure of the Orient Express, in which I played, all unwittingly, a significant part, took Pons briefly aback, for no public mention of the affair had been made.

"Thank you," said Pons.

"But you didn't come to hear that," said Bramshaw, with an affability his pinched features did not share. "Please make yourselves comfortable and tell me how we here can be of service to you. Anything we can do to help turn up the fellow who murdered Mr. Fairlie we will be eager to do."

"Mr. Fairlie had certain obligations which brought him to the plant from time to time," said Pons.

"A fine, cooperative, conscientious man," said Bramshaw. "Indeed, he came in now and then. He was Sir Charles's liaison man. I am sure you know that."

Pons surprised him with a question at a tangent. "How long has Mr. Gerald Farway been employed here?"

It took Bramshaw a few moments to recover from his surprise. "I believe it is eight or nine years," he said.

"In April, this year," Pons continued, "Mr. Fairlie inquired about the absence of Gerald Farway from his desk during August of last year."

"Yes, Mr. Pons, he did."

"Did he say what impelled his inquiry?"

"No, he didn't.

"Had he ever done so previously?"

"No, Mr. Pons."

"Or subsequently."

Again Bramshaw's reply was in the negative. The manager was now plainly at sea.

"Was Mr. Fairlie in the habit of checking up on the time employees of Farway Printers spent away from their desks?"

"Nothing of that sort, no."

"So his inquiry must have come as a surprise to you?"

"Yes, it did. I wanted to ask – but, you didn't ask Mr. Fairlie. He was a man who kept his own counsel. If I had asked, I'd have most likely been put off. He might have taken it wrong, too."

"You wrote him to say that Gerald Farway had been away from his desk for two days."

"Evidently you found my letter."

Pons nodded. "In consequence of that inquiry, can you say, was Gerald Farway reprimanded?"

"Not to my knowledge."

Pons sat for a few moments in contemplative silence. Then he changed the subject again.

"Two years ago, just before Sir Charles's death, he returned from a journey with Mr. Fairlie. Do you know where they went?"

"No, Mr. Pons."

"When they returned, both men appear to have been uncommonly busy. Among other occurrences – several men were discharged. Can you relate these discharges in any way to that journey Sir Charles took with Mr. Fairlie?"

Bramshaw was now utterly bewildered. He sat shaking his head. "Oh, those discharges had been in the works, so to speak, for some time. I can see no connection between that odd journey Sir Charles took with Mr. Fairlie and the discharges that were ordered on their return. The men discharged had been failing in their obligations consistently over a period of time – at least a year, before they were actually discharged."

"Sir Charles's interest in the business was maintained by Mr. Fairlie, I take it."

"Oh, yes."

"So that actually these people were discharged on Mr. Fairlie's recommendation?"

"No, sir. On mine. Mr. Fairlie merely carried my recommendations to Sir Charles. Of course, Mr. Fairlie was the kind of man who needed to satisfy himself that the charges were true, and he did so."

"So he went about in the plant to see for himself?"

Bramshaw nodded. "He was the last person to want to see any injustice done," he explained. "He had a horror of doing any injustice to anyone himself. It was second nature to him."

"That is consistent with the portrait we have of him, Mr. Bramshaw."

"We said, some of us, that he was too honest for his own good. Worrying about details of no significance, particularly where it concerned the Farway family. He seemed to feel that he personally owed Sir Charles more than he could repay him."

"Can you conceive of anyone who might want Mr. Fairlie dead?"

"No, Mr. Pons – I cannot."

"Yet someone obviously did."

"It is beyond me, sir – utterly beyond me."

And this was the sum total of Pons's visit to Farway Printers, Ltd. When we walked away from the plant, I could not keep from pointing out that we had drawn another blank.

"I am not disappointed," said Pons. "The negative may be as informative as the positive, as by this time you must know. Whatever Mr. Fairlie's secrets were they seem to have had little to do with the business except in the most peripheral way."

"Then why are you doing this routine police work?" I demanded. "For that's what it is."

Pons nodded amiably. "The police cannot do everything. They are all too busy. But this is part of the process of eliminating the possible and establishing the probable. Now we shall see what the inquest holds."

VI

INQUEST

Dr. Henry Littlefield officiated at the inquest. He was a man of middle age, a native of Frome. His manner was proprietary. He had been coroner for a decade, explained Sir Hugh Parrington, who had joined us. He looked out at the audience over his spectacles and seemed to be in no hurry to open the proceedings. Outside, the rain that had been threatening all morning was now falling, slowly and steadily, as if it meant to come down for hours, and the sound of dripping at the eaves and of running water filled the room.

Gerald Farway was present for the family, and Ralph Bramshaw was at his side. I observed that Pons looked from time to time toward a heavily veiled young woman, all in black, who sat alone and very still well away from anyone else and who, I concluded, must be Miss Diana Fairlie.

Once Alfred Aston, the guard, made his appearance, Dr. Littlefield opened the inquest. Evidently he had been waiting for him to come, for he now gave as much an appearance of haste as previously he had of leisureliness.

The guard told a straightforward story, with Dr. Littlefield putting in a judicious question now and then. He had known Jonas Fairlie for almost two decades. He had been a frequent traveler – not regular, no, but every little while or so. No, he could not be called more than a nodding acquaintance, but his habits were familiar to Aston, and he never slept on the train – not within Aston's experience. "So that when I saw him sitting there like that, so soon after he got on, I concluded something was wrong, and I stepped in and found him dead."

"And how did Aston know he was dead?" inquired the coroner.

"Why, he wasn't breathing," replied Aston, faintly indignant. "And there was all that smell of chloroform."

"How do you know that, Mr. Aston?"

"I know what it smells like," said the guard. "I've been in the hospital in Bath."

Since Aston showed some signs of becoming voluble, the coroner did not press the point. "Go on, Mr. Aston."

Aston set forth his actions on his discovery of Jonas Fairlie's body and presently finished. He was allowed to leave the stand and Dr. Lucas Everdene, the medical examiner, followed. The medical evidence was set forth succinctly. The smell of chloroform was still evident when the doctor arrived. There was no sign of the pad or cloth or whatever had been used to cover Fairlie's nose and mouth, but the typical reddening of the skin was plainly to be seen. The doctor, however, would not say that Fairlie had died from the effect of the chloroform or from fright or failure of his heart as a result of the attack. "The attack on him, however, in your opinion, brought on his death?" asked Dr. Littlefield.

"No doubt of it."

"You did an autopsy?"

"Of course. There was some heart damage. It appeared recent. The precise cause of death would be immaterial in this case," said Dr. Everdene. "He was an aging man, and the sudden attack killed him."

"If a man had chloroform clapped over his nose and mouth, how long would it take him to die, in your estimation?"

Dr. Everdene made a gesture of impatience. "Five minutes of chloroform would kill anyone in such circumstances", he said testily. "But the point is that Fairlie could have died in less time from shock. Just shutting off his oxygen for five minutes would kill him, in all likelihood."

Dr. Littlefield excused him.

Police Sergeant Arthur Bates took his place and gave his evidence in a skilled, professional manner. He had been summoned from the station and in the absence of the Superintendent, he had gone to where the car had been sidetracked at Westbury. There had been some question about the scene of the crime, but Mr. Aston's evidence seemed to place it within the boundaries of Somerset rather than in Wiltshire. A hasty conference between the Chief Constables of the two counties had resulted in returning the body to Frome in the carriage in which the crime had taken place.

Dr. Littlefield bore down sharply on all the sergeant's evidence, picking and pecking at it with some deliberation. He seemed to think that Bates ought to offer more details about motive. How could he be certain nothing had been taken from the body? for instance.

"Not knowing what Mr. Fairlie carried with him, I couldn't say, sir," said Bates.

He was allowed to leave the stand presently, and a succession of witnesses followed – two police officials from Westbury, primarily to verify the meeting with the Chief Constable, Sir Hugh Parrington, and Nichols, the booking-clerk – but it was evident that if the police had anything in the way of formal evidence pointing in any specific direction, it was not being offered. In just short of two hours, the inquest was adjourned. Pons had not shown much interest in the proceedings. He had kept his attention on Miss Fairlie and when he saw that she had risen and was about to make her way out of the room, he was on his feet and off to intercept her. He reached her side at the entrance.

"Miss Fairlie?" he asked. "I would like a word with you."

Without lifting her veil, she answered, "You have the advantage of me, sir. I don't know you."

She had a pleasant, well-modulated voice. After Pons had introduced us, she hesitated for a few moments, with people milling around her, then said, "Let us just sit down at the rear here," and led the way to the now abandoned chairs at the back of the room.

There she sat down, careful to arrange herself so that her back was to the people still passing out of the room, and raised her veil. She was indeed a beautiful young woman. Not yet thirty, she had what country folk call a peaches and cream complexion, out of which looked hazel eyes rimmed with an edge of green; her hair was a lustrous chestnut, her lips were full and inviting.

"We are looking into your father's death, Miss Fairlie," explained Pons. "Perhaps you have something to tell us."

She shook her head, biting her lower lips. "I find it very hard to believe Father was – " she hesitated, as if it were difficult for her to say the word, " – murdered. I cannot imagine why. And such a desperate act, too!"

"Your father came to visit you frequently?"

"Yes, I suppose you would call it frequently. At least once a month, sometimes twice. There is no other family, Mr. Pons. My father had a younger brother, Howard – but Howard was a rascal, to hear my father tell it, and the two couldn't get along."

"Still alive?"

"Somewhere."

"Last heard from?"

"Australia, two years ago." She hesitated again, as if in doubt whether or not to speak. "He wrote Father for money. He wanted to come back to England. Father didn't send it."

"You don't seem to have come here to visit your father?" said Pons then. "Why?"

"There were good reaons for that, Mr. Pons," she said steadily. "The same reasons for which I left Frome. Even if there were not such reasons, I am employed half-days, and I have obligations."

"I observe, Miss Fairlie, that you wear a wedding ring."

"I am not married, if that's what you want to know," she answered at once. "It isn't a wedding ring. I wish it were. It was given to me as a friendship ring – a token of our engagement – by the man I had hoped to marry."

"Peter Farway."

"You could hardly escape knowing about it if you came here," she said. There was no bitterness in her voice. "He gave me the ring just before he went to Scotland. I am sure you know all about it."

"No. It was your father's death I was asked to investigate. But since you have opened the subject, perhaps you will not mind a question or two." At her gesture, he continued, "I take it your intention to marry was general knowledge here?"

"We saw no reason to keep it secret."

"We have been told that Sir Charles Farway disapproved of your plans," said Pons.

At this point Miss Fairlie's tight control gave way. Tears came to her eyes. She turned her head away, fumbled for her handkerchief, and held it for a few moments to her eyes while she fought to regain her composure. When she looked up again her lips were fixed with determination.

"Forgive me," she said. "I loved them both so very much – Peter and my father. It is very hard for me." She sighed heavily.

"But no, Mr. Pons, I'm sure it was not like that. Sir Charles wanted Peter to be sure, to be absolutely certain that he wanted to marry me. True, he sent him to Scotland, but Peter explained that to me. I too wanted Peter to be certain. I was sure in my heart that he was – as I was."

"I submit, however, Miss Fairlie, that some doubt about Sir Charles's motives remained, " said Pons.

She gazed at him full for a long moment before replying. "I suppose that would be inevitable in the circumstances. Peter's death affected us all very much, all of us who loved him. And he was their only child. They've tried to fill the void with nieces and nephews. But you must know that, too – there's no need my saying it."

"Returning to your father," said Pons after a thoughtful pause. "Had he ever spoken to you of enemies?"

"No."

"Of danger?"

"No."

"Of anything troubling him?"

She shook her head. "But something was troubling him. I began to notice it not long after Sir Charles's death. At first I thought it had to do with problems of the estate, but I came to think otherwise."

"He never spoke to you about it?"

"No, Mr. Pons. Not so much as a hint. But that was his nature. He was much given to keeping things to himself – until he was sure that the time had come to speak." Her frown deepened. "But I know he was troubled – deeply troubled. I asked him several times what bothered him, but he brushed my questions away. That was like him, too."

Pons gazed at her for a long time, until she began to stir uneasily. Then he spoke, gravely. "Miss Fairlie, I dislike to alarm you, but you may be in some danger."

Her eyes flashed. She was startled.

Pons went on. "Your father was killed to prevent his telling what troubled him."

"How can you be sure of that?"

"There is nothing other so far that offers a tenable motive. He was on his way to see me, we believe, when his life was taken."

Miss Fairlie lost a little of her color. Her hands clenched.

"It must sooner or later occur to his murderer that you may have been in his confidence, and that you too may know the secret to prevent telling which he was killed."

"But – I know nothing."

"The killer may not know that. I do think that for the time being you are safe. In time you may not be. Do you have any objection if Sir Hugh arranges for some kind of surveillance?" Miss Fairlie did not know what to say. She was disconcerted rather than alarmed. She kept on clenching and unclenching her hands. She looked away. Presently she swung her head back.

"I'd hate to be kept under surveillance," she said. "Tell me frankly, Mr. Pons, do you really think it is necessary."

"If the murderer knew your father as well as I suspect he did, no. But we are bound to consider the possibility that he may not have known him well enough to be fully aware of his secretiveness."

She smiled, reassured. "Then, if you don't mind, I'll take my chances. You've warned me. I'll be wary."

Her eyes fixed suddenly on someone beyond us. A faint smile touched her lips. She gave a little nod.

Gerald Farway stood across the room, in the act of tipping his hat to her. Behind him stood his cousin Rebecca, her face a dark mask. She stared at Diana Fairlie without any sign of recognition. As Diana looked toward her, she turned abruptly and walked out of the room. Gerald clapped his hat to his head and followed.

"Miss Fairlie," said Pons again.

"Yes, Mr. Pons?" She turned to look at him once more. It was impossible to determine what she might have thought of Rebecca Farway's deliberate cutting of her.

"Once more – what troubled your father? If he never said anything to you, how did you know?"

"Oh, a woman always knows these things," said she. "Father was restless – he couldn't sit still – he was preoccupied – and he had never been that when he came to see me before Sir Charles's death." She broke off abruptly. "But, truthfully, Mr. Pons, I'm afraid I can't tell you anything you want to know, I really can't. I would, certainly, if only I could."

"If I find myself in Cheltenham, I may call on you," said Pons then.

For some reason, Pons's suggestion disturbed her. I saw her fingers tighten on the handkerchief she still held.

"Unless there is some reason you would rather I didn't," continued Pons.

"I'm sure," she said, choosing her words carefully, "I am at your service. No one – more than I myself – wants to see my father's murderer caught. I could come to Frome at any time you need me. You have only to send word."

"Thank you, Miss Fairlie."

She stood up, lowering her veil once more. She walked quickly away, pausing to say a few words to Sir Hugh Parrington. Then she was gone and Sir Hugh stood waiting for us.

"A fine girl, Diana," he boomed. "A tragedy they didn't marry."

"It occurs to me to wonder," said Pons, as we walked out of the building into the now thinning rainfall, "now we've heard all about Sir Charles's reaction to that projected marriage – how did Mr. Fairlie react to it? Does anyone know?"

"I would suppose the idea would have appealed to him – with his closeness to the family and all," said the Chief Constable. "I don't recall that he ever said, one way or the other." He shrugged. "But that's not important. I've had some reports that are. Let's just step around to the station. We've turned up the clothing – hat, coat, even the false beard – just as you guessed we might. Found along the tracks – one piece here, another a bit farther on, and then the last. As thrown out of the train from another compartment somewhere along."

"I am not surprised," said Pons dryly.

"Well, come along and see what you can make of them."

The Chief Constable strode briskly through the rain with never a thought of the weather, always a step or two ahead of us, until he drew up at the police station, where he stood aside to let us pass.

Superintendent Ian Rossiter, a tall man whose portliness did not offer any impediment to the quickness of his movements, took us directly to the garments found along the railway line beyond Frome, recounting precisely where they had been found, and by whom – information which appeared to be lost on Pons, who seemed neither to know the places Rossiter mentioned nor care about them, save to point out that the discovery defined, relatively, where the attack on Robert Farway had taken place.

The garments and beard were on a table in a locked room. They had evidently been discovered before the rain had fallen for, though damp, they were not wet. The coat was long – of a length that on a man of medium height must come well below the knees; it was of a rough cloth, loosely woven, but for all that it looked like the kind of coat that might be worn by a countryman – even a shepherd out among his sheep, it was not an inexpensive garment.

Pons examined it with care, looking in vain for any mark that might identify its maker. There was none; it had been cut carefully away from both the collar and the rim of the inner pocket, for the coat, surprisingly, had such a pocket in the lining that went down three-quarters of its length. Pons felt the cloth, pressed the coat to his nostrils.

"Hrumph! Chloroform," said Sir Hugh. "I caught a smell of it."

"Oh, there is more," said Pons. "This coat has been worn outside in open country – hillsides. It has a pungence about it over and above that medicinal odor you've already detected. Try it again." He thrust the coat at the Chief Constable.

Sir Hugh raised it to his nostrils in turn.

"Try the hem, the hem," said Pons impatiently.

"Yes, of course," agreed the Chief Constable. "So it has been worn by someone in the country. And Frome is a market town – it could be anyone."

"I submit it could not," said Pons. "The coat is not, despite its appearance, an old one. It has not been well cared-for, but it shows none of the signs of wear. The hem of it, which shows some discoloration, has been frequently brushed against something wet – I suggest it was dew; that would account for the pungence so evident to us. The cuffs and one pocket – the right side – we may postulate a right-handed man..."

"No fancy tricks here, eh?" put in Sir Hugh.

"These are the source of the medicinal odor, which you say is chloroform," Pons went on.

"Let me smell it," I asked.

Sir Hugh handed the coat to me. Pons now took up the hat and turned it round and round in his hands. I smelled the coat in turn – hem, cuffs, pocket. The typical sweetness of chloroform was unmistakable. I said as much.

"Yes, yes," said Pons brusquely. "Nothing more?"

"A medicinal odor, yes," I said.

"Not chloroform?"

I shook my head. "No, this is not chloroform. Quite possibly chloroform was spilled here – and on the cuff, but that is sweet. This is not."

"What does it suggest, Parker?"

"Some kind of antiseptic. I cannot determine what was used here. One other thing. Rubber."

Pons chuckled. "Of course, he wore rubber gloves. Thrust them into his pocket."

"To avoid being burned by the chloroform, obviously," I said.

Pons was still turning the hat over in his hands. "Used by an angler," he said now. "Dry flies have been attached to the band."

"We saw that," said the Chief Constable.

"The hat has been worn more consistently than the coat," Pons went on. "The signs of wear are everywhere – on the brim, the sweatband. It is the kind of hat used again by countrymen – particularly by hikers, anglers, sportsmen. And not inexpensive." He held it to his nose.

"Not a medicinal smell again," said Sir Hugh.

"No – the other."

"Well, it is like leaves of some kind, foliage," said the Chief Constable, smelling it. "There is a bed of herbs at Farway Hall that has something of the same pungence."

"Yes, it is herb-like," agreed Pons. "But not specifically of rosemary or thyme or any herb commonly found in herb gardens."

"All of them together," said Sir Hugh.

"Heather," said Pons.

He took the hat again. "How would it come to have such a pungence? Surely not because it was dropped to lie in a bed of herbs! No, I submit it was taken off along a trout or salmon stream when in use by an angler, and left to lie perhaps for hours at a time in heather which imparted its pungence to it. Not just on one occasion, but habitually. The fragrance is strongest along the brim. If it had been packed away in a scented place – with a sachet of herb-leaves, for example – the entire hat would have been permeated with it."

The beard was plainly of commercial manufacture. Unlike the garments, however, it looked new.

"Bought for the occasion," said Pons. "Any shop the length and breadth of the isles, specializing in supplying masquerade or dramatic costumes or the paraphernalia of mummers could have supplied this beard. It is very probably a standard piece, and there is nothing to identify it, to set it apart from any other like it."

"So that we'd have a hard time – an impossible task to find where it was sold," said the Chief Constable.

"Not impossible, no. Improbable as of now. But once a suspect clearly emerges, you should have but slight difficulty associating its purchase with him. The same thing is true of the hat and coat."

"We'll set inquiries afoot," said Sir Hugh. "Neither hat nor coat appears to be of local manufacture."

"Look farther abroad," said Pons cryptically. "No local man bent on murder would acquire a disguise here in Frome." He turned from the beard and garments and stood looking out of the window. The rain had begun to fall again, a heavy, sodden downpour. "What have you done about tracing the chloroform?" he asked without turning.

"No trace," said Superintendent Rossiter. "We've been all over Frome and Westbury. We're looking into other nearby sources. We can't find any source for it."

"And the murderer? Where did he get on the train."

Sir Hugh cleared his throat. "We can't seem to find that, Pons. We've sent descriptions of him all the way back along the line as far as Exeter. There's no report of such an old man's taking the train anywhere. No booking-clerk remembers him – and he was distinctive enough to have been remembered. Nichols here recalled him quite clearly when old Fairlie was done in."

"So he carried his disguise on to the train in his bag," mused Pons, "and put it on when he wanted to use it."

"He must have known, then, that Robert Farway would be on the train," said Sir Hugh.

Pons nodded. "He knew that, beyond doubt. But there was no secret about that. Everyone at Farway Hall knew it, including the servants."

"And then, having worn these things," put in Rossiter, "he got rid of them because he knew he couldn't use them again."

Pons turned. "Let me draw your attention to the significant alteration in his pattern."

"What alteration?" asked Sir Hugh bluntly.

"On the initial occasion – the prelude to the murder of Jonas Fairlie – he came to the booking-office wearing his disguise. On this occasion he carried his disguise concealed in his bag. That is the significant alteration. I commend it to you. Meanwhile, I have another small line of inquiry to explore, if you will excuse us."

"You can't walk in this rain," said the Chief Constable. "We'll run you over."

On the way back to the George, Pons said nothing. Sir Hugh was voluble, but Pons only nodded once or twice by way of reply. At the hotel he mounted rapidly to our quarters and began to pace the floor. I observed that he took from an inner pocket a folded paper; he looked at it from time to time, frowning, until at last he came to a stop in the middle of the room.

"Fool that I am!" he cried.

"What is it?" I asked.

"It is plain as a pikestaff," he answered. "Parker, whenever I am prone to praise my poor powers, remind me of the murder of Jonas Fairlie. It is all here," he went on, tapping the paper in his fingers.

I had lain down on the bed; now I came to my feet and strode to his side. The paper he carried was that on which he had written down the initials copied from the scratch-pad found in Fairlie's room at Farway Hall.

"We have been proceeding – without adequate thought – on the assumption that these are initials," he said.

"Surely they cannot be anything else!"

"Surely they are," retorted Pons. "Why should they not be? Let us just separate them."

So saying, he took a pencil and drew a line down between them, separating the initial letters from the secondary ones.

"They are still," I said, "initials."

Pons shook his head impatiently. "Yes, yes – of a sort. We are misled by Farway's intended helpfulness. Hattrays and Ainslie, indeed! Let us just forget for the nonce any but the first row of letters."

"Yes," I said, "G, R, and J. What do you make of them? They still remain the initials of Ainslie and the Hattrays."

"But that is not all they remain," said Pons. "Forget these cousins of the Farways."

I stood mystified.

"Come, come, Parker. Are these not also Farway initials?"

"There is not an F on the page," I protested.

"G could stand as well for Gerald, could it not? And R for Rebecca or Robert? And J for Jill?"

"What of that? A mere coincidence," I said.

"No, no. Ainslie and the Hattrays made up the coincidence."

"Well, then, what of the second row of letters?"

"We agreed, did we not, that the indecipherable letters above these initials were numerals?"

"Yes, we did, though we couldn't be sure of them."

"Very well, supposing Fairlie set down a date."

"I accept the premise," I said.

"Capital! Then of what possible relationship could these initials be? Think, man!"

"I am thinking," I said. "Of course, they are related – I can see that."

"Then you must see how."

"Well, Pons – let us see. Fairlie puts down a date. Beneath it he writes – if you say so, Gerald Farway's first initial. And then Rebecca's or Robert's – I suppose it is Rebecca's. And then, Jill's. He means to discover where they were on that date!"

"Ah, Parker, you do not disappoint me! It is almost two decades since you have observed my methods, and since they are really quite simple, you should be able to continue."

"Of course," I cried. "I see it all now. What Fairlie meant by that second row was the place – the place they were. Of course. Gerald – 'A' – means that Gerald was absent from home on that date. And 'H' means 'at home' – so Rebecca or Robert and Jill were at home – or not away from the place they might have been expected to be." And, now I had got started, I was not to be outdone. "And that upper line – those numerals – " I went on, "must have been a date, like August 17, 1937 – however old Fairlie put it down!"

Pons positively beamed.

"So now, Parker," he cried, "you know one of Mr. Fairlie's secrets."

My enthusiasm faded. "I have to confess I do not," I said, "any more than you know the identity of the murderer!"

He made an impatient gesture with one hand. "Oh, I know the identity of the murderer," he said. "That is not the problem. The problem is to prove his guilt in court."

"You do!" I cried, astounded.

"You ought not to confuse knowledge of the identity of a murderer with the legal evidence needed to convict him. These are two different matters. It is one thing to make what appears to be a brilliant deduction, but quite another to marshall evidence in so convincing a manner that a jury has no alternative but to find the defendant guilty. The former is relatively easy – the latter anything but easy."

I knew better than to ask Pons for the name of the murderer. "I still do not know – as you put it – the one of old Fairlie's secrets."

"The reason he was coming to see me? Surely that is now obvious, Parker."

"Not to me."

"Now consider. Since Sir Charles Farway died – perfectly naturally, so much cannot be gainsaid – two people in the family died – Sir Charles's brother Austin fell to his death – his nephew Ronald was drowned off the coast of Wales. Prior to the old man's death his son Peter died – shot in an accident with his own gun. Is that not a remarkable sequence of accidents?"

"Pons, you cannot mean...?"

"Ah, but that is what Mr. Fairlie came to think, did he not? He began to nose about – to make a great number of journeys. He made inquiries, however discreet, in Frome. He went to Wales, to Scotland – and I have no doubt he made inquiries there, also. He must certainly have found some ground for his suspicions, and the more he found, the more troubled he grew. He must have become convinced that someone was attempting to wipe out the family, taking infinite pains and a great deal of time to do it. But all that activity on the part of one who had not previously been so active could not have gone unnoticed. Somewhere in the course of his inquiries he attracted the attention of the murderer. And at about the same time he began to come uncomfortably close to establishing his identity and the fact distressed him so much that he wanted to shift that responsibility."

"To you."

"It would seem so."

"But the motive?" I protested.

"Could it be other than greed? Sir Charles's estate. It must have been known that the property would be left, after Lady Farway's death, to the surviving nieces and nephews."

"But Sir Charles had changed his will," I pointed out.

"The murderer cannot have known that, can he?" said Pons, his eyes dancing. "Or she," he added, chuckling. "It now becomes more than ever necessary for us to learn where Mr. Fairlie went on that mysterious journey with Sir Charles, after which the old man changed his will so precipitately. I think, for one venture, we will take a little journey ourselves – to Cheltenham first – and then perhaps to Wales."

VII

A VISIT TO CHELTENHAM

The inquest having freed Jonas Fairlie's body for burial, brief services were held early the following afternoon. The Chief Constable appeared at the George to take us to the church and subsequently to the cemetery. Once again the family was represented by Miss Rebecca and Gerald Farway; once more Ralph Bramshaw came from Farway Printers, Ltd. This time, however, Diana Fairlie did not sit alone; she was in the company of Douglas Abercrombie, whose dour countenance lent itself fittingly to the services.

The coffin was kept closed. Miss Fairlie did not once raise her veil, nor did she look around to see who might be there. At the cemetery she accepted condolences from the two Farways and Bramshaw. Pons made no attempt to speak to her; he had observed that Rebecca Farway had glanced in his direction several times, both in church and at the cemetery, uneasily, sometimes almost with hostility.

It was therefore not a surprise to me when Pons walked over to her as she and her cousin were on their way to his car.

"I would like a few words with you, Miss Farway," he said.

"Hadn't you better be about, with the others, catching the man who attacked my brother?" she asked coldly.

Gerald's hand tightened warningly on her arm.

"When is it convenient for me to see you?" pressed Pons.

"This is as good a time as any," she answered. Her face, patched with sunlight and shadow thrown by the elms that towered overhead, was both proud and defiant, and also, I was certain, betrayed some disquiet.

"Very well," said Pons. "I want to ask specifically about the obligation of seeing to it that the doors and windows of Farway Hall were secure at night. Whose was it?"

"It was either Pyatt's or mine. Pyatt is the butler, as I think you know."

Pons nodded. "Thinking back to the night Mr. Fairlie was murdered – who saw to the doors?"

"Pyatt did it first. And when I went to bed I went around to the front and the back." She hesitated, they added, "I didn't see to the side doors, but they aren't usually unlocked once uncertain weather begins."

"And when you had done so, you retired to your quarters?"

"Yes, I did."

"And did not stir from them?"

Her eyes flashed angrily. "I haven't said so. No one asked me. I did go out again – to see to Aunt Ellen. I thought I heard her moving about; I went to see if she needed me."

"Did she?"

"Well, yes, she did. She hadn't been moving around, no – but she did want some hot milk. I went downstairs for it."

"You encountered no one?"

"No." Once again there was a curious hesitation in her voice.

It did not go unnoticed. "I put it to you, Miss Farway, that you heard or saw something you didn't think to report to the police."

"Perhaps that is so," she answered.

"What was it?"

"It was something I thought I saw – I can't be sure..."

"Go on, Miss Farway." Pons's voice had hardened a little with his growing impatience.

"I thought I saw a light under the door to Mr. Fairlie's rooms," she said then. "I believed, naturally, that Mr. Fairlie had come in, and I dismissed it from mind. But the more I have thought about it – I suppose it must have been someone else..."

"His murderer searching his room," said Pons bluntly.

"I suppose it must have been," she said.

"You heard no one moving about later – as, for instance, someone you might have thought to be Mr. Fairlie leaving his quarters?"

She shook her head. "Nothing. When I brought Aunt Ellen's milk up to her, Mr. Fairlie's door was dark. I naturally thought he had gone to bed. It was late."

"What time?"

"It must have been one side or the other of eleven o'clock. Not far away from that hour."

"Thank you, Miss Farway."

We stood aside to let her pass.

"She is apprehensive," I said.

"I daresay," agreed Pons. "She has not told all she knows or put into words what she suspects."

The Chief Constable disengaged himself from Diana Fairlie and the lawyer, and came walking leisurely toward us. The afternoon had grown unseasonably warm, and Sir Hugh was fanning himself with his hat. Chaffinches sang from the far edge of the cemetery, and now Diana Fairlie and Abercrombie began to move away from the graveside so that the men there could go about their work.

"I have one or two little tasks I would appreciate your performing, Sir Hugh," said Pons, as the Chief Constable came up. "And, once done, I rather think we need only sit back and wait upon developments."

"Whatever you say."

"It may upset Rossiter a little, but he'll get over it," continued Pons. "Before anything else, however, I want to pursue some enquiries elsewhere – Glasgow, Cheltenham, perhaps Wales."

"Oh, those are the places to which old Fairlie traveled," said the Chief Constable. "Though I'm blessed if I can imagine what you might turn up there. We don't even know precisely where he went."

"In Scotland, perhaps not," agreed Pons. "But in Cheltenham certainly to visit his daughter – and in Wales to his own cottage. He may have gone farther afield in those places – that remains to be disclosed."

"When do you go?"

We had now reached Sir Hugh's car. Before getting in, Pons paused to reply. "I think there is little time to be lost. We expect to leave later this afternoon. We'll be back, however, as quickly as events permit. In any case, we'll retain our quarters at the George."

I was not destined to accompany Pons into Scotland, however, for a trunk call caught me at the George while we were making ready to leave; my locum had encountered complications in one of my patients, who in turn demanded to have me in attendance. There was no alternative – my patient was one of long standing, and I could not refuse his request. We parted company at Paddington, where I promised to meet him as soon as possible at the George.

It was two days before I rejoined him. He had preceded me by only a few hours.

"You are just in time, Parker," he cried. "We are off to Cheltenham in an hour."

He was animated and looked freshened, as if he had been tramping the highlands.

"What did you discover in Scotland?" I asked, as I unpacked.

"Nothing I had not previously assured myself could be discovered there," he said.

"Evidence?"

"I leave that to the province of the police," he said. "When I am engaged in one of these little inquiries on my own, I will pursue every piece of evidence, no matter how small or trivial; but when I am associated with the police, I prefer to leave the routine work to them."

"You found trace of Fairlie?"

"I did, indeed. I fancy, though, I made considerable more show of myself than Mr. Fairlie did."

More than this he would not say, but this was to be expected of him if he were not quite convinced that what he might say were beyond question. In good time he would speak. Within the hour, we were on our way to Cheltenham. "This is one of England's loveliest cities," reflected Pons as we rode into it almost two hours later. "Situated as it is between the Severn valley and the high Cotswolds, it is ideally placed for visitors to this part of England. You know what a warm place it has in my affections."

"I have heard so before this," I said. "But why are we coming here now?"

"Ah, Parker, you are ever a man for driving straight to the point. Here I am in the mood to appreciate the beautiful old trees, the wide streets, the classic facades of the city – and you insist upon the mundane affair of the moment." He sighed. "We are here to keep an eye on Miss Fairlie."

"You think she may be in immediate danger, then?"

"Not as much so as we are likely to be in a day or two," he replied cryptically.

"What then?" I persisted.

"Why, I am curious to know how she lives. We know very little about her. Miss Fairlie, everyone tells us, lives in Cheltenham. She says she works half-days. Now that is curious, is it not? Why not full days? Moreover, she has withdrawn so effectively from Frome that little is known of her in Cheltenham, which is but sixty miles or so from her former home. Granted that her father was secretive, it is no less uncommon."

"Oh, come, Pons," I said. "It is only natural. Despite what she says, she was wounded by what must have been some opposition to the marriage they planned – and she now wants nothing more to do with Frome."

"Did she not seem to you eminently sensible?"

"I thought so."

"Certainly not the kind of woman to indulge in such romanticism as you suggest as reason for her cutting herself off from Frome. She must have had friends in Frome. We have heard nothing of them. Her father visits her. She does not visit him."

"She has plainly made a new life for herself here in Cheltenham," I protested. "One finds, as one goes on through life, that it becomes impossible to maintain all one's former friendships and acquaintances."

"True, true," agreed Pons testily, "but it is easy to begin anew, to cut one's self off when there are no ties. I submit that she had the strongest of all ties to Frome and to Farway Hall, for her father still lived in that city, indeed, in the Hall itself, now that she had left him, and he was an important factor in the lives and business of the Farways."

"She struck me as a woman of independence and spirit," I said. "It is the sort of thing that kind of woman would do."

Pons smiled. "Perhaps I ought to defer to your superior knowledge of the fair sex. After all, you have married one of them, and you are clearly in a more authoritative position than I."

"Ah, that is elementary," I said.

"But here we are in the center of Cheltenham."

We were now walking along the Promenade, having come on foot from the station along tree-naved streets, but none so fair as the Promenade itself, one of the most beautiful streets in all England, green with trees, colorful with flowers, flanked by handsome buildings, ranging from the municipal offices to rows of shops.

"Now there is a telephone booth," said Pons. "Let me just step into it and see whether Miss Fairlie is listed."

He suited his actions to his words, while I idled on the kerb.

In a few minutes he returned. "We seem to be within a block or two of her apartment. I believe it is on the first floor above one of the shops near the Neptune Fountain just ahead. Let us just pay her a visit."

Miss Fairlie's apartment was indeed above one of the shops along the Promenade near the Neptune Fountain, a particularly attractive area of the street, though the immediate quarters adjacent to her apartment were not singular but rather ordinary, however neat in appearance.

Miss Fairlie, however, was not at home. There was no answer to our assault on the bell.

"It is almost noon," I said. "Mornings may be her half-days. Or she may be out to lunch."

"Let us sit down over across the street near the fountain and watch the outer entrance," suggested Pons.

Accordingly, we crossed to the benches arranged between the fountain and the street, and sat down facing the entrance to the stairs that led to Miss Fairlie's apartment. "I have been thinking," I said reflectively.

"Commendable!"

I ignored him. "Did not Mr. Abercrombie say that Sir Charles Farway had settled a sum of money on Miss Fairlie?"

"I have not forgotten it."

"There you have the explanation for her working only half-days. Why should she wear herself out at some task which may be little to her liking when she has funds enough to be comfortable without working all day long five or six days a week? It is all very simple when you look at it that way."

"It is, indeed," said Pons.

I waited to hear some withering comment follow, but I heard none. Pons sat in contemplative silence, his head cocked a little to one side – though his eyes remained fixed upon the street – as if he were listening to the songs and chirpings of birds; for the masses of foliage on the Promenade invited them, – robins, a mistle thrush, blackbirds, dunnocks, a greenfinch; once one managed to shut out the sounds of the street, which was not difficult to do here, the voices of the birds could be heard very pleasantly.

So we sat in silence, contemplating the surroundings. I saw, I thought, a great many American tourists; I had spent enough time in the States to find it easy to pick them out in any crowd, for they were much less reserved, indeed at times almost boisterous, and less conservative in their selection of clothing. There were, too, some people manifestly in Cheltenham for the waters; these could be identified almost as readily, though, to be sure, most of them were past middle age.

Pons's eyes never once left the entrance to Miss Fairlie's apartment.

Presently he spoke. "There she comes, Parker. She has come directly from her work."

I saw Miss Fairlie walking along the street toward the shop above which she lived, and watched her, as Pons watched.

"Let us give her a moment or two – to remove her wraps, but not enough time to prepare lunch," said Pons.

Miss Fairlie vanished into the building across the street. I followed her in my thoughts – up the stairs – along the hall – into her apartment. Hat and coat off.

"Now," said Pons.

We crossed the street and mounted to Miss Fairlie's apartment. Pons pressed the bell button.

We waited.

Miss Fairlie crossed to the door, slipped a night-latch on to chain the door, and opened it a trifle. She looked out, cautiously.

"I am pleased to see you have not taken my warning lightly, Miss Fairlie," said my companion.

"Mr. Pons! And Dr. Parker! You surprise me."

She slipped the night-latch off again, and threw the door open wide.

"Please come in."

If there were any hesitation about her invitation, she quickly concealed it under the customary apologies I have found women prone to make – the quarters were not in order for lack of time, and that kind of talk; though, as far as I could see, her rooms were in immaculate condition, just as she had left them for work earlier in the day.

The central room into which we walked and where, at Miss Fairlie's invitation, we sat down, was modestly but not cheaply appointed, revealing every evidence of good taste. Nevertheless, Miss Fairlie made a show of cleaning up – moving around to pick up a copy of a book and restore it to her shelves of books – of which there were a good number, picking a small peaked cap off the top of one of her two bookcases and carrying it into an inner room, straightening a chair – all those little actions I have seen my own wife perform innumerable times in the face of visitors.

For once she was at no lack of words, talking constantly as she moved about setting her room to rights, as she thought it ought to be, but finally, having finished, she sat down herself. "You are surely not guarding me," she said then.

"No, Miss Fairlie," answered Pons. "It is only that, finding ourselves in Cheltenham, it occurred to us to call."

"Have there been new developments then?" she asked.

"Yes, but I am not at liberty to talk of them," said Pons. "I would like to assure myself that you will be at our disposal if we should send for you at any time."

"Of course. I told you as much."

"And at your work?"

"Sir Hugh knows where to reach me if I am called from there." She did not offer this information to Pons, however.

"I have been attempting to trace your father's routes," Pons went on. "I have been to Scotland. Tomorrow Dr. Parker and I will go to Wales."

"I don't know what Father did at Glasgow, but there is no secret about his place in Merioneth. He went there to think out his problems – which I suppose were principally those of the Farways – and to rest. That part of the coast is quite secluded. Father had access to the beach, and he loved to walk the hills. He was quite a naturalist, Mr. Pons. When I was a child he taught me much of what he knew about the birds and animals."

"He seems to have been something of an enigma, Miss Fairlie – reclusive and secretive."

"Why, I suppose Mother's death was a great shock to him. He turned inward. People do this sort of thing – they retreat into themselves. Father was more sensitive than most people suspected, and – like so many sensitive people – he did his best to hide it."

"As you do," said Pons.

She acknowledged this with a brisk nod.

"You live very quietly here," said Pons. "I see little evidence of theatre programs."

"I spend my evenings at home, Mr. Pons."

"With books. I saw, when you picked it up, that you are fond of *The Wind in the Willows*."

"It's one of my favorite books," she said. "I have read it twice – once aloud." She smiled.

"Few such charming books have come out of England," agreed Pons. "And T. S. Eliot, too – that is surely *The Waste Land* I see on the near shelf, is it not?"

"I like to keep up with what is new in books, Mr. Pons. Reading is one of my chief pleasures."

"And there is *From a View to a Death*," Pons went on, his eyes moving from one book to another on Miss Fairlie's shelves.

"Yes, Anthony Powell is one of the newer novelists. I admire his style."

"And Milne – charming." He gazed again at Miss Fairlie, with an enigmatic smile haunting his lips.

"May I offer you tea, Gentlemen?"

Pons came to his feet so abruptly as to seem rude. "No, thank you," he said briskly. "We have imposed on your good graces long enough – overlong, Miss Fairlie. We must be going."

She was too startled to protest, and by the time she found her voice, Pons was at the door.

"I cannot understand you, Pons," I said as we were going down the stairs toward the street. "You were – well, *rude*."

"Perhaps. But it would have been more rude to stay. That young woman was tense with fear that we might."

"You cannot mean it!"

"Indeed I do."

"I saw no evidence of it."

"You were not looking for it. I was."

We gained the street, and I started up on the way to the station.

"Not yet, Parker. Let us not be too hasty. We are bound across the street from the place we left but a few minutes ago."

"What on earth for?"

"Ah, I enjoy the sylvan beauty of the Promenade near the Neptune Fountain. Need there be a better reason?"

"There needn't – but I'm sure there is," I said. "I have lived in your company too long to be deceived."

"That is either intuition or inductive rationalization," said Pons, chuckling.

"It is neither," I said. "It is professional knowledge of the subject."

"You almost said 'patient'."

We crossed the street as we spoke, and found ourselves once more facing the row of shops on the side we had left.

"You will have observed that Miss Fairlie's was one of at least four apartments on her floor," said Pons. "I have some slight curiosity about her neighbors, if you will bear with me."

"Aha! I knew it. 'Sylvan beauty' indeed!"

"So let us just observe for a time who goes in or out over there. It is the noon hour, and we may expect the tenants to make an appearance."

"To be precise," I said, "it is a quarter to one."

Pons did not respond. He had settled himself and was now keeping an eye on the entrance across the street. As it was in full view – and we were not as easily discernible from the street – watching the entrance was not difficult, except for the number of people who passed constantly up and down the Promenade.

We sat there for perhaps forty minutes. In the course of that time six people entered the stairway to the apartments above – an elderly man and woman, a young mother with her small son, a man I took to be young, though I could not see his face clearly for the hat pulled low over his eyes, and a gentleman of perhaps thirty-five.

"Did that not look like Gerald Farway?" I asked.

"He had the general appearance, yes," agreed Pons, "but that appearance is presented by a very high percentage of men in that age group in England. And if he intended to call on Miss Fairlie, why, he has made an ill-timed visit, for here she comes now."

Miss Fairlie was indeed emerging from her quarters. She carried a market basket.

"She's going shopping," I said. "Perhaps she means to have lunch in her apartment."

"Let us wait on her return."

She was back in but twenty minutes, her basket filled.

"We may as well return to Frome," said Pons then.

"If ever I was on a wild goose chase," I grumbled on the way up the street, "this was it."

"We shall have to be content with a few feathers, will we not, Parker?" asked Pons, with that irritating air of having added significantly to his knowledge while I manifestly had not.

VIII

JONAS FAIRLIE'S RETREAT

When I woke the following morning – the day of our departure for Jonas Fairlie's retreat in Merioneth – Pons had already gone out. I got up and dressed leisurely, since I had packed the previous night, on our return from Cheltenham, and then descended to the hotel restaurant for breakfast. As it happened, I sat near the wireless, which carried soft music to the breakfasters, for I was not alone in the restaurant.

Thus it was that I heard the newscaster's announcement of the morning news and was astounded to hear Pons's name coming over the air. I listened in growing amazement.

"Superintendent Ian Rossiter announced last night that the well-known London detective, Solar Pons, who has been working in cooperation with the police in the matter of the murder of Jonas Fairlie, expects to reveal the identity of the murderer on his return from Merioneth, to which he is going today in an effort to tie up some loose ends of the case. Mr. Pons was drawn into the case at the suggestion of the Chief Constable, Sir Hugh Parrington, for certain evidence was introduced early in the case to show that Mr. Fairlie was on his way to call on the detective when he was murdered. Mr. Pons and his companion, Dr. Lyndon Parker, will leave early today for the cottage Mr. Fairlie always maintained in Wales. Asked whether Mr. Pons had given anyone any hint of the identity of the murderer, Superintendent Rossiter was forced to admit that he had not, that Pons alone was confident of that knowledge and would not, in justice to all concerned, reveal it until the appropriate time."

Hearing my own name made me feel the cynosure of every eye. I left the restaurant hurriedly and hastened back to our quarters.

Pons had returned. As I entered, he was standing in the middle of the room looking with some satisfaction at the morning paper. Without giving me time to speak, he thrust the paper at me.

I had a foreboding of what I would see – and there indeed it was, in a prominent box on the front page –

LONDON DETECTIVE TO NAME
FAIRLIE MURDERER

– and below it, substantially the same announcement I had just heard on the wireless.

I threw the paper aside. "How could you tolerate this?" I asked.

"'Tolerate' is not the word, my dear fellow," he replied.

"Permit, then."

"Gently, gently, Parker – I myself urged it upon the press."

I was even more astonished. "This is unlike you, Pons – unworthy of you."

"Ah, there is method in it, Parker, I assure you. I could see no other course that might serve so well to bring this matter to a conclusion."

"Now that is an ambiguous statement, if ever I heard one," I cried.

"How familiarity does breed contempt!" said Pons, chuckling. "Believe me, I know what I am about."

"Why, if the murderer sees this he may be tempted to act. It is an open invitation to murder!"

"That is what I meant it to be."

"You cannot mean it!"

"Surely it must have come home to you, Parker, that we are dealing with a cold, ruthless, and resourceful murderer. I know that only the most painstaking and routine police work can assemble the evidence we need for conviction – and in the time that may take, someone else may die. We cannot risk it. We must tempt him to act. The attack on Robert Farway is proof that we have rattled him – and this announcement is calculated to rattle him further. I fancy we will not long be alone at Jonas Fairlie's cottage."

"It's hardly a method of which I can approve," I said. "If that is what you mean to do, we should go armed, at the very least."

"Sir Hugh has provided us with small arms. I have them packed. But I fancy we are in no danger of that kind of violence. Simulated accident is his forte – bullets may be traced, and are in themselves proof of homicide. The contrived accident always leaves a residue of doubt, if indeed it ever comes under suspicion."

"Where is this cottage of Fairlie's?" I asked then.

"Why, it is near Llwyngwril. From such description as I have of the area – it is not familiar to me, I should mention – the cottage is away from the village, on the coast below Barmouth Bay."

"On the seashore?"

"No, up the slopes from the shore, with access to the water's edge; a path leads down."

"Pons, I do not like this," I said.

"My dear fellow! Stay here, if you prefer."

"You know I will not. But this fellow is not playing. If all you say is true, he means to kill, not just to frighten."

"That he does," agreed Pons with equanimity I could not share.

Whatever else I might have said was cut short by a loud drumming on the door. Pons opened it to the Chief Constable, who pushed into the room booming, "Are you ready?"

"Sir Hugh is driving us," said Pons.

"We'll go up through Gloucester and Hereford, and bear on to Machynlleth and Towyn," said the Chief Constable. "Were you satisfied with the announcement?"

"It should serve," said Pons.

"Went out over the B.B.C. late last night and again this morning," Sir Hugh went on. "We've released it generally. Don't doubt that everyone who might be interested knows it by now. I don't know what you're up to, Pons, but I do hope we'll have him on your word."

"Unless I am very much mistaken, in not more than three days," promised Pons.

"I don't follow you, Pons, but we're going along with you. Another thing – you asked us to keep the family under surveillance. Gerald has left Frome, reportedly for London on business."

"I see. Was that before or after the first announcement of our plans?"

"I suppose it was after, but his plans must certainly have been made before. He left this morning, early. But Bramshaw knew he was going well before last night – he knew it two days ago.

"It might do no harm to find out where he is in London – and try to reach him."

"Right. I'll call Rossiter before we leave."

"The other members of the family are where they should be?"

The Chief Constable looked unhappy. "All but Jill. She's managed to give the French police the slip. No trace of her."

"How long has she been gone?"

Sir Hugh looked even more unhappy. "Well, Pons – the fact is, they never made contact. They can't find that she returned from England." He shrugged. "Another thing they did find out – she apparently left for England two days before she said she did. At least, she left her lodgings then."

"Ah, we make progress," said Pons dryly. "I saw too that but one newspaper carried the length of time we expected to remain at Fairlie's cottage – two days."

"The B.B.C. aired it. And some of the papers surely carried it." He shook his head. "Some of my men don't like it – you'd expect that. But at least it's better than Scotland Yard from their point-of-view."

"We had better get started, said Pons.

"Let me call Rossiter."

The Chief Constable telephoned the station and gave instructions for the police to establish some sort of contact with Gerald Farway in London. "Just make sure he's there."

This done, we carried our bags down to the car waiting in front of the hotel. Sir Hugh's driver put our luggage into the boot, and within minutes we were on our way north out of Frome, the Chief Constable filling the first hour with speculation in a vain hope of persuading from Pons some clue to the identity of the murderer he proposed to name when we returned from our sojourn in Merioneth.

But the Chief Constable fell silent before we reached Gloucester, unable to move Pons, and did not resume his attempts until we stopped for lunch at Shrewsbury.

"You have all the facts," said Pons. "You need only put them together. And once you have assembled the evidence, you can go into court with it."

"What can you hope to turn up at old Fairlie's place?" said Sir Hugh.

"Have the police been there?"

"We saw no need for it. We still see no need for it. A murder done near Frome can hardly be sufficiently related to the dead man's cottage a hundred fifty miles away. And he hadn't been there in over a month."

"Ah, well, I will concede that there may be no direct link between the cottage and the crime. Nevertheless, I intend to visit it. If I cannot turn up the evidence we need, then we will set down the lines along which the police must work at their routine assembling of the necessary evidence with which to charge and convict the murderer."

Sir Hugh turned to me. "Have you no influence with him, Doctor?"

"None, I assure you. Pons pursues his own course. He has a horror of making an error."

"Tut, tut! We all make mistakes," said Pons airily, in the manner of one who made the least. "Someone's life might be at stake here – and we owe it to all concerned not to act hastily."

That was Pons' last word. From Shrewsbury on he was engaged with the beauty of the Welsh landscape. Despite much development in the way of inns and hotels for the increasing numbers of tourists, many areas of Wales remained wild and striking to the eye. From Machynlleth we followed the Dovey River toward the coast for several miles, and from Towyn north to Llwyngwril the coast itself.

It was not possible to reach Fairlie's cottage by car. We found it necessary to leave the car at a roadside path, and walk for half a mile into the hills to the cottage itself. Sir Hugh and his driver, carrying our bags, accompanied us, the Chief Constable growling and harrumphing.

Sir Hugh had obtained the key to the cottage – a tidy little dwelling of stone and wood, more substantially built than I had supposed, and obviously old enough to have been bought by Fairlie rather than put up by him. It stood partly up a slope with a precipitous path leading beyond it to the heights behind and to the north of it, and a sort of defile leading down to a narrow strip of sandy beach, broken here and there with great boulders.

The opening of the door revealed – as might have been expected – a neatly kept interior, roughly but comfortably furnished.

Sir Hugh looked cursorily around, walking into the four rooms that made up the single floor of the cottage.

"You're not on the telephone here," he said, as if he were making a formal charge against Pons's lack of foresight.

"Well, it is no problem to walk into Llwyngwril," observed Pons, "when it becomes necessary to telephone. Fairlie obviously preferred his isolation to its possible interruption. I can appreciate his point-of-view."

"We'll expect to hear from you. If you let me know, I'll send the car for you."

"That is hardly necessary," protested Pons.

The Chief Constable went on briefly about his "responsibility" for Pons, and then at last bade us farewell and followed the driver back to his waiting car, manifestly disgruntled. At once Pons reverted to his old self. He ignored the bags we had brought – one for each of us, into which at the last we had put the arms Sir Hugh had brought – and stood looking keenly around, his eyes darting from one wall to another, scrutinizing the furniture – chairs, a desk, a table.

"It is obviously Mr. Fairlie's domain," I said. "Everything is as neat as the proverbial pin."

Pons nodded. "But there is a drawer not quite shut on the right side of the desk, a curtain awry at one window – that to the right, some papers in disorder on the clock shelf. Would Mr. Fairlie have left the room so?"

"You aren't suggesting that this place has been searched, too?"

"I rather think it has. In more leisurely fashion. There was no need for haste here. I submit that while we were looking for a murderer in Frome, he was here looking for evidence against him."

"How can you say so?" I cried.

"Not a document, I suspect," continued Pons. "But anything Mr. Fairlie might have left in writing to incriminate him. Even down to such casual notes as he might have made – as we saw at Farway Hall."

"Evidence," I said. "Of what? Surely not of his own murder!"

"Come, come, Parker," he said, not without impatience. "Evidence concerning some kind of criminal act, patently. Fairlie alive was dangerous to someone, and it was necessary not only to remove him but also anything he may have set down about the inquiry he was conducting."

"Surely this is made up of the flimsiest cloth," I said. "There is little evidence to act on."

"But enough. And there is not the slightest evidence of anything other to afford motive for his murder." He crossed to the desk, as he spoke, and pulled out the drawer. "Yes, there is some disarray here. Someone has been through these papers – not, I submit, Mr. Fairlie, who would have left them in a neater arrangement."

"What are the papers that remain?"

"Some letters." He opened one as he spoke to look at the signature. "They are from his daughter." He returned them to the drawer, unread. "Some pages of an account; they appear to be of tax computation. A list of supplies needed – doubtless for repairs he intended to make here. Nothing of importance. And, of course, there is nothing to show whether anything was taken."

Thereafter Pons examined the cottage thoroughly, room after room, inside and out, while I unpacked our bags. When he had finished, he came back in and suggested that we follow the path to the beach.

"This is undoubtedly the path taken by Ronald Farway on that fatal night," mused Pons, as we made our way along the defile, which, though steep in some places, was not long.

It opened out on the beach, which was here so narrow a stretch of sand as to be virtually under water at high tide. At the moment, however, the tide was out, and the sand sloped steeply away toward St. George's Channel. Gulls flew low over the water along the edge of sand, crying out in their companionable voices. Far out, a blue haze lay over the sea. To the north, in Barmouth Bay, several small vessels were visible, but too far away to be identified as more than fishing or pleasure craft. Great rocks jutted up out of the sand, as had they at one time become detached from the rocky hill reaching upward from the beach, and fallen there, to become lodged in the sand and washed in ever more firmly by the tides.

There were no prints in the sand, other than those we made, and those of the gulls that had but recently walked there.

"It would be a challenge to swim here," I said.

"Would it not!" agreed Pons. "And how much more of one to risk even greater danger here!" he added enigmatically. "You refer to Ronald Farway's accident?"

"We have been told it was an accident," said Pons reflectively. "The woman who was with him so reported it. He went out to swim by moonlight – he never came back. Does not that strike you strangely?"

"Not at all. The sea does not always give up what it takes."

"Or what it is given," said Pons cryptically. "But let us move in the other direction. There is a lane that leads up to the crests. I submit it is the wisest course to follow to familiarize ourselves thoroughly with the terrain. We shall be out in it to encourage him. An accident is easier to simulate up there." He pointed uphill. "We shouldn't want another drowning here. The repetition might arouse suspicion, eh?"

"You harp on that drowning," I said. "Why?"

We began to climb back up the defile.

"Young Farway was either drowned or he was not drowned," said Pons.

"That is a most elementary premise," I put in.

"Agreed. If he were not drowned, his failure to turn up proved embarrassing to the young lady – Gerald Farway's fiancée, though the accident evidently ended their engagement. If he were not – let us pursue this matter a trifle longer – his disappearance lacks any discernible motive. Can you suggest one?"

"Easily," I said. "He may have struck his head on a rock or something of that sort and suffered a loss of memory. Perhaps even of identity. He may have turned up down the coast in some backwater."

"And kept hidden in the face of the search for his body?" put in Pons. "Well, that is possible, but highly improbable. He had everything to gain by turning up alive, everything to lose by drowning."

"But suppose he deliberately vanished because he had more to gain by doing so – more than we have yet turned up?"

"That is an interesting speculation," agreed Pons, "but we have so far nothing to justify it."

We had now reached the cottage and attained the lane that led uphill beyond it. This was a steeper climb, and it was patent that the lane was little used, for it was partly overgrown. In some places it skirted dangerously close to the edge; in others it meandered inland, climbing steadily.

Our course gradually revealed a long undulating ridge of mountains, evidently part of the Cader Idris range; indeed the high peaks of the Cader Idris itself could be seen far inland, almost due east of our position, but a little to the north; while before us the rolling mountains ranged toward Fairbourne and along the Mawddach inland to the east, toward the County Town of Dolgelley. To the west lay the blue waters of the sea.

We were now perhaps three-quarters of a mile from the cottage, and at the top of the rise there. Pons, who had been walking ever more slowly, came at last to a stop at a point where the lane bent almost to the rim of the sharp declivity there. He peered over the edge, and saw below the sea dashing against rocks at its base.

"Here, I should think, is the perfect spot for an accident," he said thoughtfully. "There is a rock formation that offers concealment on the east side of the path. A sudden rush here upon an unexpected traveler, and he would be dashed to his death below."

I shuddered. "How can you speak so calmly of it!"

"Put yourself in the place of the murderer," Pons went on. "Would he not come to a similar conclusion? Can you see a better spot? We have passed none as suitable for the purpose of an accident as this."

"When is it that you expect him to come?"

"If he comes. I expect an attack tomorrow night. He will need to study our habits before he makes an attempt. We may suppose some familiarity with the place on his part. I shall make it a practise to walk out to this point and stand here to view the sea several times this evening and tomorrow. Let me see, there will be a moon this evening, if I am not mistaken – but in any case, the starlight is sufficient."

"Unless the sky is overcast," I said.

"It is clear enough now."

The sky was indeed clear, though the sun was now low and would soon set. None but a few flocculent clouds along the western rim were to be seen in all the heavens; the night promised to be clear.

"I think the idea mad, Pons," I said.

"It is just mad enough to succeed."

"How can you be sure *he* may not succeed?"

"I cannot. But forewarned is forearmed. I will not be taken by surprise." He gazed ahead. "We need go no farther. This point will suit our purpose as well as any we might find. Moreover, it is not too far from the cottage. Let us return."

We walked back down toward the cottage. I was perplexed at Pons's assurance that an attack on him would be made. He seemed not to doubt it. His "If he comes" had been merely perfunctory. He had convinced himself that his challenge would be accepted.

When we reached the cottage, I could remain silent no longer. "Pons, why are you so sure that he will come?"

"I am familiar with the pattern of his crimes."

"Crimes?" I echoed.

"Crimes," said Pons without elaboration. "Let us brew a cup of tea and take some nourishment."

"I confess to some uneasiness, " I said.

Pons laughed almost heartlessly. "Ah, the hunting instinct is less strong when one is in the position of being the quarry. There is really no difference between hunting a stag, let us say, and a human being, except that, in the latter case, the odds are less great – particularly when the quarry expects the hunter. This fellow has a singular vanity."

"It takes as much to set one's self up for his quarry," I said.

"*Touché*," answered Pons.

"Then he must already be somewhere near."

"I should think it mandatory. If he means to study the lay of the land and our habits on it, he must have at least a day in which to do it. The sun is going down now. I fancy we are safe for the night except for the possibility of fire."

"You cannot mean he might fire the house?"

"Well, it is within the range of possibility," said Pons, as if he were discussing some event remote in place and time. "And if you don't mind, we'll take turns on watch tonight.

So it was at taking turns watching that we spent the night. I myself took the first watch, saw the moon go down, and the evening stars – Jupiter and Saturn – following westward, moving from one window to another in the darkness and peering out into the landscape, which lay under the faint glow of starlight after moonset, a glow that would have enabled me to see only someone silhouetted against the sky. I saw and heard nothing, not so much as an owl, and though, for a while after Pons took my place, I was unable to sleep for thinking of the possibility of a nocturnal attack, I did presently drift off.

Nothing untoward happened in the night, and all that next day, Pons walked the paths at given intervals – to the beach once or twice, but most often to the heights, where he stood out against the sky, visible, I was certain, for miles, a lean, solitary figure, for he went alone save for one occasion when I walked with him. He was tense with expectation, and explained twice that he was anxious to be back in London, and had taken this "extreme measure" in the hope of bringing the problem to a rapid solution. But for the most part he was taciturn, preferring silence to speech.

At our spare evening meal, Pons announced that he expected an attempt to be made during the dusk hour. "Putting myself in his place," he explained, "I would consider that my last and best opportunity. The light will be right. The vista to the west – with moon and planets over the sea and afterglow, would certainly attract the eye of any walker along the lane and so divert attention from anything else. A sudden rush – a skilfully planned push – and all would be over. It would have the look of an accident, particularly if he took time to crumble away part of the edge at that point in the path."

I tried at that point seriously to dissuade him from his rash plan, but he would not be moved. Indeed, he rather looked forward to it, and there was a certain deviousness in his manner I did not understand until later. When he set out on that final walk along the heights, he clapped me on the back and bade me a reassuring farewell.

"What am I to do?" I asked.

"When once I have reached the top," he replied, "it might be well if you came along as far up the path as possible without showing yourself. You are not visible from the top for at least half the way. Anyone concealed up there – and I expect our friend to be there – would not be able to see you. His attention will in any case be concentrated on me and, seeing me come alone, he will conclude that you are remaining behind."

"You never think he might anticipate you," I cried.

Pons chuckled. "His concern is with murder – not its thwarting."

I watched him go with a heavy heart. The sun was now well down, the waxing moon shone, the evening star was visible in the heavens, and so, too, stars of the first magnitude. A smouldering afterglow still lay along the western rim, as if great fires burned far below the horizon and cast reflections of the flames up on the smoke-like clouds that lay there, just within sight; but on the surface of the earth now dusk was closing in, and Pons was a dark figure moving up the lane toward a foreseen assignation I hoped would never take place.

In but a little while I followed cautiously, leaving a light burning behind me, so that if anyone were to look down – supposing that anyone were to come far enough from the crest to see – he might be misled into thinking the cottage occupied. Pons was out of sight when I started up the lane, and by this time almost all the afterglow had faded save for a single band of smoky old rose; only the light of the moon illumined the lane, though it was adequate to guide me, even though I was not as familiar with the lane as Pons, who had walked it at least a dozen times in the course of the day.

I had just come within sight of him – standing at the place he had chosen, looking out into the west, the moonlight showing on his aquiline face – when there came hurtling out of the darkness behind him a black shape, bearing directly toward Pons. I meant to cry out, but before I could raise my voice, Pons, alert to the attack, had moved toward him, and instantly the two men were grappling there. Pons's advancing to meet his assailant was clearly designed to move the struggle away from the point, but the force of their meeting inevitably carried both to the very brink – and there they stood, grappling almost soundlessly.

I ran forward, climbing toward them, my heart beating wildly, praying that Pons had not miscalculated.

I had almost reached them when one of them went over the edge with a wild, anguished cry – and then, merciful heavens! – the other tottered and fell! I flung myself forward, seeing him half on the one side of the point, hanging over the edge, half on the other – and grasped one hand, and then the arm, and pulled back with all my might.

Slowly, between his endurance and the strength I mustered, born of dire necessity, Pons came back up over the edge and sprawled for a moment there, breathing hard. It was the other who had gone over.

"A near thing, Parker," said Pons, heavily, as he sat up. "Are you hurt?" I asked anxiously.

"No, no – only a scratch or two and a bruise perhaps – and my natural vanity is a trifle shaken. No more." He got to his feet, his breathing becoming more regular, and said, "We shall have to go down at once – the tide, I think, is out far enough to permit our walking along the edge."

The journey back down the lane, past the cottage – where Pons paused only long enough to light a lantern which was among the effects left there by Mr. Fairlie – and down the rocky defile to the beach took half an hour; and the sand beyond was still wet, but Pons walked ahead, eager now, unmindful of the wetting of his shoes – and mine.

And at last we came upon his assailant, sprawled like a bundle of clothing among the rocks at the base of the precipitant slope, one hand outflung into the sea that washed gently at it, soaking his coat past his elbow. Pons held the lantern high.

"There he is," said Pons – "the murderer of Ronald Farway and Jonas Fairlie, and, unless I am sadly mistaken, of Austin Farway and Peter as well."

The man who lay there was ruddy of complexion, like a countryman, with a thick shock of black hair, bushy eyebrows, and a natty moustache. His clothing, too, was flashy, if dark – of plaid, in brown hues, with black and tan and dark grey in it.

"Your show, Parker," said Pons, stepping aside.

It needed only a cursory examination to know that he was dead. "Neck and back both broken," I said, "as well as one leg." I stood up. "But I have never seen this fellow before."

Pons handed me the lantern. "I think you have, Parker. Let us have a closer look at him."

He leaned forward and tore away the moustache – the shaggy eyebrows – the dark hair: a wig.

An involuntary cry escaped me. There lay before us none other than young Robert Farway!

"And now," said Pons, "the amenities of the situation must be observed – the local police – a trunk call to Sir Hugh, and all that. Come along, Parker – he is safely lodged until the police get here."

"Robert Farway!" exclaimed Sir Hugh as we rode back into the dawn toward Frome. "I cannot believe it even yet! Why, he was himself attacked!"

"That was his fatal mistake," said Pons. "If at that point I had had any serious doubt about his guilt, I would have lost it at once, because it was apparent that the murderer had revealed his master design. Jonas Fairlie was only an incident in it – his real quarry were the members of the Farway family. I daresay

Peter was his first victim – a murder committed on the spur of the moment, out of the necessity imposed upon him by the impending marriage which would forever remove his uncle's wealth from his grasp. It is perhaps not easily capable of proof at this late date. And it may be that Peter's death was a genuine accident, and that that accident put Robert in mind of the result that might be attained if the remaining heirs were removed.

"He clearly had a penchant for the contrived accident – I cannot believe that Austin Farway's death was caused by a genuine accident – or that Ronald Farway died in any other way but that of Robert's hand – Robert, who swam out after him and drowned him in the sea."

"But how could he know that Ronald would be at Fairlie's cottage? Hrumph! It's entirely too fortuitous."

"Obviously someone informed him."

"Ha! but who?"

"I fancy it was his sister."

"Rebecca?"

"She could surely have written him – not with the intent of preparing him to commit a crime, but simply to relay gossip common enough to the household."

"And Fairlie – what about him? How did Robert come to be here at the moment Fairlie set off for London?"

"He made it his business to be. Fairlie's nosing about at Glasgow and Edinburgh – perhaps word of his traveling to Wales – information about questions the old man had asked – all these certainly put the wind up him, and he decided that Fairlie had to die. He couldn't know how little actual proof Fairlie had managed to disclose. I daresay you men will be able to trace Farway's movements easily enough – at least, his absences from his work, which will certainly coincide with the time that Austin, Ronald, and Mr. Fairlie died." He shrugged. "Like so many clever criminals, once challenged, he lost a little of his self-assurance. He couldn't know Fairlie was bound for 7B. He couldn't know that Fairlie had only suspicions – profound, to be sure – but nothing tangible enough with which to go to the police. He believed that this might have been the case, no doubt, but he couldn't afford to take the chance that he might be in error; and once an official inquiry began, his absences from Edinburgh would surely come to light."

"And all simply to increase his inheritance!"

Pons nodded. "He was in a fair way to collecting most of Sir Charles's wealth. Small wonder he was so genuinely solicitous for his aunt's health. Once her death took place Sir Charles's wealth would have been divided and he would lose all opportunity to expand his share. He moved with care – Austin, then Ronald – and Jill was marked as the next victim. With suitable intervals between."

"How can you know that?"

"I took the number of that little car she rented – a habit of mine, gathering up all kinds of knowledge, most of it useless. That car was involved in a near fatal accident two days after she returned it. I saw the account in the papers. The police verdict was that it had been 'tampered with'. You'll recall Robert's firm refusal to ride to London with her. That tampering was done at Frome, but Robert miscalculated."

"Monstrous!" cried the Chief Constable. "But how did he manage to get around?"

"In these days, Sir Hugh, cars are ubiquitous. No one notices them. He could drive down from Edinburgh and back without anyone's taking notice of his car."

So it went for mile upon mile, with the Chief Constable putting in questions and Pons answering them. Neither of them had slept through the night, nor had I – but at last I could stay awake no longer and fell asleep to the hum of the motor and the sound of their voices.

IX

THE SECOND SECRET

Back at the George I woke only long enough to go to our quarters and get into bed, leaving Pons and Sir Hugh still talking below. I slept soundly until noon, when Pons's hand at my shoulder brought me awake.

"Come, Parker, we have still one small mission to perform," he said. "We'll expect to take the 4:39 for London."

He was listening to the wireless as I rose to dress. The news of Robert Farway's death was out, and the circumstances of it, and Pons listened to the wireless account with a wry smile, for credit for solving the mystery of Jonas Fairlie's death was now as surely being given to the local police and Sir Hugh Parrington, as two mornings ago the promise of that solution was credited to Pons.

Pons turned off the wireless. "I have sent Sir Hugh on an errand, and expect to meet him at Farway Hall. We have an appointment with Lady Farway at one. There is time for something to eat, if you like."

"I want nothing," I said. "I'd prefer something on the train, if you don't mind."

"Then let us set out for Farway Hall. We have time enough to walk, and I rather fancy walking."

"You have had enough of it in the past two days!"

"I never have enough of it. And I have a sentimental fondness for these old market towns. Who knows but that Frome under another name might not have been the setting for a scene in a novel by Thomas Hardy, whose 'Wessex' lies little more than a half hour away."

We made our way out of the George and down Bath Street to Christchurch Street West, Pons pausing from time to time to admire some ancient architectural feature, or the Parish Church of St. John the Baptist and the tomb of Bishop Ken – who pled in vain for the Monmouth revolutionaries condemned by the Bloody Assize. As we walked along, Pons discoursed on the history of the area and the beauty of the countryside.

In this leisurely fashion we reached Farway Hall at one o'clock. Pons charged the butler Parr send word to Lady Farway's quarters when Sir Hugh Parrington arrived, and we were then shown upstairs by Rebecca Farway, whose eyes were manifestly inflamed with tears.

"How has Lady Farway taken this dreadful news?" asked Pons before Rebecca knocked at the old lady's door.

"It has been a terrible shock to all of us," said Rebecca.

"And to you," said Pons. "I am sorry it had to be."

"I understand. And I understand now, too, why Robert always plied me so with questions about all of us here. He wanted to know every little thing – especially after Uncle Charles died."

She knocked at the door, opened it, and looked in to say, "Mr. Pons and Dr. Parker are here, Aunt Ellen."

"Please send them in, Rebecca."

She threw the door wide and we went into the room. Rebecca withdrew behind us.

Lady Farway sat in a handsome Chippendale wing chair, making a commanding, almost regal presence. Her eyes, too, indicated that she had been weeping, and she still held a handkerchief in one clenched hand. But it was clear that she had reserves of strength invisible to her family.

"I regret the necessity of intruding at so trying of time, Lady Farway," said Pons, "but since we hope to leave or London this afternoon, we have little alternative."

"This has been a dreadful shock, Mr. Pons, a dreadful shock. I find it very, very difficult to believe even now."

"I fear there is no doubt of Robert's guilt, Lady Farway."

"Dreadful, dreadful," murmured Lady Farway, shaking her head.

"I am all the more regretful since I am afraid yet another shock cannot be avoided," Pons went on.

She looked at him with apprehension. "Surely I am not to be asked to endure more – after all I have been through?"

"There is no alternative, Lady Farway," said Pons firmly.

A knock sounded on the door, and Rebecca looked in, a baffling expression on her dark face. "Mr. Pons, Sir Hugh Parrington has arrived."

"In five minutes, Miss Farway. Sir Hugh will know the order." Rebecca withdrew, and Pons turned again to Lady Farway. "You will recall that mysterious and upsetting journey Sir Charles took with Mr. Fairlie two years ago?"

"I do, indeed. How could I forget it! It inaugurated all the events since then."

"And you may know that Sir Charles at that time changed his will and settled a sum of money on Diana Fairlie."

"No, Mr. Pons, I do not know that. But I am happy to hear it. Sir Charles knew he had treated her unfairly."

"Sir Charles had an experience you are now about to share. Will you brace yourself, Lady Farway?"

She looked at him with mounting uncertainty. "I have seen so much of death in the past two years, Mr. Pons, that nothing can come as a greater shock to me."

"I am not so sure," said Pons.

He turned toward the door and called out, "Now!"

The door opened.

But it was not Sir Hugh Parrington who came walking into the room. It was a small, very handsome little blond boy who could not have been quite seven years old. He came in diffidently, walked half way across the room, and stood there looking inquiringly from one to another of us.

The effect on Lady Farway was extraordinary. She half rose from her chair, the color draining from her face. Then she fell back, and a long, wailing cry came from her lips. And at the last a heart-rending, "Peter!"

Since that appeared to be the lad's name, he went directly to her side, and, after but a moment's hesitation, the old woman folded him into her arms, tears streaming down her face.

"This boy, Lady Farway," said Pons, "is the heir in whose favor Sir Charles changed his will. I am sure you know why. It was this he strove so hard to tell you at the time of his fatal seizure."

The resemblance between the boy and the portrait of the dead Peter Farway that stood on the mantel nearby was extraordinary.

The old lady fought for control and looked past the boy in her arms. "Is Diana here?"

Diana Fairlie, who had been waiting outside with Sir Hugh, came slowly into the room. She met Lady Farway's eyes without flinching.

"Daughter," said the old lady with great dignity. "Thank you for bringing my grandson home." She glanced toward Pons and added, "And thank you, Mr. Pons, for making it possible."

"The crux of the problem," said Pons, as we sat in the restaurant car of the train carrying us back to Paddington, "was the matter of motive for Jonas Fairlie's murder. Passion and primary greed seemed at the outset unlikely, so what remained was vengeance or danger to someone in Fairlie's remaining alive. But vengeance seemed, on the face of the matter, improbable, for no one bent on vengeance would have cause to search the body or the quarters occupied by the dead man.

"It was not improbable that Fairlie was killed for the same reason that he intended to call at 7B – whether or not his murderer were aware that he was actually setting out for London to do so. Whatever the problem he intended to lay before us, it manifestly involved someone else. A mere matter of a threat of vengeance could have been handled by the local police. And, since Fairlie's entire life from adolescence onward seems to have been involved with the fortunes of the Farway family, it was not unreasonable to conclude that the problem in some way concerned the Farways.

"There was nothing amiss at the printing plant – or with the financial affairs of the business; therefore the matter must be something of a highly personal nature – so personal, in fact, that Fairlie felt his loyalty to the Farways to be in challenge, and wanted to thrust the entire matter into my hands and so free himself of the onus.

"Somehow – by what means we cannot now know – Fairlie stumbled upon evidence that suggested foul play in someone's death – in all likelihood Ronald's. He began painstaking investigations, correctly assuming or soon coming to believe that the motive for Ronald's murder lay in the terms of Sir Charles's will, which divided the estate among his surviving nieces and nephews. He attracted Robert's attention and doomed himself, for Robert suspected, clearly, what he was about, and killed him, after which he destroyed every particle of writing that might pertain to the investigation Fairlie was conducting.

"In his haste, he did not tear away enough pages from Fairlie's scratch-pad, as you know, and we were able to make out something of what he had jotted down there, even if I drew erroneous conclusions about those letters at the outset. When I saw them in their proper relation and meaning, however, then it was inescapably clear that Fairlie suspected some member of the Farway clan of having committed at least one, possibly more murders in order to increase his inheritance.

"There were, of course, certain obvious indications at once. Plainly, Robert had not intended to see the police called in – hence his care with the chloroform used to kill Fairlie, for only minimal burning of the skin was observed, as you noticed. But the use of chloroform in itself suggested someone with access to it, and as the routine police inquiry continued and failed to turn up any source from which it could have come, Robert became the primary suspect. And then, rattled by the activity of the police, and motivated too by his desire to cover himself if something happened to Jill Farway – that motor accident he had planned for her – he made the mistake of fabricating that attack upon himself, after which he disposed of the disguise he had worn on the previous occasion, as we have seen.

"But his mistake lay in this – the attack on himself betrayed his own real motive – the plan to eliminate his cousins from the succession to Sir Charles's will; for until that point, no one had thought of murder directed against any member of the Farway family. I was certain that I could count on anyone who had committed so rash an error to find it impossible to resist the challenge I offered him at the cottage in Merioneth."

"But the will had been changed," I said.

"Yes, yes – of course, it had been changed. Miss Fairlie left Frome not out of anger, but out of pride and perhaps some shame – for the father of the child she carried was dead, and she could not bring herself to throw herself on the mercy of the Farways. Only her father knew of the child's existence – that was his second secret – and he ultimately, fortunately, took it upon himself to take Sir Charles to see their grandson.

"It is one of life's little ironies – those little ironies that never cease to move me to some sardonic contemplation of human endeavor – that all Robert Farway's careful planning was for naught, simply because he did not know of the existence of his young cousin!"

"And how did you know?" I asked. "I was as shocked and surprised as Lady Farway to see what was obviously her grandson walk into that room."

"Ah, that was the most elementary of all. You will recall the brevity of Sir Charles's new will – it suggested at once that the bulk of his estate was no longer to be divided – oh, undoubtedly some legacy was set down for each of the nieces and nephews – but to go to one person. That one could hardly have been someone less close to him than his brother's children. Our visit to Cheltenham confirmed it.

"Miss Fairlie had in her room a small peaked cap – plainly too small for her to wear, equally plainly a boy's cap. She also had children's books – true, of the kind that many adults enjoy – I myself among them. But she said she had once read *The Wind in the Willows* aloud. One hardly reads a book aloud to one's self, and that fine masterpiece by Kenneth Grahame is just precisely the kind of book to be read to a child.

"And then, of course, while we sat there in the Promenade, we saw the boy himself returning from his half day at nursery school. Miss Fairlie was on needles lest we stay long enough to see him."

Assembling the greatest detectives all together

Covering the full range and history of detective fiction.
From Zadig, *The Moonstone*, and Dupin through Sherlock Holmes, Loveday Brooke, Montague Egg, Lord Peter Wimsey, *The Thinking Machine*, Father Brown down to Solar Pons.

John P. Marquand
MR. MOTO
VOLUME 1
Louis Joseph Vance
THE LONE WOLF
Maurice LeBlanc
ARSÈNE LUPIN Vs. HERLOCK SHOLMÈS
Melville Davisson Post
MASTER OF MYSTERIES
M.P. Shiel
PRINCE ZALESKI AND CUMMING'S KING MONK
Gaston Leroux
THE ROULETABILLE OMNIBUS
R. Austin Freeman
THE EYE OF OSIRIS
A. E. W. Mason
AT THE VILLA ROSE
Aleister Crowley
THE COMPLETE SIMON IFF STORIES
Algernon Blackwood
THE JOHN SILENCE COLLECTION
Peter Cheyney
THE SLIM CALLAGHAN OMNIBUS
Baroness Orczy
THE OLD MAN IN THE CORNER
Patricia Wentworth
GREY MASK
Raymond Chandler
THE PHILIP MARLOWE OMNIBUS
H.C. Bailey
CALL MR. FORTUNE
Josephine Tey
THE DAUGHTER OF TIME
Anna Katherine Green
THAT AFFAIR NEXT DOOR
Sexton Blake
THE SEXTON BLAKE COLLECTION
VOLUME 1
S.S. Van Dine
THE BENSON MURDER CASE
Freeman Wills Crofts
THE CASK

Yellowback range available...

1. The Old Man in the Corner by Orczy, Baroness Emma
2. The Complete Max Carrados Vol 1 by Bramah, Ernest
3. The Complete Max Carrados Vol 2 by Bramah, Ernest

THE ARSÈNE LUPIN SERIES BY LEBLANC, MAURICE:

4. Arsène Lupin 1: The Extraordinary Adventures of Arsène Lupin - Gentleman Burglar
5. Arsène Lupin 2: Arsène Lupin vs. Herlock Sholmes
6. Arsène Lupin 3. The Hollow Needle
7. Arsène Lupin 4: 813
8. Arsène Lupin 5: The Crystal Stopper
9. Arsène Lupin 6: The Confessions of Arsène Lupin
10. Arsène Lupin 7: The Teeth of the Tiger
11. Arsène Lupin 8: The Shell Shard (aka The Woman of Mystery)
12. Arsène Lupin 9: The Return of Arsène Lupin (aka The Golden Triangle)
13. Arsène Lupin 10: The secret of Sarek (aka Island of Thirty Coffins)
14. Arsène Lupin 11: The Eight Strokes of the Clock
15. Arsène Lupin 12: The Secret Tomb
16. Arsène Lupin 13: The Countess of Cagliostro (aka Memoirs of Arsène Lupin)
17. Arsène Lupin (bonus book): Arsène Lupin (novelised by Edgar Jepson from LeBlanc's original play)

18. The Complete Raffles by Hornung, E. W.
19. The Mysterious Mickey Finn by Paul, Eliott
20. You Play the Black and the Red Comes Up by Hallas, Richard
21. The Mr. Moto Omnibus Vol 1 by Marquand, John P.
22. The Mr. Moto Omnibus Vol 2 by Marquand, John P.
23. The Complete Father Brown Vol 1 (with original illustrations) by Chesterton, G. K.
24. The Complete Father Brown Vol 2 (with original illustrations) by Chesterton, G. K.
25. A Peter Wimsey omnibus: Murder Must Advertise & The Nine Tailors by Sayers, Dorothy L.
26. Was it Murder? by Hilton, James
27. The Complete Just Men Volume 1 by Wallace, Edgar
28. The Complete Just Men Volume 2 by Wallace, Edgar
29. Carnacki by Hodgson, William Hope
30. Grey Mask by Wentworth, Patricia
31. The Case With Nine Solutions by Connington, J. J.
32. Murder by Matchlight by Lorac, E. C. R.
33. The Crossword Mystery by Punshon, E. R.
34. The Cask by Crofts, Freeman Wills
35. The Bells of Old Bailey by Bowers, Dorothy
36. Crime Unlimited by Hume, David
37. The A. A. Milne Mystery Omnibus (contains: The Red house and Four days' wonder) by Milne, A. A.
38. She Faded into Air by White, Ethel Lina
39. The Wheel Spins by White, Ethel Lina
40. The Spiral Staircase by White, Ethel Lina
41. Murder of a Lady by Wynne, Anthony
42. Thirteen Guests by Farjeon, J. Jefferson
43. The Daughter of Time by Tey, Josephine
44. The Man in the Queue by Tey, Josephine
45. A Shilling for Candles by Tey, Josephine
46. The Franchise Affair by Tey, Josephine
47. Tragedy at Law by Hare, Cyril
48. The Moonstone by Collins, Wilkie
49. The Woman in White by Collins, Wilkie
50. The Circular Staircase by Rinehart, Mary Roberts
51. The Benson Murder Case by Van Dine, S. S.
52. The Philip Marlowe Omnibus by Chandler, Raymond
53. Monsieur Lecoq by Gaboriau, Emile
54. Aurora Floyd by Braddon, Mary Elizabeth
55. The Big Bow Mystery by Zangwill, Israel
56. Dossier 113 (aka The Blackmailers) by Gaboriau, Emile
57. The Mystery of a Hansom Cab by Hume, Fergus
58. The W Plan by Seton, Graham
59. Inspector French's Greatest Case by Crofts, Freeman Wills

60. Mr Bowling Buys a Newspaper by Henderson, Donald
61. A Voice Like Velvet by Henderson, Donald
62. The Deductions of Colonel Gore by Brock, Lynn
63. The Rogue's Syndicate by Froest, Frank
64. The Middle Temple Murder by Fletcher, J. S.
65. The Millionaire Mystery by Hume, Fergus
66. Below the Clock by Turner, J. V.
67. The Rouletabille Omnibus: The Mystery of the Yellow Room and The Perfume of the Lady in Black by Leroux, Gaston
68. The Complete Dupin by Poe, Edgar Allan
69. The Complete Thinking Machine Vol 1 by Futrelle, Jacques
70. The Complete Thinking Machine Vol 2 by Futrelle, Jacques
71. The Complete Thinking Machine Vol 3 by Futrelle, Jacques
72. The Complete Montague Egg by Sayers, Dorothy L.
73. The Complete J. G. Reeder by Wallace, Edgar
74. The Complete Charlie Chan Vol 1 by Biggers, Earl der
75. The Complete Charlie Chan Vol 2 by Biggers, Earl der
76. The Dr Nikola Omnibus Vol 1 by Boothby, Guy
77. The Dr Nikola Omnibus Vol 2 by Boothby, Guy
78. A Prince of Swindlers: The Simon Carne collection by Boothby, Guy
79. The Slim Callaghan Omnibus by Cheyney, Peter
80. The Fu Manchu Omnibus by Rohmer, Sax
81. The Bulldog Drummond Omnibus: The Complete Peterson Rounds by Sapper
82. The Avenging Ray by Seamark
83. The Richard Chandos Omnibus by Yates, Dornford
84. The Alan Quatermain Omnibus: King Solomon's Mines & Allan Quatermain by Haggard, H. Rider
85. The 39 steps by Buchan, John
86. At The Villa Rose by Mason, A.E.W.
87. The Eye of Osiris by Freeman, R. Austin
88. The Weapons of Mystery by Hocking, Joseph
89. The House of Dr. Edwardes by Beeding, Francis
90. The Seven Secrets by Le Queux, William
91. Call Mr Fortune by Bailey, H. C.
92. The Three Taps by Knox, Ronald
93. The Girl at Central by Bonner, Geraldine
94. The Experiences of Loveday Brooke, Lady Detective by Pirkis, Catherine Louisa
95. Mary Louise by Baum, L. Frank
96. That Affair Next Door by Green, Anna Katherine
97. Dead Letter by Regester, Seeley
98. The Tragedy of Pudd'nhead Wilson by Twain, Mark
99. The Big Clock by Fearing, Kenneth
100. The Woman in the Window by Wallis, J. H.
101. The Sexton Blake Collection Vol 1 by Hal Meredeth (or many?)
102. The Complete Simon Iff Stories by Crowley, Aleister
103. The Castle of Otranto by Walpole, Horace
104. The Adventures of the Infallible Godahl by Anderson, Frederick Irving

THE COMPLETE SHERLOCK HOLMES

105. A Study In Scarlet
106. The Sign Of Four
107. The Adventures Of Sherlock Holmes
108. The Memoirs Of Sherlock Holmes
109. The Hound Of The Baskervilles
110. The Return Of Sherlock Holmes
111. His Last Bow
112. The Valley Of Fear
113. The Case-Book Of Sherlock Holmes

114. Graustark: The Story of a Love Behind a Throne by George Barr McCutcheon
115. Beverly of Graustark by George Barr McCutcheon
116. Truxton King: A Story of Graustark by George Barr McCutcheon
117. The Prince of Graustark by George Barr McCutcheon
118. The Complete Zenda Omnibus by Anthony Hope
119. The Mad king by Burroughs, Edgar Rice
120. The Fantomas Omnibus by Souvestre, Pierre

121. The Problemist by Clinton H. Stagg
122. The Dorrington Deed-Box by Morrison, Arthur
123. The Lone Wolf by Vance, L. J.
124. The Complete Martin Hewitt Collection Vol 1: Martin Hewitt, Investigator & Chronicles of Martin Hewitt by Morrison, Arthur
125. The Complete Martin Hewitt Collection Vol 2: Adventures of Martin Hewitt & The Red Triangle: Further Chronicles of Martin Hewitt by Morrison, Arthur
126. Seven Keys to Baldpate by Earl Derr Biggers
127. No Pockets in a Shroud by McCoy, Horace
128. The John Silence Collection by Blackwood, Algernon
129. Lady Molly Of Scotland Yard by Orczy, Baroness Emma
130. Skin O' My Tooth by Orczy, Baroness Emma
131. The Wrong Box by Stevenson, R. L. and Lloyd Osbourne
132. Tutt and Mr Tutt by Train, Arthur C.
133. The Clue by Wells, Carolyn
134. The Complete Trent Case Book by Bentley, E. C.
135. The Luck of the Vails by Benson, E. F.
136. The Rome Express by Griffiths, Arthur
137. The Complete Curious Mr Tarrant by C. Daly King
138. Rope and Gaslight (2-in-1 text) by Hamilton, Patrick
139. Prince Zaleski and Cumming's King Monk by Shiel, M. P.
140. The Assassination Bureau Ltd. by London, Jack
141. Introducing Clubfoot by Williams, Valentine
142. Master of Mysteries: The complete Uncle Abner collection by Post, Melville Davisson
143. The Red Redmaynes by Phillpotts, Eden
144. Thrilling Stories of the Railway by Whitechurch, Victor L.
145. The Grey Wig: Stories and Novelettes by Zangwill, Israel
146. The Lodger by Lowndes, Marie Belloc
147. The Man from Manchester by Donovan, Dick (Joyce Emerson Preston Muddock)
148. Mr. Meeson's Will by H. Rider Haggard by Haggard, H. Rider
149. Devlin the Barber by Farjeon, B. L.
150. Checkmate by Joseph Sheridan Le Fanu
151. Recollections of a Detective Police-Officer by Waters
152. The Widow Lerouge by Gaboriau, Emile
153. The Expressman and the Detective by Pinkerton, Allan
154. Zadig and Vathek by Voltaire
155. The Stillwater Tragedy by Aldrich, Thomas Bailey
156. The Memoirs of Constantine Dix by Pain, Barry
157. Ashes to Ashes by Ostrander, Isabel
158. The Jewel of Seven Stars by Stoker, Bram
159. The Thomas Love Peacock Collection by Peacock, Thomas Love

THE COMPLETE DERLETH SOLAR PONS

160. In Re: Sherlock Holmes - The Adventures of Solar Pons
161. The Memoirs of Solar Pons
162. The Return of Solar Pons
163. The Reminiscences of Solar Pons
164. The Casebook of Solar Pons
165. The Novels of Solar Pons: Terror over London and Mr. Fairlie's Final Journey
166. The Chronicles of Solar Pons
167. The Apocrypha of Solar Pons

168. The Triumphs of Eugene Valmont
169. The Female Detective by Forrester, Andrew
170. Cain's Jawbone by Torquemada
171. The Great Impersonation by Oppenheim, E. Phillips

THE DASHIELL HAMMETT COLLECTION

172. The Complete Sam Spade
173. The Complete Thin Man
174. The Complete Continental Op Vol 1
175. The Complete Continental Op Vol 2

Love Golden Age crime fiction? Have you checked out the full yellowback range?

From Locked door mysteries to blind detectives through first women detectives, the yellowback reissues is one of the largest selections of classic crime fictions, in the original format with a modern clean easy read page layout. A sampling below.

For more details and a full list of titles:
visit https://www.hachetteindia.com/home/yellowbacks

H. Rider Haggard
MR. MEESON'S WILL

Melville Davisson Post
MASTER OF MYSTERIES
THE COMPLETE UNCLE ABNER COLLECTION

Jack London
THE ASSASSINATION BUREAU LTD.

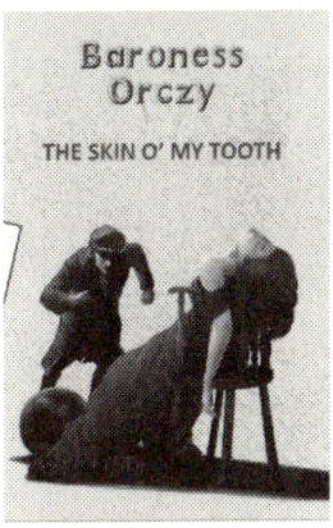
Baroness Orczy
THE SKIN O' MY TOOTH

Earl Derr Biggers
SEVEN KEYS TO BALDPATE

Horace Walpole
THE CASTLE OF OTRANTO

Sexton Blake
THE SEXTON BLAKE COLLECTION
VOLUME 1

Francis Beeding
THE HOUSE OF DR. EDWARDES

A. E. W. Mason
AT THE VILLA ROSE

Fergus Hume
THE MILLIONAIRE MYSTERY

Donald Henderson
A VOICE LIKE VELVET

Richard Hallas
YOU PLAY THE BLACK AND THE RED COMES UP